MW01029627

The Auction

KINGS OF RUIN: BOOK ONE

L KNIGHT

The Auction
Kings of Ruin Book One
By L Knight

Published by L Knight
Copyright © January 2023

Cover: Clem Parsons-Metatec
Editing: Black Opal Editing
Formatting: Black Opal Editing
Cover Photographer: Wander Aguiar

This is a work of fiction. Names characters places and incidents are a product of the author's imagination or are used fictitiously and are not to be construed as fact. Any resemblance to actual events organisations or persons—living or dead—is entirely coincidental.

All rights reserved. By payment of the required fees, you have been granted the non-exclusive non-transferable right to access and read the text of this eBook on a screen. Except for use in reviews promotional posts or similar uses no part of this text may be reproduced transmitted downloaded decompiled reverse-engineered or stored in or introduced into any information storage and retrieval system in any form or by any means whether electronic or mechanical now known or hereafter invented without the express written permission of the author.

First edition January 2023 © L Knight

Acknowledgments

I am so lucky to have such an amazing team around me without which I could never bring my books to life. I am so grateful to have you in my life, you are more than friends you are so essential to my life.

My wonderful beta team, Greta, and Deanna who are brutally honest and beautifully kind. If it is rubbish you tell me, it is and if you love it you are effusive. Your support means so much to me.

My editor—Linda at Black Opal Editing, who is so patient. She is so much more than an editor, she is a teacher and a friend.

My UK PA Clem Parsons who listens to all my ramblings and helps me every single day.

My ARC Team for not keeping me on edge too long while I wait for feedback.

Lastly and most importantly thank you to my readers who have embraced my books so wholeheartedly and shown a love for the stories in my head. To hear you say that you see my characters as family makes me so humble and proud. I hope you enjoy Linc's and Lottie's love story as much as I did.

Cover: Clem Parsons @Metatec
Editing: Black Opal Editing
Cover Photographer: Wander Aguiar

Prologue: Lottie

I SKID AROUND THE CORNER OF THE HOUSE, TRYING TO FIND A HIDING spot from my mom. My foot catches on a stone as my body goes airborne and I land with a grunt on the gravel of the drive. Pain stings the skin of my knees and hands from trying to save myself, and tears prick my eyes, but I shake it off and swallow down the pain as I jump to my feet and race off.

I can't be found here, I need to hide. I have homework to do and it's stupid. I don't want to do reading, it's too hard and I hate it. I round the wall that leads to my favorite part of the grounds and sigh with relief. Everything about the rose garden makes me happy. The pretty colors, the sweet smell, even the harsh thorns fascinate me, but it's the peace I get here that I love the most.

Dipping beneath the arch of trailing roses, I head towards the back, where the potting sheds are, and slump down in the fragrant grass. It's wet beneath my bottom, but I don't care. I'm safe here, free to daydream, free to be me without having to prove anything.

I examine my hands seeing the broken, scuffed skin and then tentatively glance at my knees. I hate blood, it makes me feel all funny inside, like I might be sick, and my head gets all funny, like my brain is trying to fall asleep. I abandon the idea of cleaning myself up after a glance and hope it will just scab over.

My nose wrinkles and stings and my chest feels heavy as I think about what my teacher said today. That I was stupid and it was a waste of time trying to teach an idiot. I hate that school; it's full of rich kids with fancy clothes and toys. Rich people can be mean and nasty. Mr. Coldwell is mean; he never says anything to me, but I see it in the way he looks at me, as if I'm a nuisance, as if I'm a fly he wishes he could swat away.

Mrs. Coldwell is nice though, but she always seems sad, as if she might cry. Maybe her teacher was mean to her too. But she can read, I see her in the library sometimes and I envy her. She can see the words my mother insists are there in the books, but I'm dumb and the letters move every time I try.

The gate that leads down to the lake on the other side of the rose garden creaks, and I tuck my body closer to the side of the wall, hoping whoever is there won't see me. I listen as the steps get closer and closer and close my eyes. If I can't see them, maybe they can't see me. The sound moves closer until I know they are near to me, and I open one eye and look up and into the eyes of Lincoln Coldwell.

"Lottie, what are you doing?"

Lincoln is three years older than me at nine and everyone loves him, even the teachers. They all talk about him, the girls giggle around him, and the boys are all his friends and laugh at everything he says or does. I wish I could hate him for it, but he's nice to me and always takes the time to wait for me when we're dropped off at school. He hunkers down on his haunches and I see his dark brown hair fall over his brow as he pushes it back with a sweep of his hand.

"Lottie!"

I jump at the sound of his shout and he immediately looks contrite as he sinks onto the grass beside me. His knees are bent up as he rests his elbows on them. "Are you going to talk to me and tell me why you're crying and bleeding?"

"I fell over." I sniff and try to sound brave.

"How?"

2

"I was running and trying to hide."

He offers me a hanky from his pocket and I take it, wiping my face and I grimace when I see the dirt I've left behind. "Sorry."

His handsome face creases into a warm grin. "It's meant for boogers and tears, Lottie. It hardly matters if it's dirt."

I giggle, some of the lightness returning to my heart. "You said boogers."

Lincoln rolls his eyes at me, but he smiles. He looks so much older than his brother, Clark. He's my friend too. We're the same age, but we aren't in the same class, he's really, really clever and I'm just stupid. My mood sours as I think about earlier at school and how everyone laughed when the teacher said those things to me. It makes me want to cry and I choke it back, not wanting Lincoln to see me cry and think I'm a baby.

"Hey, why the long face?"

I shrug, not wanting to tell Linc what they said. "Nothin'."

"Doesn't look like nothing if it's made you cry."

"I hate school."

"Why?"

"Because I'm stupid."

I hear his indrawn breath and angle my head to see his face. His brows are slashed low over his blue eyes, his lips pinched. "Don't say that."

"Why? It's true. My teacher said so today. I wish I could leave that school and become an astronaut."

"An astronaut?"

"Yeah, then I can see the stars up close and find out if the moon is really made of cheese. I love cheese."

"That would be a cool job."

"What job do you want to do when you grow up?"

Lincoln looks up into the sky, the late summer sun warm on our skin, and I admire his profile. He's always nice to me, but he can be different when his father is around, colder, as if he's scared of upsetting him. I still like him though. Clark doesn't seem to care what his dad thinks, he's always my friend.

"I want to be a dinosaur hunter."

I wrinkle my nose. "Dinosaurs are scary."

He laughs as he puts his arm around me. "Don't worry, Lottie, I'll protect you."

"You will?"

He looks down at me and I see the truth of his words in his eyes. "Always."

The moment stretches between us as I let my head fall to his shoulder and wish he could be in my class at school; nobody would bully me then.

Suddenly he jumps up from the grass and I tense as I watch him disappear into the potting shed. Mommy said I'm not allowed inside there as it has dangerous stuff for the plants to help the bugs stay away.

I sag back in relief when he comes back out a minute later with a green box in his hands. Sitting in front of me, he pops the box on the grass and opens it. Mommy has one of these too, it's for fixing boo boos up.

"Let's clean you up."

Gently Lincoln pulls my leg flat and takes out a wipe to clean the blood. I look away and bite my lip as the sting makes my eyes water.

"Still hate blood, Lottie?"

Lincoln is the only one who calls me Lottie, everyone else calls me Vi or Violet, but I like that he does. It makes it special. Clark called me Lottie once and I didn't like it and told him not to. I think I hurt his feelings but he wasn't mad for long. Clark is never mad for long. He's my best friend in the whole world, but I like Linc a lot too. He's just different. He makes my tummy feel weird and jumpy.

"There, all done."

I was so busy daydreaming I didn't feel him put a Band-Aid on my knee. Now it's all clean around my knee, leaving the dirt everywhere else looking even worse. "Thanks, Linc."

He nods and goes to put the first aid box away leaving the wrappers and wipes he used on the grass.

He comes back and I sigh, knowing I can't hide forever, but I wish

I could. I wish I was big and then I could decide if I wanted to read or go to stupid school.

"We should go back to the house. Your mom will be worried."

Mom is the housekeeper here at the Kennedy Estate and we have our very own place just for us. It's pretty neat and I love my room too, it's violet like my name and I have my very own desk so I can draw and stuff.

He holds out his hand and I take it as he pulls me to standing. As we walk back toward the house my tummy knots the closer we get and I slow my steps until I almost stop.

"I wish I could run away."

Linc turns to me, his head cocked so that the curl at the front falls over his forehead. "Why?"

"I don't belong here, Lincoln. I'm not like the other kids. My mom isn't rich and I don't have a daddy. I'm stupid and I wear old clothes. Everyone hates me."

"I don't hate you and you're not stupid."

"I am. I can't even read."

A hot stain of shame creeps over my face at the admission and I want to fall through the earth and disappear. Why did I tell him that? Now he'll hate me too.

A hand on my shoulder, makes me look up through my eyelashes at him so tall and handsome. He'd never be called stupid. He has everything, and yet he's nice to me still.

"I can help you. Reading is hard at first and some people have this thing where the letters move when they try to read and it makes it even harder. My friend Peter has it and he has some special-colored glasses to help him."

"He does?" Hope swims inside me and I feel lighter, that maybe I'm not stupid after all.

"Yes and special books with different fonts and stuff. Now he can read really good."

"And you'll help me?"

"Sure, but only if you don't run away."

"Okay."

I jump up and wrap my arms around him and he laughs as he hugs me back.

"Come on, let's go see if your mom made any of those millionaire shortbreads I like."

She has. My mom loves Lincoln and Clark and Mrs. Coldwell, but she doesn't like Mr. Coldwell. She never said it but I know, I can tell. She gets this look on her face that's all pinched, like my math teacher on a Monday morning.

I glance at Lincoln, beside me and feel all warm. I hope we're always friends and that he doesn't ever leave me.

"Linc, when we get older, can I marry you?"

He walks beside me toward the kitchen. "Why?"

"Because then you won't leave me."

He scrunches his nose and I wait for him to answer me. "I'm not sure I want a wife, but if I do, I'll pick you, okay?"

"Deal."

I turn and hold out my pinkie to him. He links his with mine and squeezes gently.

"Now let's go. Your first lesson starts after I get back from my piano lesson."

"Urgh, do I have to?"

"Yes. You promised."

I look at his serious face and hope he does change his mind about a wife. We could travel and find dinosaurs in my space ship and he could protect me and maybe we could take Clark too.

1: Lottie

"VI, THERE'S A CALL FOR YOU."

I pour the third cup of coffee for the suited man in my section and frown at Joe, the owner of the diner where I work in Central Park. Nerves pump through me, tightening my belly and I wonder how much of it is hunger and how much is good, old-fashioned stress. "Coming."

I smile at the suit, hoping he'll at least leave a decent tip for all the attention he keeps demanding and knowing he probably won't. You learn to spot the type pretty quickly in this job, but I have to be nice, just in case. Money is tight, and I need every cent I can get.

Picking up the receiver of the phone, I brace for whatever is coming at me, and it will be something, it always is. "Hello."

"Is this Violet Miller?"

"Yes."

"This is Mrs. Cantrell from the Riverdale School."

Anxiety tightens its hold on my chest and I struggle not to panic as I feel my heart begin to race like I've run a marathon. "Is Eric okay?"

"That's why I'm calling. He had a hypoglycemic attack. I've called an ambulance and they're taking him to Riverdale General."

My vision tunnels as fear grips me tight. Eric is sick. I need to get

7

to him. This is the mantra suddenly rattling around my brain on a loop as I try and remain outwardly calm. "I'm on my way."

"Someone will stay with him until you arrive at the hospital."

"Thank you."

My hand won't stop shaking as I hang up and reach behind me to untie my apron. "Joe, I'm sorry to do this to you but I have to go. Eric had a hypo at school. They're taking him to Riverdale General."

Joe waves his hand toward the door. "Go, go. We'll manage."

Grabbing my bag from behind the counter I rush toward the door, only stopping to go up on tip toes so I can kiss Joe's weathered cheek. He's so good to me. Gives me way more leeway than he should and I'm so damned grateful for him, I feel tears threaten behind my eyelids. "Thank you."

Rushing out the door, I run toward the station and stop when I see a cab slow just in front of me and let someone out on the side of the street. I can't afford it, but worry for Eric is snapping at my heels. I need to be with him, to hold his little hand and tell him it will be okay. I'm all he has in the world, and I won't let him be alone for this a second longer than he needs to be. Making the snap decision I rush toward the yellow cab and dive into the back seat.

"Riverdale General, please."

The cab driver looks me over and I can feel the judgment and censure as if he knows I can't afford the fare and he's right, I can't. It will mean another night with no food for me, but I don't care. Eric is all that matters to me.

"I have the cash." I wave a handful of bills at him that I know I would've used to buy food, and he nods, hitting the gas and speeding us toward the hospital. I watch the spring rain fall outside, not realizing I'm soaked to the skin until this very second. A shiver runs through me, and I'm not sure if it's from worry or cold.

Ever since my mom died and left me with the sole responsibility of my baby brother, I've been numb. It's been three years and it still feels like it was yesterday that she was taken from us, leaving a void that I'll never be able to fill, but I promised her I'd take care of Eric and that is what I'll do.

The cab stops and I thrust the cash at the driver and jump out, running toward the entrance. Warm air hits me as I enter the reception area. The emergency department is packed, but I have one focus as I rush toward the desk, and that's to get to Eric.

"Eric Miller, he was brought in by ambulance." I try not to think of the cost or how I'll pay the bills this time. I'm a hair's breadth away from failing my dead mother and my brother. My throat clogs as the weight of responsibility almost cripples me, but a breakdown is something else I just can't afford to have. Rolling my shoulders back, I wait impatiently for the woman to click her keyboard to locate my brother.

"Are you family?"

"Yes, I'm his sister and legal guardian."

"Okay, Miss Miller. He's been taken up to pediatrics, through the door on the left."

I run, my wet feet squelching on the grey vinyl floor of the hospital as I head towards the lift. It closes as I get there, and I want to bang my fist on it in frustration. Looking around I spot the sign for the stairs and push through the door.

Taking them quickly I find myself on the pediatric floor and go through the same rigmarole as before, speaking to reception and finding my brother. When I spot his teacher I rush toward her, skidding to a stop and diverting my attention as Dr. Stanley steps out of the room.

"Ah, Violet, there you are."

"How is he?"

The kindly doctor who's been treating Eric since he was diagnosed with type 1 diabetes two years ago, smiles trying to reassure me. "Let's go somewhere quiet and talk."

Dread churns my stomach at his words, which can't be anything good. "Okay. Can I see him for a second first?"

"Of course."

Dr. Stanley pushes open the door and steps aside. I see my brother looking so small in the huge hospital bed, the white of the sheets almost the same pallor as his skin. His eyes are closed as I move closer and brush my fingers over his short dark hair. Heavy lids drift open and

9

he gives me a smile. At nine, he's small for his age and I worry that he's not getting the nutrition he needs to grow. I try my best, but I'm failing him. Yet he still looks at me with love and devotion in his blue eyes.

"Hey, buddy."

"Vi, I don't feel so good."

The churning of my stomach moves up my chest, lodging in my throat and choking me. I fight the tears of dread and worry and paste a reassuring smile on my face. This little boy means everything to me and seeing him sick wrecks me. "I know, buddy, but we're going to get you all fixed up."

I brush a kiss over his head, closing my eyes as I breathe in his scent. He's home to me. He will *always* be home. I'm his protector now. I'll fight until the body God gave me gives in before I'll let him down again. There's nothing I wouldn't do for him, not a single damn thing.

"I need to speak with Dr. Stanley. Why don't you rest and I'll be back in a few minutes to read to you." The thought of reading Eric his favorite book makes me think of *him*, but I shut it down. I can't afford to let him have a second of the softness I still feel inside me, because it will break what's left of my heart by reminding me of who he was before.

"Okay, Vi."

The tiny voice breaks me out of my stupor, and I smile again. This raucous little boy who is usually so full of energy is lethargic and exhausted from the hypo and it flays my skin to see him this way.

I step back into the hallway and see Miss Powell still waiting and feel awful for ignoring her. "Miss Powell, thank you so much for staying with him."

Her kind smile is like sandpaper on the raw edges of my nerves. I'm holding it together by a thread and if she's kind, I'll cry, and I can't afford a mental breakdown right now.

She seems to sense it and just squeezes my arm. "I'm going to head back to school. Let us know how he is in a few days."

"I will, thank you."

As she walks through the doors, I turn to Dr. Stanley and know I'm going to have to pull up every ounce of strength I have to get through this next part without falling apart.

He ushers me into a quiet room two doors down from where Eric is sleeping and motions for the chair. I sit, grateful for the opportunity to rest my aching legs. Waitressing keeps me fit, but it's hell on your feet and legs. "Hit me with the worst, doc, I can take it."

He smiles kindly and my stomach sinks.

"Eric had a bad hypo. He's very lucky not to be in a coma right now. We're monitoring him closely and will for a few days, but either his medication isn't working, or he isn't having it."

I'm grateful for his bluntness, even if I resent the implication, which is that Eric isn't getting his meds. He isn't being a dick about it, but anyone with eyes can see I'm scraping the barrel financially and insulin is horrendously expensive. "He's getting his medication." My voice is firm, as I enunciate every word. Determination and pride make my spine stiffen under his gaze.

"I wasn't implying…."

"Yes, you were, and honestly, I get it, Dr. Stanley. I know what we look like and God knows I wish I could say you have it all wrong, but you don't. I'm dirt poor but even if I have to sacrifice everything I own, Eric gets his medication."

"Well, in that case, it would seem we'll need to adjust his current medication. Increase the dose and monitor him more closely."

"Do what you need to do, doc. I'll find a way, I always do."

I can't even think about the cost of this stay and how I'll be drowning in so many medical bills that even eating will become a luxury. Perhaps I can get a cheaper apartment and more shifts at the diner, but deep down in my heart I know it won't be enough. At this point I need a miracle. My stray thoughts are cut short by Dr. Stanley speaking again.

"Does your insurance cover any of it? We have programs you can try, and medical aid."

I appreciate his kindness, but I've tried them all, and it still isn't enough. I still have my mom's medical bills that I'm paying off. They say cancer is a death sentence to the poor in America and they're right. Getting sick is too expensive, having good health is a rich person's game. I don't say any of that to Dr. Stanley though. He's a nice man, but he won't understand because he's part of the rich person's club.

I grip my bag tighter, my knuckles turning white as I fight to stay upbeat. "I'll look into it."

He nods and goes on to explain the details of what will happen and what he wants to try, and I take most of it in, but part of me is swimming against the tide, trying to keep myself from screaming at the sheer unfairness of it all.

Later, as I sit by Eric's bed through the night watching him breathe deeply, I rack my brain for a way out of this mess and find nothing. I could try going to his father, but I know I'd rather die than ask that bastard for anything. He'd likely say no anyway, which means I have one option.

I have to give up the only two things I have left, my pride and my dignity, and do the unthinkable. I have one asset left and that's my body. Looks like it's all I have left to sell.

2: Linc

꩜

I DOWN THE SCOTCH AND LIFT MY GLASS TO THE BARMAN AGAIN. IT'S Friday night at Club Ruin, my favorite night of the week as the excitement and anticipation of the weekend is hyping the vibe on the floor. I have a meeting scheduled with my business partners to discuss club business. Harrison Brooks, one of the partners and the man responsible for Club Ruin's success, called earlier saying he needed to speak with us. It was Harrison who found this building as part of his enormous property portfolio.

The man has property all over the world, having made his money from the stock markets and then diversifying into buildings and land, but now he runs Club Ruin and has a manager handle his huge property portfolio. I think Harrison gets bored too easily and that's why he needs the constant challenge, but that's a boon for us because he's taken our little club and pushed it into the stratospheric success it is today.

The beat of the music is pounding, and I can feel a headache coming on. I can't be mad though, Harrison doesn't usually ask for a meeting unless it's important or sensitive, letting the rest of us stay in the shadows as silent partners for the most part. That's why, when he called, I cancelled my date for the night and came here instead.

Honestly, I wasn't feeling it tonight anyway. I shake my head and wonder what the fuck is wrong with me. Sienna is a sure thing with big tits and a curvy ass who's always happy to get down on her knees and suck my cock like it's her job, without me even having to ask. The fact I'm not bothered makes me wonder if perhaps I've grown tired of the nameless fucking. Women are a dime a dozen, always eager and willing, and I miss the chase and the way my blood would sizzle at the thought of making a woman submit to me. Perhaps I can head for the third floor after the meeting and have some fun there.

Club Ruin was formed one night five years ago, between me and three friends from college, then my cousin Audrey got involved too. We knew nothing of this scene then and it started out as just a normal club, a place to drink, dance, and meet people. Then two years ago it became so much more. Audrey suggested we make use of the third floor and although we'd been cautious, wary of the way it would be received, she'd been right.

I wasn't exactly happy that my cousin had suggested a sex club on the top floor, but she's a smart businesswoman and not someone you say no to, so we'd gone with it and the money had come flooding into our already laden pockets.

Now with three floors, Club Ruin offers something for everyone.

The first floor is a normal club, for partygoers, who just want to dance and have fun. Only the best-looking people get into Club Ruin, we're elitist and unconcerned who that offends. We have a brand and if people don't like it they can fuck off someplace else. We're not here to cater to the whims of people who take offense as if it's their job. We have a very strict policy and dress code. If you let in the riff-raff, you won't get the clientele we're looking for, the kind that doesn't mind dropping thousands of dollars on liquor. The queue that goes around the block suggests it was the right move.

That's not the fun part though, it's the top two floors where the real fun happens. The second floor is the VIP section with waitress and waiter service only. The girls and guys are all smoking hot, with a very different uniform from the bar staff on the first floor. Normal bar staff wear tight black t-shirts with the Ruin logo and black denim skirts or jeans. VIP girls wear short black dresses and are required to have more on show, to entice the customers to spend their hard-earned cash. The men wear black slacks and are shirtless except for a black bow tie. It's pretentious but it works and that's all we care about.

My musings are interrupted by Ryker Cabot, tech genius and social media mogul extraordinaire, and one of my best friends since college.

"Lincoln, you're early for once." Ryker pats me on the shoulder and I turn to lift my brow in greeting. "Chatty as ever, I see. What bug's up your ass now?"

"Apart from wasting my Friday night with you bunch of assholes?"

Ryker claps a hand over his heart. "You wound me."

Ryker is the joker of the group, the one you can rely on to lighten any mood or situation. He comes across as the easy-to-read one of our foursome but you'd be wrong to think that. He lets you see what he wants you to see.

I rub my thumb and forefinger together. "Hear that, Midas, that's my violin playing."

He laughs. "Dick."

"Never claimed to be anything else."

Ryker is tall and broad with blond hair, which needs a damn cut, and blue eyes that women seem to swoon over. Ryker is the flirt, the man who has a different woman on his arm every night and yet they all end up in love with him, no matter the fact he rarely sees them more than once.

He's a playboy, but anyone who makes the mistake of thinking that's all he is would be a fool. He's the slickest IT whiz on the planet and there's nothing he can't do with code. He built a social media platform that has made him richer than Midas, hence the nickname.

"You have any idea what Harrison wants to see us about?"

Ryker lifts a finger at the barman, Marc, who nods and goes about pouring the vodka Ryker loves to drink.

"Not a fucking clue."

He gets distracted as a group of women in short skirts and huge smiles walk past. "Ladies."

"Hey, Ryker."

They stop and I idly let my eyes move over them, assessing if I can be bothered to put in any work. Not that it involves a lot, money and good looks make it easy to get laid or get your dick sucked, but I find myself bored with the constant, meaningless sex.

Perhaps I should date, but the thought alone makes me wince. My last girlfriend was so needy, always texting and wanting to see me, and demanding we do things together. I don't want to have to base my decisions on someone else. Plus, they always think dating means they have access to me at all times and get the right to sleep over. I don't spend the night with anyone. I'm not a cuddler, I like my space and prefer if they just fuck off home after we fuck. Apparently, that's too much to ask, and makes me cold and emotionally stunted, at least according to the last ex.

Though I may not have much choice going forward, thanks to my family. I frown, my mood darkening to thunder as I think back to the conversation with my father last weekend.

"Hey, let's head up and get this meeting started. The sooner we talk business the sooner we can have fun."

I follow Ryker through the club up to the VIP section, which is manned by four bouncers that would make anyone think twice about causing shit just from their size, and move to the stairs at the back for the third floor. I don't make eye contact with anyone as we pass through, and they wouldn't dare look at me. My wrath isn't something they want and I've been known to fire someone just for having a hair out of place. My standards are exacting and if people can't meet them, then they're gone. I've got no time or patience for imbeciles.

Club Ruin is dark with black walls and a high vaulted ceiling that goes right up to the roof four stories higher. It allows for the long statement lighting and the mezzanine from the second floor to overlook the club below it. Audrey designed it with Harrison and they did a fantastic job, taking each of our ideas and melding them into something that we're all proud of.

As I reach the third floor I see six more security members near the door. It's discreet up here, just black walls and black, soundproof doors. We offer our patrons on this floor full discretion and privacy.

Stepping into the large, shared office that's mostly used for meetings, I feel irritation prickle under my skin. I'm a moody bastard, I know that, but something is making me irrationally angry and I can't shake this mood or the jaded feeling inside me.

Taking my seat at the end of the glass conference table, I watch Harrison, Audrey, and Beck walk in behind me and Ryker.

"Cuz" Audrey kisses my cheek as she sits beside me.

"Audrey. Any idea what the fuck this is about?"

"Third floor."

"Ah."

Harrison takes the hot seat and looks at us all. "Thanks for coming, I'll keep it short."

"What's up, Harry?"

I smirk as Harrison gives me a raised eyebrow for calling him Harry. He hates it and that only makes me do it more.

"We need more girls on the third floor. Our wait list is growing, and demand is high, so we need to capitalize on it."

"So, hire more girls for the third floor." I shrug, wondering why the hell he called us in for this.

"It's not that simple. The ones being requested are of a certain type. These men and women want innocents."

I lean forward. "No fucking way are we hiring underage girls for this club. I don't give a fuck what perversions these men have."

"I'm not suggesting they be underage, but they need to be virgins."

"Well, good fucking luck finding pretty girls over twenty-one who suddenly find they want to fuck rich, fat pricks." Beck sips his drink after saying his piece.

"I don't know, Beck, you do okay."

I smirk at Audrey's dig as I sip my drink.

"Just because you want some of this."

"In your dreams, asshole."

Their flirting used to bother me until I realized that Beck and Audrey only flirted with each other because it was safe. They had zero chemistry and I was relieved. I didn't want this business I'd grown to love wrecked by those two fucking and then falling out.

"That's the issue. I have an idea but it needs your approval," Harrison interrupted as if they'd never spoken. He had a gleam in his eyes which usually meant he was about to hit us with a proposal that would make my hair stand on end.

"Go on." Audrey sits forward and I can see the gleam in her eye.

"We advertise a virginity sale or auction, the girls get to sell their virginity to the highest bidder from our members' list, and in return, she keeps fifty percent of the proceeds but she signs a contract to work for Club Ruin exclusively for twelve months."

"Is that legal?"

Beck nods. "I'll have to check with the attorney but yes, barely. Just like everything we do upstairs, it skates just this side of the line. The contract will have to say she's receiving a signing bonus."

Beck is a world-renowned heart surgeon but he has a brain that never stops moving and he likes details, so when he isn't reading medical journals on new techniques, he's making sure this club we love is safe.

"Exactly. Her contract will be the same as anyone on the third floor. They offer an escort service and what they do behind those doors is up to them."

"Fine, do it, but my suggestion is you make it a once-a-year thing, with only five girls. It will drive the cost and desire up."

Audrey nods. "Good idea. We'd need to vet them, make sure they're aware of what this is and are okay with it."

Harrison nods his agreement. "I suggest we get all five potential girls to work the third floor for a week beforehand so they can make sure they're really aware what goes on up there."

"I think that's a good idea. Have them shadow one of the original girls so they know what to expect. We know some of these men and women have some very specific tastes that might scare the life out of an innocent."

My cock thickens at the thought, and I wonder if that's what I need to pull myself out of this funk. Some fresh, juicy innocent pussy.

Harrison dips his head. "We can arrange that."

"Will we be allowed to bid?"

Ryker gives me a cocky grin and I scowl at him. "I think it's best if we don't. We don't want people to think it's rigged in any way."

I acknowledge his comment and remain silent.

"So, is everyone in agreement?" Harrison looks around the room and I nod, as do the others.

"That's settled then. I'll get on it and have more details by Monday."

I head back down to the second floor and snag the attention of Monica, one of the girls working the floor. Her hand lands on my chest as she curls into me. I let my fingers graze the skin of her smooth thigh. She's taking a liberty touching me without permission and she knows it.

"What can I do for you, Mr. Coldwell?"

Her voice is a purr and I consider asking her to take a break. This girl is wild and up for almost anything, and she doesn't cling afterward which makes her perfect for a quick fuck. "A scotch on the rocks."

"Is that all?" Her hands wander down my body and I catch her wrist in a brutal hold, throwing it off me before her hand gets to my cock.

"For now."

I watch her pout before she seems to snap out of it and sashays off to get my drink. I head over to the mezzanine balcony and lean against the waist-high reinforced glass, looking over the club.

I'm proud of Club Ruin. It's something we built together with no money or input from my father or family. Its success is because of us and nobody else. I let my eyes move over the dance floor, scanning the crowd who are letting loose. Bodies undulate in an erotic rhythm as they let the stresses of the work week disappear. That's what we offer, fun for all, depending on your personal preferences.

When we talked about the club, it was Beck's idea to have an exclusive VIP floor with members only, but it was Audrey who introduced the top floor where anything goes as long as it's consensual.

The men and women we hire to work there are all vetted thoroughly with health checks every month, and a strict policy on the use of condoms. We don't want any blowback if one of these men gets someone pregnant. They also have a rigorous background check to look for any red flags before they're offered a twelve-month contract. We want longevity in our staff but also the ability to keep things fresh and it's a fine balance. It's why each member is asked to fill in a form once a year rating the staff, and the bottom two are fired and new blood is brought in to fill the void.

The top floor is similar to the rest of the club in that it has a small dance floor and bar where they can be seen and socialize, with a stage for those wanting a more public experience, with a St Andrews Cross in the center and secluded booths mixed in with high-top tables. The real draw though is the private rooms. Each room is themed, with all the toys you might need for fun, and they're cleaned and sealed by our staff after every use. Some have viewing windows and others are completely private. We also have a high-security presence, both physical people walking the halls and cameras inside, and although discreet, they're there for the safety of everyone and no violence is tolerated.

We have a stringent selection process for our members, with only the most elite getting access. Actors, musicians, politicians, business moguls, and even professional athletes are members here. It's not a new idea, but it's one we've put our own spin on, and everyone benefits. But all the money and fame in the world doesn't give these people the freedom to be violent without consent and then only up to a point. If someone wants pain, that is one thing, but we don't allow knife play or someone to inflict wounds that bleed.

That's a whole other nightmare we want no part of and the lawsuit should something go wrong isn't worth appeasing the small group of people who request it.

My eyes scan the bar, and I freeze, my gaze sliding back toward the end of the bar where Marc is speaking to one of the new hires. My body goes stiff, every muscle stilling as I wait for her to turn around and confirm what I already know.

My Lottie is here, and she's working the bar in my fucking club.

3: Lottie

I MIX THE COCKTAIL, ADDING THE STRAW BEFORE I TURN TO MARC. "Better?" Tending bar is harder than I thought, and the pace is so much quicker than working the diner.

He offers me a sexy smile. "You'll get there, gorgeous."

I blush. Marc is handsome and fun to be around and he's good for my ego with his flirty winks and sexy remarks, but I'm here for one reason only and that's to make more money.

Eric is doing better since his hypo last week but the bills coming in are staggering and if I think about them too long, I'll drown, so I just keep plugging on. Tending bar at Club Ruin pays well but my aim isn't this floor. I need to get onto the second floor where I know the tips will be better, but apparently, everyone starts on the main bar first.

"Hey, Marc, how long does it take to work your way up to the second floor?"

His pierced brow rises as he looks at me. "You want to work on the second?"

"No, she does not."

The world seems to tilt as I feel the air leave me at the sound of a voice from my past. A voice I never thought I'd hear again. Slowly I turn and I'm rendered speechless at the sight of the man who broke my heart and threw me away like I was trash.

Lincoln Coldwell.

"Lincoln."

The slash of his brow, and the tick in his jaw, don't detract in the slightest from the full sensual lips or the blue eyes that look greyer as they stare at me with open contempt.

"What the hell are you doing here?"

I see Marc slink away as if he's worried about getting caught in the crossfire of whatever this is, his face a mask of concern as if he's frightened of the man glaring daggers at me.

No hello, or how have you been, just straight in with the hostility. He's such an arrogant prick. I wonder if the boy I loved ever existed or if he was all a figment of my overactive teenage imagination.

I steel my spine, finding the spirit that has kept me upright these last few years, and tip my chin up. I won't show this man how much his words cut me. "I work here."

"No, you don't."

I laugh as my temper flares, and I turn my back on him. The last thing I need is to get fired from this job over an argument with a rich prick I once knew. *Be honest, Vi, you more than knew him, at one time he was everything to you.*

Marc is shaking his head as if he's trying to warn me of something as he looks behind me before busying himself cleaning a glass.

"Go away, Lincoln, I'm working. We have nothing to say to each other."

"The hell we don't."

I gasp as he moves around the bar and grabs my arm, dragging me behind him as I try and keep up on the stupid heels I'm wearing.

"Lincoln, what the hell are you doing? You're going to get me fired."

As we reach the coat check, he shoves me through a door to a staff-only cloak room and I wrench my arm away from his scalding touch. I step back putting as much space between us as I can.

This man is nothing like the boy I remember, he's dangerous on a whole other level, cold and cruel as he looks at me with contempt. Yet my body still reacts to his touch, my wrist feels tingly like a current is running through it and I rub the spot he touched to try and erase the feeling.

"Why are you here, Lottie?"

"Don't call me that, my name is Violet."

"Not to me, you'll always be my Lottie."

Anger burns through me, but it's driven by the hurt of him calling me his. There was a time when I would've sold my soul to the devil to be his but that was before he took what I gave him and crushed it. Now, as I stare into his expressionless face, it seems he's become the devil. "I'm not your anything, mister." My finger pokes his chest, his rock-hard pecs unmoving as he smirks at me, but it's not the sexy smirk I remember, it's devoid of warmth and compassion.

"Still can't keep your hands off me, Lottie?"

I snatch my hand away but not quick enough as he grabs my wrist in his firm grip and places it back on the pristine white shirt, which is warm from his body beneath.

"In your dreams. You repulse me."

I let out a strangled gasp as I find myself pressed up against the wall, with his hand beside my shoulder, his hard body pinning me so tight I can feel his erection against my belly.

"Really, Lottie? You'd lie to me after everything we were to each other." His words talk of the past as if he didn't chew me up and spit me out.

"We were nothing to each other." His jaw flexes in anger at my words and I feel a tiny tendril of fear snake up my spine before I force it away. Whoever this man is now, I don't believe he'd physically hurt me.

"Is that so?" He cocks his head and I try again to pull my hand away, but he tightens his grip, so it's almost painful. "I think you're lying."

How can this be happening? Isn't my life bad enough right now without adding Lincoln Coldwell to the mix?

"I'm not lying, we were nothing to each other. I was your plaything until someone more suitable came along."

"Bullshit."

His voice is calm, controlled, and deep like a purr on my skin.

I have the urge to ask him why but I hold my tongue and try not to push against the hard evidence of his desire for me, no matter how much my body craves the feel of it. Reacting will give him what he wants, and I vowed to never let Lincoln Coldwell take anything from me ever again.

His hand skims down my arm, and I shiver despite myself, making him smirk like the devil he is now. I tip my chin up and glare at him, only making him smile wider, his even white teeth flashing.

"So feisty, Lottie. I'd forgotten how much of a fucking turn-on your temper was."

"Drop dead."

"Oh, not before I find out if you lied to me."

Before I can ask the question, my body seizes at the touch of his fingers against my pussy. This damn short skirt has made it easy for him to confirm my lie. A growl escapes his chest as he leans in closer and my eyes fall shut, overwhelmed by everything that is Lincoln Coldwell.

His fingers push aside the thin fabric of my panties, and he runs them through my folds, coating him in the evidence of my lie. I want to squirm as desire hits me like a runaway train.

"Fucking soaking for me."

"Not for you." I hate the idea of him thinking I want him still.

His thumb circles my clit as he watches me.

"Then who? One of the customers?"

I remain silent hoping my hatred of him is clear as he continues to torture me with his magical fingers. My hips rock slightly, seeking more as desire pools heavy and slick on his fingers.

"Perhaps the barman, Marc?"

I grit my teeth, forcing the whimper in my throat away. "Yes," I lie, wanting him to think it's someone else who makes my body respond this way. Not wanting him to think he has any hold over me at all.

I should push him away, kick and scream at him for touching me like he owns me, but I can't because Lincoln Coldwell has always owned my body and it seems he still does, but I'll never let him know it.

He puts pressure on my clit as he toys with me and a whimper escapes without my consent, as need builds inside me. I'm already on the edge of an intense orgasm, and he's barely touched me. It's been too long since I've felt anything and now it feels like the stopper has come off and I want, no I need, to come so badly that it feels like I've been drugged.

"That's it, Lottie, ride my fucking hand. Come all over my fingers."

His words are harsh against my neck, where his lips are resting over my pulse. He's not kissing me or touching me anywhere else, and this feels wrong but oh so right. I crest the ridge of desire as stars burst behind my closed eyelids.

"Look at me."

His deep demand has my eyes flashing open to see Linc watching me with so much heat and fire it's a wonder the club isn't burning down around us.

"Come for me, Lottie."

My body responds to his dark command and I stiffen before every sensation is overwhelming me. I cry out, my hands scrabbling for purchase on his suit as my climax makes my legs give way. Only the feel of his body against me is holding me upright.

As I come down from the pleasure he forced on me, I hate him even more than before, because deep down I know he would've stopped if I'd asked. Linc is a lot of things, but he isn't a man to force a woman against her will. It's my will that's the problem and shame spirals through me as I look down and away from his heated glare. His fingers force my chin up and I watch as he slides the two fingers that were inside me into his mouth.

His eyes close and his nostrils flare as his hips rock against me, causing a pulse of desire to shoot through my clit.

"That doesn't taste like I repulse you, Lottie."

I need to get away from him, he's scrambling my brain and I can't think or breathe for him. "Go to hell, Lincoln. I have to get back to work."

Lincoln's eyes close and when they open again, he's different, cold, with no trace of the man who just made me come harder than I ever have before. He steps back and walks to the door, leaving my skirt pushed around my hips as his eyes scan me from head to toe.

"Perhaps you're right. The Lottie I knew would never dress like a whore and let a man touch her so intimately."

Before I can offer him any kind of retort, he's gone, leaving me shaken and angry, with him and myself.

I smooth my skirt down and head back to the bar, avoiding the worried look from Marc as I keep my head down and work my ass off for the rest of the night, all under the cool gaze of Lincoln Coldwell, who watches me with a scowl from the second-floor balcony.

Around ten, Marc disappears and I don't see him again for the rest of the night. Perhaps he was sick, he did look a little peaky when I got back.

I make it home around three am and creep through the living room where I sleep, and where Mary, my neighbor, is snoring on the couch, to the bedroom where Eric is sound asleep. His face is relaxed, his body star-fished with the covers falling over the side. I tuck him in so the covers keep the cold out and head to the bathroom to undress. I won't wake Mary, she needs her rest as much as I do. Taking off my make-up, I tiptoe to the chair in the corner and huddle up with a blanket and try and force my mind to clear so I can sleep for a few hours.

I have the morning shift at the diner in a few hours and then another night at Club Ruin. I'm exhausted in body and mind and still, I can't sleep. My mind is too preoccupied with the man who broke my teenage heart. The man I've spent the last ten years hating and missing.

I should be over him by now, but I know Lincoln was never just a teenage crush for me, he was my world, and I was his until one day I wasn't good enough and he discarded me like trash, making me feel like I was less than nothing

One thing I know for sure after tonight is that he's more dangerous to me than he ever was, because this man has none of the warmth I remember, only the cold determination of a man who gets what he wants, and he sure looked like he wanted to take a bite out of me.

I fear I won't stop him, even though I hate him with every fiber of my body.

4: Linc

I DON'T KNOW WHY I'M HERE TORTURING MYSELF, BUT I CAN'T SEEM to stop. I've been positioned at this balcony every night for three solid weeks, watching her, wanting her, and knowing that I can't have her. She's a window to my past, to a man who doesn't exist anymore, and I closed the door on him a long time ago. Yet the taste of her on my fingers after I made her come still makes my mouth water. She was fucking stunning when she climaxed around my fingers and I thought I might shoot my load in my pants like a teenage boy with a porn mag as I watched her.

My dick is raw from fucking my fist, trying to pound the vision of her from my mind, and yet here I am waiting, watching like a fucking stalker. I tried to convince Harrison to fire her but after I'd already fired Marc for daring to look at something I considered mine, Harrison was pissed. He refused without a good reason, which I couldn't give him, especially as I couldn't give a sound reason for firing Marc. So, I'd had Ryker scan her social media looking for an excuse to get rid of her, to get her out of my life and he found almost nothing. She's a ghost, a beautiful ethereal mystery, and I find I want answers. I want to break her, to ruin her, and yet, there is an infinitesimal part of my soul that still finds it wants to protect her, to claim her and I need to stamp it out, eradicate that weakness that she's exposed in me.

Grown men fear me, my friends know that I'm not to be pushed, and yet she faced me with her head held high. That intrigues me, so maybe I'll let her stay and work herself to the bone until she quits. I'll enjoy watching that from my place looking down on her.

My little Lottie has grown from a sweet child and a curious shy teen into a breathtakingly beautiful woman. There's a quiet confidence about her as she moves and yet I see the vulnerability she's trying to hide and it's that chink in her armor that makes me pause. I should stay away from her. I hurt her once and I don't want to do it again, even though she broke my heart, but I can't seem to get my conscious mind to talk to my emotional one. She's a risk to me. She has the power to make me weak and I won't allow it.

Harrison comes up to lean beside me at the balcony railing. "You still stalking our new barmaid?"

I frown at him, wanting to stew in my bad mood alone. "I'm not stalking her. I'm watching her."

He chuckles, making me turn to him with a glare. "What the fuck has she ever done to you to make you even more of an asshole than you usually are?"

Only a select few would be brave enough to speak to me in such a way, and now I regret allowing even that. "I don't trust her."

"Why? She seems perfectly hard-working. The customers love her, the staff love her, she's never late and is a quick learner."

I have no intention of telling him of my history with Lottie, so I just grunt in response. "Did you come up here to give me shit or did you want something?"

"Yes, I have the new staff rosters and it's your turn to sign them off this week."

I put out my hand for the clipboard he's carrying. Harrison can be so old school sometimes, with his paper and pen obsession. It drives Ryker crazy, which only makes Harrison do it more. We take it in turns to oversee the roster; there is no need, but Harrison insists so that we're aware of the staff members.

I scan down the paper and my eyes lock onto a particular name as if drawn to it without my consent. A frown creases my brow when I see she's scheduled to begin working the second floor next week. Having her closer isn't a temptation I want, and yet I have the strongest desire to play with her, to see if I can get a reaction. She's ignored me since the night I made her come on my hand and I don't like it.

Scrubbing through her name, I replace it with one of the other bartenders and move her back to the first floor. If she wants this, she'll have to come and ask me.

I hand the roster back to Harrison who looks it over, before raising his eyes to me.

"I promised her the second floor this week."

"That was your mistake, not mine. She's not ready and if she has a problem, she can come to see me about it."

Harrison shakes his head. "What's your problem with her?"

"I don't have a problem. I just don't think she's right for the club."

"Strongly disagree."

My eyes wander over the bar, seeking her out and I scowl as I watch her laughing easily with the other staff. I know what she's doing. She's trying to tempt me and it won't work. She had her chance, and she blew it. I offered her the world, and she threw it in my face without a second thought. Lottie will learn I don't give second chances to anyone. You cross me once and once only, and then you're dead to me.

Yet a tendril of desire snakes down my spine as I watch her, mixing with a doubt that I've never felt before. There's a reason nobody crosses me. I don't lose and that's because I never second guess myself, yet since Lottie came barreling back into my life like a hurricane, I've felt seeds of doubt infiltrate my thoughts at every turn.

"If she has a problem, send her to me. I have no problem firing her if you haven't got the backbone for it."

"Fuck you, Lincoln. I have no problem doing my job, but I won't sack a perfectly good member of staff just because you have a hard-on for her."

I glance across at him with a hard glare. "Careful, Harrison." Anger ripples through my body and I clench my hand around the glass I'm holding. I don't want to fall out with my friend, but I won't tolerate his tone.

He holds my stare, not backing down an inch. It's why we're friends. We're the same, but it's also why arguments are inevitable.

Finally, he breaks my gaze and flips the page on his clipboard, and I let out the breath I was holding.

"We have three sign-ups for the auction so far. I'm going to schedule it for the middle of June if that works for everyone. It gives me time to set up the promo and get some interest building with the members. I thought we could begin one girl a week working that floor as a waitress and then, the week before the auction, all the girls work it. Having them seen should get the juices flowing and the wallets nice and loose."

"Fine by me. Send me pictures of all the girls when you have them."

"Okay, well I'm going to break the news to your girl that she can't work the second floor—yet, and then get started on the drinks orders."

I look back to the bar and see her smile at some sleazy asshole as she passes him his drink. Her head goes back, exposing that long neck, and she laughs at whatever the prick said, before leaning in close as if to hear him better. My hand clenches around the glass I'm holding and I place it on the table beside me so I don't crush it.

From up here I can see the creamy curve of her breast in the tight t-shirt, and suddenly, I get the urge to change the entire uniform so they have to wear baggy, polo-neck sweaters It wouldn't matter though, Lottie would look like a goddess in a bin liner. She's just that beautiful.

I've noticed how thin she is from my spot here in the corner and the dark circles under her eyes, which no amount of makeup can hide. Zooming in on the security cameras every night to get a better look before going home to my penthouse and jerking off like a creep, is a compulsion I can't seem to break. It makes me hate her more.

"She isn't my girl."

"Perhaps you just need to get laid, Lincoln."

"Maybe you're right. Perhaps I just need to find some quality pussy."

Harrison claps me on the shoulder. "That's my man. Beck has a few girls in room six if you want to join him."

I shrug, the idea of sharing with Beck tonight leaving me cold. We've shared before, more than once, and more than just Beck and I, but the idea leaves me restless. "Maybe."

"So, she stays off this floor?"

"Yes." I can't tolerate her this close. She'll try and bewitch me again and I won't have it.

"I'll let her know, and I have to say it's a shame. I think she would've been popular."

I grit my teeth so hard it's a wonder they don't crumble in my mouth as a growl escapes me. "Fuck off."

Harrison shakes his head and moves back down the stairs as I watch him head to the bar and speak with Lottie. I have this over-whelming need to claim her, to mark her as mine so every man and woman knows who she belongs to. It's out of character, and I know I need to walk away but it's not as easy as it looks. The desire to claim her is fighting with the desire to hurt her like she hurt me, but then maybe I should thank her. Lottie leaving made me the man I am today, and I'm proud of what I've achieved so far. I'm filthy rich, get grade-A pussy whenever I want, and more importantly, nobody fucks with me. Probably because they know I have zero fucks to give about anyone other than my family, and grudgingly, I add my friends to that list.

Lottie's eyes fly to mine and I know Harrison has told her. Her cheeks turn pink and I don't know if it's anger at me for getting in her way or embarrassment for getting rejected. All I know is that it makes me hard. I want to find out if the rest of her skin is that sexy pink color.

I raise my glass to her, baiting her and having no clue to what end, yet I can't help it. She consumes my every thought and I want to punish her for it. Punish her for leaving me, for making it so I can't fucking forget her.

I watch as she storms toward the stairs, arguing with the bouncer before Harrison nods at him to let her through. I turn, leaning on the balcony with my elbow as I watch her approach. Lottie has always had a quick temper, and it's a beautiful thing to watch. I swallow the last sip of whiskey as she reaches me and place the glass aside. I see Harrison hovering just behind her, concern on his face and it makes my blood boil. She doesn't belong to him.

But she's not yours either, a tiny voice whispers in my ear and I shove the thoughts aside. "Can I help you?"

Lottie moves fast as she slaps me hard. No, not a light slap, a full-on whack across the face. It barely hurts, just stuns me as I rock back. I reach up to touch my cheek as Harrison dives to grab Lottie, but I put my hand up to stop him and he pauses. He looks aghast, unease on his face as if he knows what's coming. I have the exact excuse I need to fire her now. Lottie crossed a line and he knows that. Yet I find I'm enjoying this far too much to give it up just yet, despite the sting tingling my cheek.

"You fucking asshole. How dare you poke your nose in my life. You have no fucking right."

I watch her chest heaving, her face wild and all I want to do is pin her against the wall and kiss her until I consume all that fire. "I have every right. You work for me."

Lottie throws her hands in the air. "Oh, is that how it works? I work for him too. Doesn't he have a say?" She points at Harrison who puts his hands up and steps back with a raised brow.

"Don't fucking test me, Lottie."

"Or what, you big prick? You gonna try and wreck my life more than you have already? You don't own me, Linc."

Hearing her call me Linc after all this time is like a balm to my soul. She's the only person who calls me that, and up until now, she's kept me as Lincoln or Mr. Coldwell.

I move closer, crowding her as people walk past, their eyes seeking the drama and the show we're providing for them now.

I know Harrison is confused by the familiarity between us and he'll have questions but for now, I need to shut this down before I do something stupid like kiss her treacherous lips. "I have no wish to own you either."

I see my words have hit their mark and smirk as a feeling of satisfaction moves through me. "You'll go home and if I decide you can keep your job, you'll be on a final written warning for gross misconduct."

I feel every nerve in my body buzz with the knowledge she's about to tell me to shove my job, giving me exactly what I want. Yet instead of the jubilation of knowing I've gotten my way, I feel a small whisper of regret that this has come to an end so soon.

I see a plethora of emotions cross her face, anger, hate, and suddenly defeat, and it twists my gut in a way I hadn't expected.

"Fine, I apologize for hitting you."

Her eyes are on the floor, as she speaks, and I don't like it. "Look at me when you speak." My bark makes her chin lift, her eyes finding mine and I see the burning hatred I feel reflected in her eyes, but it's preferable to the defeat of a few moments ago.

Her fingers twist around each other as she speaks, and I know she hates this. Lottie is a prideful little thing and still has no control over her emotions. "I said I apologize for hitting you. It was out of line and uncalled for. I should never have lost my temper."

"Go home, and someone will be in touch about your position and if you'll resume your job here."

Lottie nods and rushes away and I know what happens next. She'd always cry after losing her cool, the tension too much for her. I want to taste those tears on my lips and know that it was because of me.

Harrison moves toward me. "You want me to sack her?"

I feel the bite of resignation in his voice. "No, she can continue, but maybe now you'll agree she isn't cut out for the VIP floor."

Harrison studies me and I won't give him the satisfaction of looking at him, especially as I'm watching Lottie pick up her bag from the back of the bar. Her eyes lock on mine once more and I'm sure I can see the tell-tale glint of tears in her eyes, and it makes my dick stiffen.

"I don't get you, Lincoln. She just handed you the perfect reason to get rid of her and you don't take it. And if anyone else had done what she just did, they'd be facing a police cell or worse. Yet you let her get away with it. Why?"

"None of your business."

"Wrong, this is my business when it affects Ruin."

I turn to him my stare cold. "Leave it, Harrison."

He shakes his head. "Whatever."

He walks away, leaving me to ponder his words. He's right. Nobody speaks to me like that, for certain nobody lays their hands on me and gets away with it, but despite my better judgment, Lottie gets away with it.

I feel the web I'm weaving tighten and wonder for a second if I'm the spider and she's the fly or if I'm going from prey to victim.

I text my security to ensure they're following Lottie home. She's taking the bus each night, which is stupidly irresponsible and dangerous. I have no care for her as such, but I wouldn't want her to get hurt, at least not before I've had my fun with her.

5: Lottie

I FOCUS ON MY BREATHING AS I LET THE WARM WATER FROM THE shower ease the tension from my shoulders. Mary was surprised to see me home early, but she seemed to sense I needed some space and, instead of asking the hard questions I could see on her lips, she squeezed my shoulder and left to go home.

The woman is sixty-five years old and has three grandchildren she never sees. I know Eric fills a hole in her life, but I'll never be able to repay her for the things she does for us.

Without her I'd be lost. She's a shining example of kindness and yet I hate the sympathy I saw in her eyes when she looked at me tonight.

This is all Lincoln's fault, that man is the devil incarnate. Ever since the first night when he'd shown me how weak he thought I was, he's been fucking with me. Watching me like a stalker hunting his prey and that was how he made me feel, like prey.

He never spoke to me or approached me again, but I felt it and I also know he was the reason Marc was fired. I'd wanted to confront him, but when I spoke to Marc about it he denied it and said he had been offered a manager's position elsewhere, so I had no proof, just my assumptions. To prove a point to me, that he has power and I have none. It's the same as it always was before. I'm weak and don't belong, only last time he was on my side and now he's my adversary. The other difference is I now have a hell of a lot more to lose than just my pride and my heart.

Turning off the water, I wrap my hair in a towel and pull on the old, faded nightshirt I've worn since I was a teen. It's ratty and thin, but it's also soft and comforting and reminds me of my mom.

God, I miss her.

There are days when I think I can't go on without her to guide me, to show me what to do but I'm her daughter, and she gave up everything to protect me and keep me safe and I won't let her down.

I check in on Eric once more, smoothing his hair from his face as he sleeps soundly. He's always had the ability to sleep like the dead. As if he doesn't have a care in the world and I thank God that didn't change with the loss of our mother.

It's still early for me, barely eleven, and I should take the opportunity to sleep while I can, but my eyes stray to the mountain of bills on the side table, and I know I have to face this head-on and not behave like an ostrich, as much as oblivion tempts me.

Two hours later, I've run the numbers again and again and still I know that even with my added wages I can't make the payments. Defeat weighs heavy and I shrug it off with a wiggle of my shoulders. I can't give in to despair, I won't.

I navigate the old laptop, which Mary very kindly gave me, and begin to surf the internet. I've been avoiding this, the thought of selling my body makes me feel physically sick, but the alternative is we end up on the streets and I won't let that happen.

I click through different sites, my nausea growing as I see the requests some of these men make. Sickness churns in my belly as my fingers scroll through the sites. After about an hour I'm about to close the laptop when my eye catches on an advert.

It's asking for applicants for a virginity auction and the logo at the bottom is one I recognize all too well. I press on the application form where there are more details. Reading through, I feel hope burn a little brighter. This could be exactly what I need. I'd get to keep half the revenue for the auction. I'd only have to sleep with the winning bidder once to fulfill the contract and then I'd sign an exclusive contract to work in the member's section of the club for a year and that would involve just bar work. Anything else would be voluntary.

Before I can chicken out, I fill in the form and pray that Lincoln doesn't get to see them. The humiliation would be one thing, but I could take that, my pride would just have to take the hit for my sweet baby brother, but what if he put the brakes on it out of spite like he did tonight? I hit send and close my eyes. I have a moment of panic where I want to snatch it back, to change my mind but I can't, and perhaps that's for the best.

Be brave, Lottie, be strong, and you'll become everything you're meant to be. My mother's last words to me whisper through the air as if she's there beside me and I feel comfort from them.

Finally, I curl up on the couch and let exhaustion pull me under. Tomorrow is a new day and a chance for hope.

I wake with a gasp hearing the phone by my side ringing. I'm disorientated as I grab for it, my voice still husky with sleep. "Hello?"

"Violet, it's Harrison Brooks."

My heart thunders in my chest as I wait to hear my fate. "Hello, Mr. Brooks."

"I got your application."

I swallow around my dry tongue. "I see." I wait for him to shut me down.

"Are you sure this is something you want to do?"

I pause. Of course I'm not but beggars can't be choosers. I don't say that, I won't air any more of my dirty laundry to him like I did last night.

"Yes, I'm sure." I try and imbue my voice with confidence and I'm not sure if I pull it off.

"Very well. We'll discuss it at the next managers' meeting and let you know if you've made it through to the next round."

"Next round?"

"Yes, there are over fifty applicants to pick through and we only want five girls."

My excitement from last night falls. "Oh."

His voice softens. "Violet, I want you to know that I'm rooting for you."

"Why?"

He chuckles and it's deep and throaty and I wish I could be attracted to him, not the evil spawn Lincoln Coldwell.

"I see the spirit in you, and it reminds me of someone I once knew."

"Thank you."

I'm hesitant to ask, afraid of the answer, but I have to know if I still have a job, especially as the auction is becoming less likely. A virgin auction suggests younger girls and I'd probably be the only geriatric virgin in the lot. Taking a deep breath I ask, "Is my job still open?"

Harrison sighs and I close my eyes as tears sting the back of my nose.

"Last night was gross misconduct, Violet. I have to say I'm surprised Mr. Coldwell didn't have you dismissed and arrested for assault. Believe me when I say he doesn't tolerate that kind of thing and neither do I."

I try not to sniff and alert him to my dismay. "I understand."

"That said, you still have a job if you want it."

"I do?"

Excitement and hope bloom in my chest as I jump from the couch noticing it's still only eight am.

His voice is tinged with warmth when he answers. "Yes, Violet you do. But I suggest you stay out of Lincoln's way. I have no idea what the beef is between you two, but I don't want it spilling out into the club."

"It won't, I promise."

"And you won't be given any shifts on the VIP floor. We feel your temperament is a tad too short for some of our more excitable guests."

Disappointment tightens my shoulders and I had to roll them to ease it. "I understand." And I did, the optics were such that it looked like I was the problem as far as Harrison was concerned and he'd always side with his partner. I got that. I didn't like it, but I got it.

"Good. We'll see you tonight for your shift and, Violet, a word of warning. Lincoln isn't a man to be crossed. You'd do well to remember that."

"Thank you, Mr. Brooks."

Hanging up, I do a little dance and try not to let the relief send me giddy. It might seem silly but even the small victory of keeping my job is cause for celebration.

When Eric wakes, we decide to spend the day at the park with a picnic of homemade sandwiches and chips. As the late spring sun bakes the day in warmth, I hope that maybe things might go my way this time, pushing aside the fact I've agreed to auction off my body in exchange for this small reprieve is something I don't examine.

6: Linc

I GRIT MY JAW, GRINDING MY TEETH TO THE POINT MY DENTIST WILL have a coronary as Harrison speaks. We're at a meeting to go over the five candidates for the auction and the final image on the screen sends my blood pressure through the roof. His eyes are on me as he goes over Lottie's application.

"As you all may be aware, Violet is one of our bar staff. She's twenty-five, unmarried, and her background checks are clear. She's agreed to the medical but there are no red flags."

"Don't you think she's a little old to be a virgin?"

Ryker frowns as we all look at the image she sent in with her application. She's holding a sun hat on her head as the wind tries to blow it away. She looks fresh-faced and so beautiful it makes my chest ache before I swallow the feeling down.

Harrison nods. "I'd considered that, but I mean, look at her. She's gorgeous and she has a sweetness about her which our customers on the ground floor love. She makes more in tips than any other bartender."

"I have to admit, I'd definitely tap that given the chance."

Beck smirks and I have the overwhelming urge to punch my friend in the face. "Have some fucking respect, Beck," I snarl. Instant regret at showing my hand making me even angrier than I already am. I don't want Lottie doing this damn auction, but she's nothing to me so why should I care?

"What's your problem, Lincoln?"

I lock eyes with my friend. "I don't have a problem. Do you?"

Beck holds my stare, never one to back down, and the tension in the room rises until Audrey breaks it.

"Okay, children enough with the pissing contest. I think Violet is perfect and as you say, she's charming and sweet. I think she'll be a huge draw."

She's charming and sweet. She's also a liar, but if she wants to sell her body then who am I to stop her?

"Whatever, just sort it out. I have a meeting to get to." I stand abruptly, pushing my chair back and leave the room. I have no interest in hearing the details and I'm regretting we even started this auction. As I make my way down the stairs, I spot the woman who's consumed too many of both my waking and sleeping hours.

She's shaking a cocktail, concentration on her face, allowing me the freedom to watch her close up without her seeing. As if pulled by a magnet, I walk toward the other end of the bar and order a beer from one of the other girls. I sit there like a goddamned stalker watching her for almost ten minutes before she spots me.

Her spine stiffens and her head turns as if she senses me. Her features still and her eyes lock on mine, and I hate that I can't read her expression. There was a time when I knew every thought in her head but not anymore. This Violet Miller is a mystery to me, and perhaps I should let it stay that way, but I just can't seem to walk away when I know I should.

As the bar fills up, I move closer to her section and hold up my glass when she looks at me. I see her bite back her reaction and paste a false smile on her face. It makes me want to laugh out loud for probably the first time in as long as I can remember.

"Mr. Coldwell, what can I get you?"

I cock my head, subtly inhaling the sweet scent of cherries that is, and has always been, Lottie to me. I drink her in from head to toe and fight to curb my natural response. Which is her, splayed out naked on this bar for me.

"What do you suggest?"

I study her pretty face, wondering how the hell this woman is still a virgin and have to bite my tongue to stop the question from slipping out.

"How about a Liquid Viagra? You look like a man who could do with one of those."

With anyone else I'd be fuming at the insult, but this woman has some kind of invisible hold on me and instead, a bark of laughter erupts from me, startling us both.

I leaned forward when my mirth had subsided and watch the pulse in her neck hammer silently, but she doesn't back down. She's still mad as hell at me and getting her licks in as best she can. Lottie was always scrappy, even when she was a tiny little thing in pigtails.

"I can assure you, Lottie, I don't need Viagra in any form and if you wanted to ask about my sex life, then you should have just come out with it."

I see her cheeks pink at the point I scored, and she huffs.

"Not if you were the last man on earth."

"How could you possibly know that since you're so..." I let my gaze slide over her in slow perusal loving the way her body responds seemingly against her wishes, "innocent."

Her eyes flash to mine and I see mild panic as she freezes as if waiting for the ax to fall. She gets jolted by another barmaid, and it seems to snap her out of her trance.

"Trust me, I know."

Her words sound like a challenge, and I smile. She seems to have forgotten that I never back down from a challenge and the woman in front of me is the sexiest I've had in a long time. "That sounds like a challenge, Lottie." I quirk a brow at her and she pales.

Spinning, she begins grabbing different liquors and I watch as she measures and pours, adding ice before she shakes the cocktail shaker like it's someone's neck she's wringing and by the vigor she puts into it, I think it's mine she's imagining.

When she finally pours the bright blue liquid through a sieve over a glass full of ice, I wonder what the hell, kind of poison she's trying to give me.

"There you go, Mr. Coldwell."

I glare at the drink with apprehension.

"This is a Liquid Viagra?"

"No, I changed my mind. It's an Adios Motherfucker."

With that, she smirks, turns on her heel, and moves to serve the next customer at the crowded bar. I'm left with a feeling in my chest that's almost happy, a smile trying to force its way past my lips.

AFTER THE EXCHANGE WITH LOTTIE, I TAKE MY DRINK TO THE OFFICE we share with Harrison and find it thankfully empty, which is a blessing. Logging into the Club Ruin system, I find the file I'm looking for and skim over the other applicants' details before I get to the one that I'm truly here for.

Violet Miller.

I wrinkle my nose at her address, hating that she's living in such a dangerous part of the city I love. My eyes scan the details, looking for information and insight into the woman who is equal parts intriguing and infuriating to me.

Age, height, weight, all mundane things, and then I get to the part where it asks about her dating history and why she wants to do this. Beck insisted on these questions as we need to know if we'll be facing any jealous boyfriends and also what the motivation was for selling something so personal.

A frisson of delight lights up in my chest to see she doesn't have a boyfriend and she hasn't for the last two years. For some reason the thought of Lottie with another man makes me seethe with anger and possessiveness. I know it's a holdover from when we dated as teenagers, but I'm a very demanding person and with Lottie it's different. She was the first and only person to break my heart and that experience shaped me and made it so I never made the mistake of letting a woman close to me again.

I slam the laptop closed in anger, wondering what the hell I'm doing. I don't want Lottie or care about her so why am I obsessing over her? Is it just a nostalgic trip down memory lane, to a time when life was simpler? Yes, that must be it, that, and the fact I haven't gotten laid in months.

Standing, I decide to head home. My phone rings in my hand and I glance at the screen to see my mom is calling. I hesitate, debating whether to answer or not, but I've sent her last three calls to voicemail, and she'll be banging on my door in the next twenty-four hours if I don't answer. "Hey, Mom."

"Darling, you finally answered my call."

I scrub my hand over my face, guilt weaving a heavy shroud over my shoulders. "Yeah, sorry. I've been busy with work."

"You work too hard. You need to get out and have more fun in your life."

This is the same conversation we always have, my mother worries, as is her right according to her. "I have fun."

"When was the last time you smiled?"

"Tonight, actually," I answer with delight at the fact I don't have to lie to her.

"Oh, tell me more?"

I hear the glee in her tone and want to keep that joy from dissipating. My mother, despite her luxurious life and the ladies she lunches with regularly, is lonely. I see it when she thinks I'm not looking. My father is a faithless pig who doesn't deserve her and, more and more, he leaves my mother alone so he can run around with his floozies. I have no clue as to why she puts up with it, and I've given up trying to get her to leave him.

"I saw Violet Miller earlier in passing and we chatted." I have no idea why I said that and regret it the moment the words fall from my lips.

"Oh, my little Violet. How is she?"

"Good." I don't say more because what can I say? She's more fuckable than ever. I can't get rid of the hard-on in my pants since I met her. She's about to auction off her virginity.

My mother laughs. "Oh, my darling, as descriptive as ever I see. Is she married?"

"No, Mom, she isn't."

"I always thought you two might get together, you know."

This surprises me. "You did?"

"Yes. You always looked at her like she hung the moon, and she'd follow you anywhere."

"We were kids."

"Oh, I know that, sweetheart, but still. She was a lovely girl. I was sad when they left the way they did. How is her mother?"

I realize I haven't asked her a single thing about her life, too captivated by her attitude and the way she makes my dick hard. "I have no idea."

"Oh."

I can hear the disappointment in my mother's voice and hate that I put it there. "I'll ask her next time I see her."

"You're seeing her again?"

God, when will I stop my brain from spewing out words to her? My mother has always been the one woman who can wrap me around her little finger. Well, she and Lottie, but afterward it was just my mother. She's the only woman I trust or will ever trust again.

"Perhaps, I frequent the place she works, so maybe." I know her next question and want to cut it off at the knees before she has the chance to sink her teeth into this conversation. "Mom, I have to go. I'll come over on Sunday and we can have lunch. Love you."

I hang up before she can respond and grip the back of my neck. Now I've gotten myself caught in a predicament of my own making and it's Lottie's damn fault.

That woman is the bane of my existence.

7: Lottie

Since the night I made Lincoln the Adios Motherfucker cocktail he's stayed out of my way. A big part of me is grateful and relieved but a small part I don't want to acknowledge is disappointed. I hate that he can still evoke even that amount of feeling in me.

On the positive, I've signed the contract for the auction, and it's now confirmed. I'll be one of the five girls up on the podium on the night. My belly flutters with nerves even though it's two weeks out.

I push that aside as I wipe my hands over the short, silver, backless dress I'm to wear tonight. Harrison informed me that I'd be required to work a week on the third floor where the auction will be held. I hadn't known a lot about that part of the club until he explained it was a sex club.

I was a little shocked, to say the least, but I shouldn't have been, given the auction. I signed the non-disclosure agreement forbidding me from discussing the third floor or anyone I might see up there. I didn't care about that, who would I tell? I have no life apart from the club, the diner, and Eric, and I'll go to the grave before I tell him what I'm doing.

Exiting the bathroom, I run straight into the last person I want to see. "Mr. Coldwell."

He looks dashing in a grey three-piece suit, his blue eyes bright and his hair messy in a way I know he's been running his fingers through it in frustration.

"Lottie."

We stare at one another for a moment, the electricity arcing between us as strong as it's ever been but now tinged with an undercurrent of mistrust and wariness.

His eyes sweep over me from head to toe and I try not to fidget even as I feel my nipples bead in the flimsy dress. His eyes, so expressive in the past, give nothing away of how he's feeling. He's a closed book now, so far from the boy who'd tell me his dreams and desires with excitement and hope simmering inside him.

I always knew he'd do great things and everything I've read about him over the last few weeks has only confirmed that. He's successful in his own right, not just because of Kennedy Enterprises. He's also a huge benefactor for several charities, some of which are very close to my own heart.

"I should get going."

"It's your week on the third floor?"

"Yes."

He nods and I see his jaw flexing. "I'll let you go. Have a good evening."

"You, too."

I wring my hands together as I watch him turn away from me and walk away. I have the overwhelming urge to call him back but what would be the point? Too much has happened for us ever to salvage a friendship from this mess.

The third floor isn't what I imagined it to be. There's a small bar area with stools for those wanting to sit. An array of top-shelf alcohol and champagne, and the glasses here are all real crystal. It faces a small dance floor with a stage behind it and has a huge cross in the middle. Around the outside of the room are booths of seating.

The décor is all black and the lighting is moody and chic, giving the customers privacy. I try not to stare when I see a movie star, known as a heartthrob to millions of women, with his tongue down a man's throat. I have no interest in who he wants to be with but find it sad that he keeps it a secret, or maybe he wants it that way. I have no idea and as I see more and more famous people, I wonder how they manage to keep this such a secret from the world. Mixed in with the famous are the regular rich people from old to young, male and female alike.

Tonight, I'll shadow Chantelle, who has worked this floor for six months. She's lovely with red hair and brown eyes. Every part of her petite body screams sex and she uses it with an ease that I wish I had.

"When you deliver their drinks, they'll sometimes try and cop a feel. If you don't feel comfortable with that, let one of the bouncers on the floor know and they'll have a word. Everything up here is consensual, and respect is to be shown at all times. They're aware of that, but some do try and push the boundaries, but Harry is strict about it."

"He seems like a nice man."

"Oh, Harry is great. They all are, although Beck is my favorite. He's wild in the sack."

I feel my eyes widen in shock. "You've had sex with him?"

Her laugh is light and tinkling. "Yes, a couple of times."

A thought pops into my head and the question is out before I can think better of it. "Do all the owners play at the club?"

"Everyone except Harry. As he runs it, he likes to keep things separate."

"Oh."

Chantelle wraps an arm around me and smiles. "Come on, Vi. Let me show you the ropes."

I spend the night serving drinks and receiving inquisitive looks and compliments from the members. Some of them want to chat and flirt and up here it's encouraged, but so far none have pushed my boundaries past what I'm comfortable with. A squeeze on the ass at worst and even that stopped quickly after one of the bouncers had a word, although that wasn't my doing.

My tips alone have doubled my wages for the week and all I've done is smile and deliver over-priced alcohol to tables.

Around midnight, things begin to get a little wilder. Two men and a woman were putting on a show in the middle of the dance floor. I see the movie star who was kissing a man earlier with his hand up the woman's skirt as she leans back into another man who I think is an NFL player. His hands are caressing her exposed breasts as movie star man fingers her to a loud orgasm. I've watched porn, everyone has, but this feels different, more real. Probably because it is, and I find myself intrigued with how my body is responding. It feels wrong to enjoy it but at the same time so right.

Exposed pleasure is visible on the woman's face as she lets herself go, not caring that others are watching or perhaps that's only heightening her pleasure. All I know is it's hot and makes hot arousal pool in my belly.

"Does it turn you on, Lottie?"

I jump, almost losing the tray in my hand at the whispered words against my ear.

Linc steadies me with a firm hand on my bicep and I right the empty tray. His eyes are on me, and they are full of dark desire.

I don't want him to know how much this affects me. "I was just intrigued."

"Hmm."

His hand skims my exposed spine, slowly dipping lower until his fingers are on the curve of my ass. I shiver as goosebumps erupt on my skin.

"Are you cold, Lottie?"

"No." My voice sounds breathy and soft, and I swallow to clear it.

He takes my hips in his hands and spins me to face the trio of people who are now naked in the middle of the room. I feel the solid warmth of Lincoln at my back, the hard ridge of his erection through his suit pants pressed where his hands had been moments ago.

"Watch as he makes her come again and again on his hand, his face, and then his cock."

I watch transfixed by the erotic sight before me. Movie man is on his knees between the couple, his mouth moving from the NFL guy's cock to the woman's, who I have a feeling is a politician, pussy. All three look enthralled as if they're the only three people in the room.

Linc's hand moves from my hip to the edge of my dress, and I feel my breath stutter in my chest. I want this. I want to feel his hands on me. I've craved it since the first time he did it weeks ago. The memory of the way he touched me is ingrained in my brain.

As his fingers touch my exposed pussy, he stills, his lips finding my ear, his warm breath tickling my skin. "Do you know how hard it makes me knowing that you've been walking around here all night with your cunt bare?"

He slides his fingers over my pussy, working my clit, sliding a finger inside me, and stroking me until I sag against him, my legs weak. I glance around but most people are watching as the NFL guy, who is lying on the floor as the woman rides his face, is fucked by the movie guy. It's like being on the set of a porn film, only this is real and feels more sensual than dirty or sleazy.

"Watch them, Lottie. Look at the pleasure they're giving and receiving." His free arm bands around my waist and my breathing becomes raspy and uneven as Linc works my clit, the wet glide of his fingers proving to him how much I want this.

I grip his arm, the suit fabric abrasive against my skin as I feel my climax build. Pleasure coiling inside me from his touch. "Linc."

I don't know what it is I want but I know I need something.

"Come for me, Lottie. Give it to me now."

I bow forward as my orgasm hits me and clamp my thighs around his hand as he turns to swallow my scream with his mouth. Linc doesn't stop kissing me until my climax has subsided. He lifts his head and, for the first time since we met up again, I see the man I knew, his emotions raw and vulnerable. A second later I see his expression go blank as he lets me go, my legs wobbly.

Linc steps back and looks around before he pins me with a gaze. "Well, that performance should get some interest for the auction."

His words are like ice water on my skin. "You bastard."

He smirks. "Now, now, Lottie. Remember your place."

"Oh, I remember my place."

I step toward him, anger racing through me like a live wire. He humiliated me again and I let him, but that was the last time. I poke him in the chest. "That's the last time you touch me, Lincoln. Stay the fuck away from me."

He puts his hands in his pockets as he smirks. "Oh, Lottie, I don't think so."

"If you touch me again, I'll tell your mother exactly the kind of man you are. You think she'd like to know her son forces himself on a woman?"

His brows are hard slashes as he looks at me and I know we've drawn the interest of Harrison and Audrey, who are watching not five feet from us. I don't care. I don't give a fuck about anything apart from letting this man know what a bastard he is.

"Don't threaten me, Lottie. You're not playing games with a little boy anymore."

"Oh, I'm aware. The boy I knew would never have treated me like that, but then maybe the boy I knew didn't really exist."

"Let me make this clear. When I touch you again, Lottie, it will be because you can't go another second without my touch. In fact, I might just make you beg."

"Go to hell."

"I'm already there, sweetheart."

I walk away trying to maintain as much dignity as I can, biting my lip to hide the quiver. I hate that this upsets me so much. The rest of the night I steer clear of Lincoln Coldwell and avoid the gazes of the patrons.

I know why I'm doing this but at times like this I wish I could just run away and forget everything, but I can't. I have responsibilities and I wouldn't want it any other way. Eric is my driving force, my reason to keep going and that is what I'll do.

Fuck Lincoln Coldwell.

I'm changing out of my dress in the locker room when I hear heels clip on the floor and look across to see Audrey Kennedy walking toward me. My stomach trips over and sinks like a stone.

"Violet, do you have a moment?"

"Yes, of course, Miss Kennedy."

Her smile is kind as she motions for me to sit. "Please, call me Audrey."

"Okay, Audrey."

It's a classy, old-world name that suits the woman beside me. She's stunning like a Hollywood actress from the golden age.

"I saw your exchange with Lincoln."

It's on the tip of my tongue to apologize like I've done all my adult life. A habit that's hard to break, and I know the root cause, but I'll never speak of it to a living soul. "I apologize for the scene I caused but I won't apologize for what I said to him."

Her lips tip up and her eyes sparkle. "As well you shouldn't. He was out of line, and I have to say it's very out of character for him. Lincoln prides himself on his aloof control and I've never seen him behave that way with another employee, or anyone to be honest."

I give a mirthless laugh. "I guess I bring out the worst in him."

Audrey purses her lips. "Harrison says this isn't the first run-in you two have had so I looked into you."

I swallow, wondering what she's found as my heart hammers hard in my chest. "Oh?"

"Yes, I wondered when I heard Lincoln call you Lottie, but my private investigator confirmed that you're *the* Lottie Miller who broke his heart all those years ago."

My mouth falls open. "I'm sorry? I broke *his* heart?"

"Yes. I was with him after and he'd kill me for saying this but what you did changed him. It made him hard and distrustful of people."

I stand and pace because I don't want to snap at the woman who holds the fate of myself and my brother in her hands. "With all due respect, Audrey, I have no idea what he told you, but the only person with a broken heart was me. Now, I understand we were kids and shit happens but Lincoln has been nothing but a dick to me since we met up again and that's not okay."

Audrey stands, smoothing out the non-existent wrinkles in her red pencil skirt. "Look, Violet, I can see that there's way more to this than I'm aware of, and perhaps even the two of you, but I do know that for the first time in ten years, I'm seeing a side of my cousin that has been dead. He's alive and even if that is resulting in him being, as you put it, a dick, then I'm glad for it. I have a feeling you're exactly what he needs."

"I won't be his emotional punching bag."

Audrey flutters a hand to her throat. "Oh goodness me, I'd never suggest such a thing. Just give him a chance to show you who he is now, and I think you'll be surprised."

"You did a background check on me, so you know I have a brother and you must know my circumstances. I don't have the time or the energy for Lincoln's tantrums and manipulations. I respect that you care for your cousin, but I can't be the person to fix his emotional baggage, whatever that might be." I stand my ground and I hope like hell I'm doing the right thing. She could fire me and then I'm back where I started or worse.

"I do know your difficulties, and I'm sorry to hear of them. It must be very difficult for you. Just don't close yourself off from him. He isn't showing you his best side, but I have a feeling if anyone can pull him in from the cold, it's you, Violet Miller."

"And if I say no? Do I get fired or pulled from the auction?"

"Of course not. I'm not an ogre, Violet."

I smile, relief settling over me. "I think it's ogres."

Audrey grins and it transforms her from beautiful to absolutely stunning.

"Keep being you, Violet, and stand up to him. He's so used to people pandering to him and running like scared little kittens that he's forgotten what it is to be humble."

"I have no choice but to stand up for myself." I don't add that I have no one else to do it, because it makes me look sad and I like this woman. Although our positions in life are vastly different, I think, in another life, perhaps a former life, we would've been fast friends.

"I see that, but I also see a woman who's determined and hard-working. If you want out of this life, Violet, I have no doubt in my mind that you'll succeed."

"Thank you, that means a lot coming from you."

"It's the truth."

I walk out with her and see the club is empty except for a clean-up crew who are wiping down every surface with an industrial cleaner.

"Good night, Violet, and please don't worry. Your position here is safe, no matter what you decide."

I nod and head down the back stairs. I've already decided I'll be keeping a wide berth from Lincoln Coldwell. His cousin might see something in him worth redeeming but I don't. At least that's what I keep reiterating as I catch the subway home to my tiny, damp apartment.

8: Linc

I DIDN'T WANT TO ATTEND. I LEFT IT UNTIL THE FINAL MOMENT BEFORE I jumped in my car and raced to the club. It's the night of the auction and since the encounter with Lottie my temper has been the cause of many whispered words throughout the club. Everyone is avoiding me as I stomp up the stairs to the third floor like an angry bull.

Touching her again had been a mistake because now I only crave her more. Seeing the anger and hurt in her eyes after the way I behaved filled me with shame. I hadn't intended to hurt her. Fuck, I hadn't intended to touch her. It was as if my body had a mind of its own around her like some fucking super magnet pulled me towards her at every turn.

Feeling her fall apart in my arms, bringing her to climax in that way as we watched the trio on the floor, had affected me. Had me wanting her in ways I'd sworn years ago I'd never let myself feel again. I'd panicked and pretended I'd done it to drum up interest for the auction.

I was a pig and I knew it, and if I hadn't known it, my friends had made it very clear what they thought of my behavior, especially Audrey. She hadn't said anything but the disappointed looks she's speared my way landed a blow.

The room was set with the stage backlit to show the five girls off to their full advantage. The room was full to capacity with some very big hitters. Glancing around the room, I knew one of these men would take Lottie's virginity tonight and I feel my stomach roil. The thought of any of these men touching her makes me see red.

"Big night."

Beck is at my shoulder as I take the drink he hands me. "Yep."

"Still in a pissy mood, I see."

"Fuck off, Beck. Don't you have a life to save?"

"You know you could stop this if you wanted. We have a clause in the contract that says any of the owners can stop the auction at any time if they see fit."

It's so tempting I feel my muscles tense as I try to still my body from moving. "Why would I do that?"

"Oh, I don't know, maybe because you have a hard-on for the exquisite little Lottie."

My head snaps to him. "Don't fucking call her that." My tone is cold.

"Why not? It's her name, and you call her Lottie."

"That's different."

"Why?"

He's goading me and I'm falling into his trap. "Do what you want, Beck."

"Want to know what I think?"

"Do I have a choice?"

My eyes are on the stage as Harrison walks out and a hush falls over the room.

Beck leans closer, lowering his voice. "I think you really like her and you hate that. She brings out something soft in you."

"Bullshit, I'm exactly the same as I've always been."

"Wrong, she gets away with shit nobody else ever would. I mean she clocked you one and yet here she is, about to walk up on the stage."

My eyes are drawn to the stage as the first of the girls walk out dressed in white stockings and suspenders with little white lace bras

57

that leave fuck all to the imagination. It was Audrey's idea and if it had been any other time I would've been salivating with the rest of the men in here.

Yet as Lottie struts out last, her long lithe legs in three-inch stilettos, her fucking gorgeous body on display, all I want to do is run up there and throw my jacket over her to cover her from the eyes of these men.

Harrison is droning on about each girl's assets as I clench the glass in my hand until I feel it yanked from my grasp. I glare at Beck, who nods at the crack in the crystal.

"Chill, Lincoln."

"Lastly, we have Lottie, who is twenty-five, measuring in at a gorgeous thirty-four, twenty-two, with a C cup size."

I swallow the bile that's bubbling in my throat, feeling utter disgust for everything we're doing here tonight. These women might be willing but suddenly it all feels wrong.

The men around the tables are practically drooling as they leer at the women. I watch Lottie as she tries not to fidget. Her body is tense and she looks seconds away from bolting. I hope like fuck she does.

She might need the money, but I don't think she has it in her to go through with this. Granted, I don't know her motives, I never finished reading her file and I've avoided finding out about her, because I know once I do, I won't be able to help myself. I'll want to get involved and help her. She's my weakness and I won't let her use me again.

As the first two girls are auctioned at over one million dollars, I feel the hair on my neck prickle and look up to see her watching me with open hostility. I smile and wink, hoping she can see me. I know she does when her jaw hardens and her chin lifts. Damn, that backfired. She might well have been thinking of walking, but she won't now.

If I know anything about Lottie Miller, it's that she's as stubborn as a mule.

"Next up is Lottie. Shall we start the bidding at fifty thousand dollars?"

I edge forward a touch, moving down the side of the room beside the bidders as hands fly up. The bidding quickly exceeds one million and is still rising at an alarming rate. When it comes down to the last two bidders, I feel the knot in my stomach tighten. Archibald Crush is a seventy-six-year-old philanthropist with a penchant for younger women and more money than he could ever hope to spend. Cedric Chang is the other bidder and although he's much younger at fifty-one, he's into some very shady stuff and it was because of him we had to ban knife play.

Without conscious thought, my legs are moving to the stage. I see the shock on Lottie's face but I don't give her a chance to argue. Her mouth drops open as I bend at the waist, put my shoulder into her belly, and throw her over my shoulder.

"Auction's over."

With my hand covering her ass, I turn and stalk away, all the while she's kicking me and screaming at me to put her down.

"Lincoln, I swear to God if you don't put me down I'm going to castrate you."

I wince when a foot almost does the job for her, my hand lands on her ass in a hard smack, and she yelps.

I clear the room, feeling Beck watching me with a smirk. I'll deal with him later.

"Oh my god, you did not just spank me."

"Shut up, Lottie."

"No, asshole, you don't own me."

I carry her past the stairs as she kicks and screams, her tiny fists hitting my back.

"Lincoln Coldwell, if you don't put me down, I'll make you regret it."

I smack her ass again and she squeals in outrage, but when I place my hand over the warm skin to cover her from prying eyes, I find her warm and wet and my already hard cock turns to fucking stone.

I don't respond to her tirade, it only makes me want to fuck her more, so I let her rant.

"How dare you speak to me like that."

I push open the door to my office with my shoulder and see Ryker look up in surprise.

"Get out." His slow grin only makes me angrier. "Get the fuck out, Ryker." I keep a struggling Lottie over my shoulder as I glare at him.

"Violet, are you okay with me leaving?"

Bastard.

"Yes."

Her voice is shaking, and her wriggling is making me hard as nails.

"Then I'll leave you to it."

I throw her on the leather couch before stepping back. I'm fighting every primal urge I have to claim this woman and it's making me fucking crazy.

"Wrong, I do own you. I was your first kiss. I was the first man to put my fingers in your hungry cunt, and I'll be the first man to fuck you. So yes, Lottie, I do own you."

Her eyes are flashing fire as she struggles to cover her creamy body from my gaze and I can't resist licking my lips when I catch her eye. A blush steals over her cheeks and I know she's remembering how I made her come a few weeks ago.

"Why are you doing this, Lincoln?"

My eyes flash to her as I stalk closer, crowding her into the couch as I lean in, placing my hands on either side of her thighs so she's trapped. She leans back as if trying to get away, but I see the way the pulse in her neck beats wildly.

"Linc. To you, I'm Linc."

"You stopped being Linc the night you threw me away like trash."

Her words, so cold and hard, force regret like a bitter pill to flood through me. I did do that, but not for the reasons she thinks. I'd never treat her that way, but she doesn't know that, and I doubt she'd believe me now anyway.

"You were never trash, Lottie. You were always the rose among all the thorns in my life."

"Cheap words, but actions speak volumes, Lincoln."

I step back, knowing I need to come up with a new tactic. "Why are you selling your virginity and how the fuck are you still a virgin?"

I can't deny the thought that she's never let a man touch her or fuck her makes me happy because it makes me fucking ecstatic.

"None of your business."

"I'm making it my business."

"Why? Why do you even care? You have no idea what you've done by dragging me off the stage. I need to get back out there and see if I can fix this."

"Not gonna fucking happen."

She throws her hands up and I can see the frustration on her face, but also the exhaustion and it gives me the overwhelming urge to protect her, to ease her struggles, but I push those thoughts aside as I admit, "I always cared, Lottie."

She holds her palm up at me. "Stop, let's not rehash the past. I don't want to hear your lies and bullshit, Linc."

"Fine, tell me."

She stands and straightens her shoulders like a woman about to go to war. She's nearly a foot shorter than my six foot four, but still, she faces me down with her chin up and her head held high. She's spectacular.

"Fine, you want to know why?" She moves toward me until we're almost touching, and I look into her moss green eyes and see the determination there.

"Yes."

"For Eric. I'm doing this for Eric."

9: Lottie

"WHO THE FUCK IS ERIC?"

I smirk as he explodes, as I suspected he would. Lincoln Coldwell doesn't like to lose or be second. "Eric is everything to me."

His jaw ticks, and then he swallows before turning away from me and walking to the bar. Up until the moment Harrison took the chance away, I'd been going back and forth about my decision to enter this ridiculous auction. It felt humiliating and seedy standing up on stage in this virginal white lace but it was my only chance to pay my way out of the financial mess I'm in and help my brother.

"I see. Does Eric know you're doing this for him?"

"No, and he can never know."

"And why is that?"

"Because he wouldn't understand."

"But he'd accept your help and your money for whoring yourself?"

Shame and anger mix like a potent poison inside me, but it can't seem to stamp out the attraction I still feel for him. It was always strong even when we were young. I was sure I'd marry him one day and we'd live the happy life I'd read about in fairy tales. Fairy tales he'd taught me to read. Now the attraction is so much stronger but tainted with hate and betrayal.

"Why do you hate me, Lincoln?"

I watch his eyes flash to me and I know he hates it when I call him Lincoln, hiding the familiarity and affection we once had, but he doesn't control me anymore, at least not in that.

"I don't hate you, on the contrary, I'm trying to help you."

"By getting in my way?"

"I have a proposition for you."

The tiny hairs on the back of my neck rise in a silent warning and I know I'm not going to like what he says next. "Not interested."

Moving to the small table with a selection of crystal decanters, he pours himself a drink and lifts it up to me. I shake my head, the last thing I need is to have my head scrambled with alcohol when I'm dealing with him.

"I'll give you the money you need, or would have made from the auction, and in exchange, you'll marry me."

My eyes bug out and my jaw drops open as I stare at him. "Have you lost your mind?"

He smirks and lifts his eyebrows as if he isn't so sure about the answer himself. "No, I'll pay you two million dollars to be my wife for one year."

"Why would you do that?"

My brain swims with the number he just said. It might be a drop in the bucket for a man like him but for Eric and me, it's life-changing. I could settle our debts and find us a nice house to live in where we could be happy and still have some left for any medical problems that might arise for Eric in the future.

"I need to force my father to retire, and there's a stipulation in his contract that says if I marry, the position of CEO at Kennedy Enterprises passes to me, plus the board would rather see a married man take over than a single one. We can marry for a year and then we get a quick divorce and we both come out of this with what we want."

My stomach churns at the mention of his father, a hateful bully who I detest, and so did Linc and Clark. I can't be around him, and I won't have him anywhere near Eric. "Where would I live?"

"With me at my penthouse on Central Park."

"Would I get my own room?"

Am I really considering this?

Lincoln moves toward me, and I fight the urge to step back from him and show weakness. I once loved this man with my whole heart and he stomped on it like it was nothing. I wish I could say the hate I feel toward him now is all I feel. But he terrifies me because I know he could make me love him again and I wouldn't survive him a second time.

His hand lifts and he runs his knuckles down my jaw, pausing as it flitters over the pulse in my neck, before skimming the edge of my bra, lightly caressing the swell of my breast. I should stop him, but I feel paralyzed, caught in the tangle of seduction he's weaving around me.

"No, my sweet Lottie, if I'm paying two million dollars, I want to enjoy every inch of your delectable body." His voice is like gravel on my skin, and my nipples bead at the suggestion.

"Three million."

His fingers pause and he cocks his head to meet my eyes. I don't know why I made the demand, two million was ridiculous already, but the need to fight him and not give in makes me counter.

"Three million is a lot of money."

"One for the marriage, one for my virginity, and one for the right to fuck me afterward. Then I get my divorce after a year and I'm free of you."

My heart is almost beating out of my chest, and I'm seconds away from caving into his touch when he steps away.

"Deal, I'll have the contract drawn up."

Shock fills me but so does relief. I think of Eric and know I can do this. I can survive a year with this man, as long as I steel my heart and don't let myself fall for him again. Sex is sex. It doesn't have to involve emotion or love. Plenty of my friends from school had sex without love and so can I.

I hope.

I stick out my hand to shake his and he looks at it and then back to my face before his hands go to his belt. The clink of the metal is like thunder in the silence, and I feel electricity zip through my body as my heart beats out a wild rhythm.

"On your knees. Let's see if I'm going to get my money's worth."

Lincoln unzips his pants, and shoves his boxers down, exposing the hard, red, angry-looking head of his cock. I've never seen one up close and personal before. We never went this far when we were teens, just kissing and touching over the clothes. He'd always insisted we wait until I was eighteen before we had sex.

"I said. Get. On. Your. Knees." His voice is a dark command and I find myself sinking to my knees, so I'm face to face with his hard cock, the veins running up the length making me want to trace them with my tongue. A bead of pre-cum sits on the end and I find myself wanting to taste him.

Firm fingers tip my head up so I can see into the desire-filled pools of his eyes. His thumb traces my bottom lip, tugging it down as I flick my tongue out to wet my dry lips, finding his thumb instead.

"Do you have any idea how many times I've dreamed of this?"

I'm struck dumb by his words, a sensual cloud hanging over me, consuming every thought.

"Is this the first time you've sucked a cock, my little Lottie?"

I nod, unable to speak and see him blow out a shallow breath.

"Open your mouth."

I do as he says, letting him rub the end of his dick on my lips, coating me with the taste of him. It's salty but not unpleasant. Feeling braver, I lick around the head, getting a feel for the ridges along the silky velvet length of him. Like the rest of him, his cock isn't small and for a second, I'm fearful that he'll hurt me when he takes me.

As if he senses my fear, he strokes my cheek. "Relax, sweetheart. Open for me, take my cock in your sweet mouth."

I had no clue that dirty talk was a turn-on for me, but I feel desire soak my panties, an ache blooming between my legs.

I open and take him inside my mouth, bobbing my head just a little, and his groan of pleasure settles over my skin. Lincoln rubs my cheek, gently and I lean into his touch.

"Such a good girl."

I blossom at his praise, wanting to please him and earn his softness.

I dip lower, taking more and his hands tunnel into my long hair, gripping it tightly away from my face as the pinch makes me moan around his cock.

"Hmm, my dirty girl likes a bit of pain."

I bob lower as he begins to move his hips, rocking towards me, making me take more until I gag as he hits the back of my throat. He holds me there and I panic for a second, choking on his cock, until he pulls me away and I suck in air through my nose, spit dribbling down my chin as my eyes water.

"Breathe through your nose."

I take him again, doing as instructed and he moans.

"Fuck, this mouth was made for my cock."

I move faster, bobbing and sucking as he holds me, controlling my movements. I glance up, finding him watching me and the look in his eyes is dark and full of ownership, but something else too. A tenderness I recognize, a glimpse of the man I knew before.

I hold his gaze as I feel him swell inside my mouth.

"I'm gonna come. Decide where you want it."

I've never felt power like this before. This man is at my mercy, and I want it all. So, I keep going, increasing my speed until he swells again and holds me still. His seed shoots into my mouth as a roar fills the room. I can't take it all and some of his come drips down my chin.

Lincoln pulls out, his cock wet with his come and my saliva and he tucks himself away as he swipes his thumb over my chin, collecting the come I missed.

"You should have asked for ten million. It would've been worth every cent."

Holding his hand out he helps me to my feet and embarrassment washes over me. I can't believe I did that.

Linc wraps a hand around my back and hauls me close to his body, and I regret that I haven't seen the body beneath the suit yet, but the knowledge that I will sends a shiver of delight through me. His head dips and he kisses me, his tongue darting into my mouth and I know he can taste himself on my tongue and it fuels the arousal simmering in my blood.

When he pulls back, I'm a melting pot of lust and seconds away from climbing him and demanding he take me now.

"We taste like utter perfection."

God, this man and his dirty talk.

He releases me and I almost stumble as he moves to the desk and leans against it, crossing his arms over his chest and spreading his feet wide.

"I'll have the contracts drawn up on Monday. I can recommend a lawyer if you want someone to look over them for you. We'll marry next weekend."

"So soon?"

"Why wait?"

He's right but this is all happening so soon, and I can't keep up. "I need to explain this to Eric."

His brow drops and he gives me a cold look. "Do whatever you need to do but let me make one thing clear, Lottie. I won't tolerate any other man in our marriage. I require complete fidelity from you."

"Then I get the same."

"Of course."

"But Eric lives with me. I can't just leave him. He'll live with us."

"Absolutely not."

I smile, enjoying having the upper hand in this moment, but I know I need to explain who Eric is to me. "I need my bag from my locker."

Confusion and irritation cross his face. "Why?"

"Can you just get it for me, please?"

With a sigh, he walks from the room to do my bidding. He didn't ask for the combination but knowing Linc he already knows it.

I walk around the room looking at the pictures of the five of them on opening night, looking happy and proud. I spy a closet and move toward it, hoping I find something I can wear. I feel so exposed standing around in my underwear, especially while Linc is fully clothed.

I see a line of shirts and run my hands along them. I lift one to my nose and wrinkle it as I smell Harrison's aftershave on it. I move along until I find one that smells like Lincoln and slip it from the hanger. We seem to have reached a tentative truce and I don't want captain caveman going all grumpy about me wearing another man's shirt.

I button it and roll the sleeves as I wait.

When the door opens, he stops to take me in before he smirks. "I see you found the closet."

"Well, I can't walk around in my underwear."

"On the contrary, I think it should be part of the contract that you do."

I stare at him open-mouthed and ready to fight him on it until I see his lips twitch. Linc always had a dry sense of humor and I'd forgotten that about him. "Very funny."

"Don't laugh. If I thought I could get away with it I would."

"Well, you can't."

He hands me my bag and I rummage through it until I dig my old phone from the pocket. I check it for calls as I always do, I've been paranoid since Eric's last hypo. Satisfied all is well at home, I walk towards Lincoln and turn the screen to him, but he's looking at me.

"This is Eric."

He glares daggers at me and I fight the shiver of desire, which I know isn't the result he wanted. But one thing I do know about Linc is that he'd never physically hurt me. He might rip my heart out metaphorically speaking and stomp all over it but he'd never lift a finger in anger.

"I have no interest in seeing this man."

"Just look at the damn screen, Linc."

His knowing smirk as I use his shortened name makes me want to return his glare, but he looks at the screen.

Then his face falls, shock taking hold before his eyes come back to mine. "You have a son?"

The outrage on his face makes me want to laugh. "Duh, virgin remember? No, this is my baby brother, Eric." I look at the picture of us from his last birthday. We're eating a plate of nachos dripping with cheese and grinning at the camera. We'd gone to the movies for his birthday and had nachos on the way home.

"Your brother?"

"Yes. He's nine and I'm all he has in the world."

Confusion blanks Lincoln's face as he grasps my phone, taking a better look at the picture on my screen. "What about your mom?"

Emotion clogs my throat, but I force the words out. "She died three years ago from breast cancer."

His face falls and I see genuine emotion cross his handsome face. Linc has always been gorgeous, but now he's another level of God-like handsome. His square jaw, the high cheekbones, his long-lashed blue eyes, and full lips all add up to a drool-worthy man.

"I'm sorry."

"Thank you."

I take the phone back and tuck it into my bag.

"I guess I should go finish my shift on the third floor." I have no desire to go back up there, but now I'm not part of the auction, this is my regular night to work, so I should get to it.

"No, go home. I won't have you working here once we marry."

"But we aren't married yet, Lincoln, and we haven't signed the contracts either."

"No, but we will, and until then, you can take the time to spend with Eric."

It's tempting, the sheer level of exhaustion I'm feeling is like nothing I've felt before, but I won't let him think he can dictate what I can do. "Thank you but no. I'll finish my shift. You might change your mind and realize this is insane by morning and I need the money now you've screwed my chances of a big payout."

"I could fire you."

I nod. "Yes, you could." I let him know he holds that power because it's the truth, but I stand my ground, regardless. If Lincoln Coldwell thinks I'm going to sit back and let him walk all over me, then he has another thing coming. I might be a shadow of the Violet he once knew, but she's still inside me. Waiting for the energy to get out.

Linc sighs. "Go finish your shift. I'll take you home after."

"No need. I can take the subway like I do every night."

A shiver runs through him. "Do you know how dangerous taking the subway is at that time?"

"Of course I know, but I have no choice. My limo is in the shop and the Bentley is being serviced. Plus, I'm careful. I carry pepper spray."

"Still got a smart mouth, I see. Perhaps I can find a better use for it."

His eyes drop to my mouth, and I see the desire in them flare to life as he remembers what they were doing minutes ago, would be my guess. I need to go before we wind up back where we started. I want this man too much and I need some space to shore up my defenses against him.

I rush from the room, and he lets me go. The rest of the night I feel him watching me from the seat at the end of the bar, but it doesn't make me feel vulnerable and scared like it did before, it makes me feel safe. Which is ridiculous because he's the biggest threat to me of all.

10: Linc

I GLANCE ACROSS THE CAR AT LOTTIE WHO'S LOOKING OUT OF THE window. I drove her home last night and again after her shift at the diner today. She fought me at first, but she's learning quickly that I always get my way. I don't know why she insists on working at the Club or the diner now we have our agreement, but she doesn't trust I'll follow through.

She's wrong.

She doesn't know it yet but I'm never letting her go again. The night of the auction was like a reawakening for me. I quit fighting the pull she has over me and decided to control it instead. I want her, I always have so I'll have her but on my terms this time.

I'm meeting with my lawyer tomorrow morning and hashing out what I want in the contract and then tomorrow afternoon we'll meet with Lottie and the lawyer I suggested for her. Hudson Carmichael is perfect for this. He hates my guts and I hate his, which is why I know he'll look after her interests.

Proposing had been the last thing on my mind when I hauled her into the office on Saturday night. My only thought was stopping the auction, but a proposal had just popped out and I couldn't regret it. It was a sound idea, we'd both get what we needed from the arrangement. I'd be able to get my dad off my back and away from the company so he can go back to being a philandering asshole somewhere else, and I get the company I love out from under his control. My grandfather only let him have the position because of my mother, and it has to end.

My father and I haven't got much of a relationship. He's a bully and a cheat, and he rubbed my mother's nose in his infidelity for years. I wish she'd divorce him but she won't, and every time another scandal breaks, I see her die a little more inside. He's a despicable human being.

He bullied Clark all his life until my brother had enough and moved abroad. I miss him, but I know it's for the best. Clark is happy in Paris with his boyfriend, Gaspard, and they're living the dream.

I have to call my mother and tell her about the wedding, and Clark too, but I don't want my father there, so we've agreed on a courthouse wedding with just a witness each and Eric.

Lottie clearly adores her brother, and I admire her for taking on the responsibility of a child. Her mother must have been over forty when she'd had him. I can't help wondering what she was thinking having a child after such a large gap, but I liked Mary Miller so don't think too badly of her. The grief on Lottie's face when she told me about her passing made it clear that the wound is still raw, even three years later.

Harrison was furious with me for pulling that 'stunt', as he put it, but I calmed him down by telling him I'd cover the membership for both angry bidders for the next year. I hadn't told any of my friends why I'd done what I had, or that I'd proposed to Lottie, but I will when it's done. When Harrison pushed for an answer, I told him I thought she was going to faint. He didn't believe me but thankfully didn't push. That's the good thing about everyone thinking you're an asshole, they don't push you.

I turn to look at Lottie who's still watching the world go by out of the car window. "Does Eric know I'm coming to meet him?"

Lottie glances my way and pulls her lips between her teeth with nerves. It makes me want to taste her again. We haven't touched since the night in the club when she gave me the best blow job of my life.

She was so innocent and unsure, but so enthusiastic and eager to learn. It had blown my mind and I knew it would be my favorite spank bank material until I could crawl between her soft thighs and make her mine.

"Yes, he does but he's more excited about moving to a new house and getting his own room. Our apartment isn't much but it's all I can afford right now."

I see shame flame across her cheeks. "Do you share a room?" I frown, not liking the idea of her being so strapped for cash. Lottie looks away as if the view is suddenly so consuming.

"I sleep on the couch."

Her words cut like a knife through my gut, and I hate that she's living like this, and even a week seems like too long. She wants to stay until the wedding, but I'll have my lawyer amend the agreement so she moves in the second she signs the contract. Lottie is living like a sewer rat when she's a motherfucking Queen.

I don't know when it happened, but I fell head over heels for Violet Miller a long time ago. She was my first love and unbeknownst to her, my last love. She was the only woman to ever have found her way inside my cold heart. I realize now that she's the missing piece I've been searching for all this time. The second she walked back into my life I felt peace, but I fought it tooth and nail because I don't want to be that weak man who's led around by his dick. Now my feelings are only intensified as they're mixed with a sexual chemistry that is off the charts. I know she feels it, and it frightens my little Lottie to death, but I'll make her see that she's mine, she always has been.

The truth is, when I saw her again my heart recognized that I never stopped caring about the woman who was about to become my wife. I just need to convince her I won't hurt her ever again and that's a battle I'm ready for even if I must use her body's reaction to me against her to win. I just need to do it in such a way that I don't reveal how weak I am around her and expose my vulnerability.

We pull up outside an apartment in the lower east side of Manhattan and I look up to the fire escape where teenagers are hanging out smoking god knows what. I grimace and exit the car, moving toward Lottie who has already gotten out.

"Hey, Vi."

She looks up at one of the teens and waves. "Hi, Anthony."

"Who's the suit? He your john?"

I go to step forward, to teach the little shit some manners but I feel a hand clamp down on my arm.

"Watch your mouth, Anthony, or I'll tell your mother you're smoking her pot again."

"Sorry, Vi."

She shakes her head with a smile and heads inside.

"Does he always talk to you like that?"

She regards me as we head inside. "He's a good kid really, he just hasn't had a lot of supervision."

I hold my tongue, not wanting to end up the bad guy again. We've reached an uneasy truce for now and I'd like to keep it that way.

The inside of the building is no better than the outside. Damp with black mold growing up the walls and a broken lock allowing anyone inside the halls. I know people live like this, I'm not stupid or so ignorant of the world that I can't see it, but to think my Lottie has been living this way when I was enjoying every luxury known to man makes me sick to my stomach.

"It gets better."

I feel her shy embarrassment as she looks at me and follow her up the stairs. I keep my mouth shut knowing anything I say now will only anger her and make her feel worse.

As she unlocks the door to her apartment, I hear a kids TV tune and smile. The Simpsons was my favorite show growing up too. Her apartment is clean and tidy with homey knickknacks throughout including several kid's paintings and pictures on the fridge. The smell of dampness is less pungent in here, but it still lingers. From the doorway, I can see the living room, a tiny kitchenette, and then two doors which must be for the bathroom and the one bedroom she said she had.

On the couch, which is threadbare and sunken in the middle, is an older black woman who is watching me intently. At her feet is a little boy with bright blue eyes and brown hair that flops over his face.

"Eric, Mary, this is my friend Lincoln."

74

I move closer, putting my hand on her back, and feel her stiffen as I greet them.

"Very nice to meet you, Mary, and you too, Eric." Somehow this meeting feels important like it could change my life in some way, but I'm not sure how a nine-year-old boy could have such an impact. I crouch to his eye level before sitting my ass on the floor beside him. "I love The Simpsons. Have you seen the movie with spider pig?"

Eric grins wide and I feel my chest tighten.

"Ah, yeah. I love that one."

The tightness eases as we talk all things Bart and Homer. I hear Lottie seeing Mary out and then feel her come back into the room and sink into the couch behind us. Laying a hand on Eric's hair, she ruffles the waves, and he tips his head back.

"You eaten yet?"

"Not yet."

Lottie frowns. "You know the rules, young man."

"I know." His childish groan makes my lips twitch. Seeing this side of her is like being allowed a glimpse of the future we could've had if circumstance and life hadn't gotten in the way and forced me into a situation I had no control over. I would've married her. I'd had a plan in my head of how I'd do it too, but then it all went to hell. I wonder if we would've had children of our own by now and feel an ache in my chest.

"Go wash up, I'll start dinner."

"How about I take us out for pizza?" The offer is out of my mouth before I can think about it. Lottie looks wary, wringing her hands together and glancing between me and Eric.

"Can we, Lottie? Can we go, please?" Eric holds his hands out in a prayer position, and I see her softening. Her stunning smile peeks out from beneath the clouds of responsibility I see her carrying on her delicate shoulders.

"I don't know. You have school tomorrow and you have a lot of homework."

Eric scrabbles to his knees. "I done it."

"I've done it." Lottie corrects and I feel my lips twitch.

"Fine." He grumbles and I watch the interplay between them closely. "So can we, please?"

I catch the second she gives in and wonder if Eric can teach me his ways because every interaction between Lottie and I so far has been a battle of wills.

Her green eyes land on me. "Are you sure?"

I nod. "Of course."

Her gaze moves to Eric. "Fine but go change. I don't want to embarrass Lincoln."

As he runs off to do her bidding, I stand and move closer to her as she watches me warily. I hate that the easy trust we had years ago is so broken and know I only have myself to blame, but Lottie ran from me, she didn't believe in me, in us, like I did and that is what I can't forgive the ease with which she walked away. Taking her hand in mine, I step closer and I can see she's fighting the urge to step back. I make her nervous and I like that and yet at the same time, I hate it. "For the record, Lottie, you and Eric could never embarrass me."

A blush steals over her skin and I trace her cheek with my thumb, cupping the back of her neck and feeling her pulse quicken at my touch.

"You don't know that."

"Yes, I do."

I'm getting angry now that she's seeing herself in this role of downtrodden mouse. The Lottie I knew had so much fire and passion. The woman before me is broken and tired but I see the fire still simmering underneath it all and I want it back.

My body moves so we're chest to toe, her breasts pressed against me, and I want nothing more than to take her to bed and spend every second I have getting to know her until we're both spent.

Instead, I lean toward her, the scent of her body spray something so familiar that it arouses a memory of the night we first kissed. It was nothing like now, but as I catch her lips with mine, the feelings she evokes spin in my mind with thoughts of forever. Lottie has always had the ability to make me lose my mind.

Her lips are soft and pliant beneath mine and I flick my tongue through the seam of her open lips and taste her sweetness. She's so responsive, opening for me like a flower seeking the sun.

When a giggle has her jumping from my arms, I try and resist the urge to drag her close to me again.

I'm addicted to her.

The truth is I always have been and apparently ten years apart hasn't changed a damn thing.

Lottie Miller is the girl who stole my heart when I was nine years old and she's never given it back.

I. Am. Fucked.

11: *Linc*

THEN

"Do you believe in destiny, Linc?"

I'm lying on the grass of our special place, the rose garden where it all began, with Lottie's head on my chest as she sits between my legs, sprawled out as we always do. It's late and everyone else is settled for the night. It's my favorite time of day when we can just be together without me having to pretend that Lottie isn't everything to me.

I can't remember a time when she wasn't, but everything changed last summer with one simple kiss. Her first and, for me, the only one that really mattered, and since that day we've been us. We know her mother wouldn't approve and I understand it. I'm three years older than Lottie at eighteen and Mrs. Miller wouldn't understand that I want to preserve her innocence as much as she does.

Well, I guess that's not strictly true, I want Lottie with a fire that burns my soul, but when I take her virginity, it will be because it's the right time for her, not because I can't control my need for her.

A dig in my ribs has me looking down into big green eyes that see into every part of me. She's always had the ability to really see me, not the boy the world sees.

"Linc, did you hear me?"

I tickle her ribs and roll us in the cool grass until I'm hovering over her body, encased by her slim thighs. "Yes, I was thinking, give me a second, Miss Impatient."

"Really? It felt like you were zoning out."

"I was not and to answer your question, no I don't believe in destiny."

Lottie wrinkles her nose and frowns at me. "I do."

"How so?"

I trace the pattern of her initials into the bare skin of her belly where the short yellow top separates from the denim of her shorts. Goosebumps break out on her skin and I smile, loving how she responds to my touch.

"Well, what are the chances of us meeting? You're richer than Hades, go to a posh school, and run with the upper echelons of society. Then there's me, a nobody who just happened to be born to the housekeeper."

"Hey, don't fucking say that. You aren't a nobody, Lottie. You're everything to me."

If anything about this girl drives me crazy, it's that Lottie has no value in herself. She truly believes she's nothing, and it doesn't seem to matter how hard I try and tell her different.

Rolling her eyes she spears her fingers through my hair, her nails scratching on my scalp, making me groan. "I know that I'm that to you, but nobody else will ever see that and you know it."

"They will, Lottie. In time, they'll accept we're together and we can stop hiding it."

"Your father will never accept it."

"My father is a dick, and I don't care what he thinks."

"Yes, you do, Linc and I get it. He's your dad."

I push up so I'm away from her distracting touch, and look her in the eye as she lays in the grass watching me. "I don't. I mean it, Lottie. I hate him and I don't care what he thinks. There is nothing he can do to me that would make me change how I feel about you. I love you."

It isn't the first time I've said it to her, and I never tire of the softness I see come over her face when I do. She's so beautiful she takes my breath away.

"I love you too, Linc."

I hear the hesitation in her voice and want to wipe it from her thoughts. I don't know what else I can do to convince her of my feelings. Then an idea hits me. It's a big statement and I know it will be a lot, but people will see us together and know how serious we are.

"Come to senior prom with me."

Her eyes light up and I know I want to do everything in my power to keep that look on her face for the rest of my life. I might be young, but I know what I want and that's Lottie forever.

"Really?"

I grab her hands and pull her up so we're both on our knees face to face, and I cup her cheeks in my palms. "Really. Come as my date and then the world will know who you are to me."

Lottie looks away before glancing up through her lashes in a look she knows drives me crazy. She's part vixen, part innocent lamb, and I want to ravish one and cherish the other.

"Who am I to you, Linc?"

I smirk, knowing what she wants and giving it to her because I can't say no to this girl. "The girl I'm going to marry one day." I've been telling her this since we were kids but then it was fun and now I mean every fucking word. She'll be my wife and I'll love her until I die.

I know people will think I'm crazy but it's the truth. Lottie is the other half of me, she always has been. Maybe destiny is right because I truly believe she was made for me and me alone.

"I love you, Linc."

"I love you too."

"Promise me we'll always be like we are right now."

"I promise, my little Lottie."

I bend my head and kiss her and it's like sparks simmering in my body. This girl lights a fire in me, she makes me want to consume her. She makes me wish she was my first, like I know I'll be hers because everything that came before was meaningless.

Our kiss turns urgent, tongues dueling, hands reaching and searching, as I swallow her moan of desire.

"Linc."

I tear my lips away from hers and we're both panting. "We need to wait."

"I don't want to."

God, if she only knew how much I wanted to bury myself inside her, to fuck her to her first climax around my cock, but I want this to be special.

"Lottie, help me out here. I'm trying to do the right thing. We need to wait until you're eighteen."

I see her pout before she draws her bottom lip between her teeth, and I almost come in my pants from the sight.

"Fine."

I feel her disappointment, God my dick is throbbing from it.

I draw her into my arms and we lay back against the shed where I first realized Lottie was important to me. So many firsts in this place. It will always be the place where I feel the most relaxed, the most settled in my own skin.

"What will we tell your mother about prom?"

"I don't know, maybe I can sneak out and Clark can cover for us."

He will. Clark is my little brother and, apart from me, the closest person to Lottie. He's her best friend, but I'm the boy who loves her.

"I'll ask him to help us. Once we get to the prom, it will be too late. Everyone will know who you are to me."

"What if someone finds out and tries to stop us?"

I hear the uncertainty in her voice and want to dispel her doubts. "There's nothing my father can do to me that will make me change my mind about this or us. Do you understand, Lottie?"

I kiss her head as she snuggles closer to me, her leg thrown over my hips and I roll my lips to bite back the groan as she almost rubs her thigh against my rock-hard cock.

"Okay, Linc. I trust you."

Her trust means the world to me and there's nothing that would make me break that trust. Lottie is hardy, but she's also fragile and full of doubt about herself. It took me years of working with her to help her read when her dick teachers gave up on her. Now she reads the classics to me as part of our nighttime routine. She thinks it's because I want her to practice but it's not. I just need to hear her voice as the last thing on my mind before I go to sleep. Lottie soothes me, my rough edges, and the tension I always feel from being born Lincoln Coldwell.

"Read to me."

"Linc."

"Please?"

She sighs but gets her book from her bag, as I set up the flashlight so she can see. As her body weight settles against my chest, a sense of peace surrounds me. Lottie is my peace and I'm never letting her go.

12: Lottie

"ARE YOU SURE YOU WANT TO GO THROUGH WITH THIS?"

I'm sitting in the slick modern offices of my new lawyer, Hudson Carmichael. The furniture is all leather and polished glass and I feel so out of place here, but he's kind to me, although I can tell he thinks this is a huge mistake, but what choice do I have? Every choice I had has been taken away until this is what I'm left with. "Yes, I'm sure."

Hudson holds my gaze and I take the seconds to evaluate him. He's good-looking, more than good-looking, he's the kind of hot that would make any woman worth the name swoon at his feet. Yet all I can see is Linc and the way he looked at me in his office when I'd had him in my mouth.

"Well, in that case, let's go over some of the details and see if you have any counter requests."

We spend the next hour going over what Linc has asked for and what I'm prepared to give him. Some are ridiculous, and others are what I would've expected from him.

"He wants you to quit your job at Ruin and at the diner the second this contract is signed and for you and Eric to move in with him."

"I'll quit the job at Ruin, but I need to give Joe more notice so he

83

can find someone. He has been good to me, and I won't leave him hanging."

"We could add something to the contract that benefits the diner financially if you leave without notice. That way he gets what he wants and the diner is compensated?" I think about the idea Hudson is suggesting. The diner needs money for a new kitchen and that's chump change for Lincoln, and the reality is, Joe could fill my position easy enough. Hard up single moms who need money are everywhere.

I nod. "Let's do it."

Hudson grins. "Great and what about moving?"

"I won't move in with him until we're married."

"That's the other thing, he wants it this Saturday."

"Yes, he told me that, too."

Hudson leans closer, his lips pursed and I can tell he's holding something back and I want to know what it is that he dislikes about Linc.

"Are you okay with that, Violet?"

"Yes." I smooth the crease out of my dress and smile.

"Hudson, why do you dislike Linc so much?"

He sits back and his features melt into an unreadable canvas. "My feelings for Lincoln have no bearing on me being able to represent you."

"On the contrary, I think it has plenty to do with it."

Hudson places the contract on the desk between us and leans back in his chair. "It's a family beef going back to our fathers. It just bled down to us in college, we were in different frat houses, and I guess the competition transferred to us."

"So, Linc has never done anything personally to you that would make you think he'd hurt me?"

"No. I actually think the reason he hired me is because he cares for you. He knew I'd go over this contract with a fine-tooth comb."

A laugh bubbles up my throat, but it's strangled by emotion. "You're mistaken. Lincoln doesn't care for me. He doesn't care for anyone but himself. If he did recommend you for the reasons you say, it's only because he wants to feel better about himself."

"Violet, can I ask you why you're doing this? There's clearly bad blood between you, and marriage and living together is pretty intense."

"I know, but I need the money for my brother and it's only a year. I can handle Lincoln for three hundred and sixty-five days."

Hudson cocks his head and turns, his knees brushing against my own under the table as he faces me.

"If you're struggling, I'll loan you the money, Violet."

I pull away and look at this man who I barely know. He has a hard edge about him but also a softness which I don't think he shows to many people. "Why would you do that? You barely know me."

"No, but I see a woman doing whatever she can for a child she loves, and I respect that."

"Do you have children, Hudson?"

He frowns and I wonder if he'll answer when the silence elongates.

"No, I don't but you remind me of my mother."

I can't help thinking that's the most personal emotion this man has shown in a very long time. "I'll take that as a compliment."

He grins and it transforms him from handsome to devastating and he still falls short of Lincoln Coldwell, and I hate that the man who broke my heart still has such a hold over me, when he clearly never gave me another thought.

"It's a compliment. I'm a total momma's boy."

I smile and touch a hand to his knee and feel him tense. "I don't need you to be my hero, Hudson, but I do need someone to watch my back legally and maybe be my friend?"

He grips my hand and squeezes gently. "Deal."

He turns away and the private moment is gone but I do feel like I finally have someone in my corner fighting with me and I hate that it isn't Linc. But he gave up that right when he humiliated me and broke my young heart, ruining me for all other men in the process.

Two hours later I'm walking beside Hudson towards the conference room in his building. I'm surprised Linc, being the control freak he is, agreed to the meeting being held here but I'm glad he did.

The second I enter I feel the electricity sizzle on my skin as my eyes lock with the man who'll become my husband in just five days' time. His gaze is hard, unreadable, as he scans me, stopping on the hand Hudson has on the small of my back.

Linc's jaw tenses as he stands abruptly, buttoning his jacket as he walks toward us. "Hudson."

Linc shakes hands with my lawyer causing him to remove his hand from my back. As he does, Linc turns and puts his body between us. Bending his head close, his breath fans my neck tickling my hair and making me shiver.

"I suggest you discourage any man from touching what's mine unless you'd like to see me break every bone in his body."

He smiles as I freeze as if he hasn't just threatened bodily harm, and I wonder again who this man is that I agreed to marry. Linc leads me to the chair beside his and pulls it out for me. I sit because my legs feel weak and I wish I'd eaten the lunch Hudson provided, but I was too nervous about this meeting.

Hudson moves to sit beside me and Linc blocks him.

"You can sit over there."

Linc points to the seat beside his lawyer and Hudson glares at him, before turning to me with a question in his eyes. He's giving me the choice and it feels good, which is why I nod.

Once we're settled, I feel Linc lean back, his arm stretched behind the back of my chair, in a proprietary manner. "Shall we begin?"

Hudson reads out the terms I want to be added to the contract.

"Miss Miller would like it added to the contract that two of the three million will be put into a trust for Eric on the day of the wedding. The remainder is to be paid when the contract is fulfilled and paid directly to her."

"No."

I startle and turn to Linc at his vehement denial. "No?"

"I'll agree to the two million in trust for Eric to be set up exactly one year from today, but the one million will be paid as soon as the marriage papers are signed."

I know what he's doing. By adding this clause he's trapping me so that I won't be tempted to break the one-year deal. "I have no intention of breaking this deal if that's what you're concerned about, Lincoln. I don't lie or break promises like some people." I see his eyes crinkle and wonder if his dentist will be able to repair the damage he's doing to his pearly whites by grinding them in such a way.

"Well, now you have the added incentive."

I sigh and nod at Hudson, who continues.

"Miss Miller wants it stipulated that she won't be expected to act as your wife when you aren't in public. She'll share a bed, but any other wifely duties will not be fulfilled. She'd also like it that Eric not be made aware of the true nature of the situation."

I can feel him watching me like a warmth running up my side.

"I agree. Miss Miller doesn't have to fulfill any other duties, except to be available to me sexually and to sell our marriage as a happy one to friends and family, including public functions."

We carry on this way for thirty minutes as Hudson lists my demands and Linc counters until we're at the last one.

"Finally, Miss Miller will not live in the property known as The Kennedy Estate."

"Everybody out of the room. Now." Linc bangs his hand on the desk, and I jump as the silence re-settles. Linc stands and leans across the table at Hudson. "I said get the fuck out."

Hudson stands and I can see this is seconds away from getting out of hand as Linc's lawyer hesitates in the doorway waiting to see if his client will snap.

"It's okay, Hudson. Give us a minute."

Hudson pulls his locked glare away from Linc and looks at me with a question, so I give a small nod.

My nerves are fraught and I'm exhausted from running on fumes, but I can handle this conversation because it's the one thing I won't back down on. The Kennedy Estate holds too many memories, and I won't have them choking me at every turn for the next year.

As the door clicks closed, Linc spins my chair to face him, trapping my knees with his muscular thighs. The suit he's wearing today is dark navy with a white shirt and deep red tie. He looks every inch the billionaire tycoon that the magazines love and I hate it.

"Why won't you live at Kennedy?"

I don't want to tell him that my heart beats faster just thinking of what that place meant to me. Of how I dreamed it would be my home forever with him beside me as we built a life and a family. I don't want to tell him it's the scene of the worst night of my life and I still wake with nightmares from what happened that final night. So, I lie. "I need to be closer to the city."

Linc cocks his head and swallows. He knows I'm lying and I silently beg him to let me have this one thing.

He leans closer, resting his hands on my thighs and caressing the skin of my inner thigh with his thumb, moving the cheap fabric of my skirt higher and higher. "Liar."

Heat rushes through me pooling in my belly as I fight the reaction his touch has on me. "I'm not lying."

"Lottie, Lottie, don't you remember how well I know you? I can always tell when you're lying to me."

"You used to know me, Lincoln. Now we're nothing but strangers to each other."

"Don't fucking lie to me."

His anger wasn't something I expected, but it shows a chink in his armor that I wasn't expecting. "I'm not lying, Lincoln. There was a time when I thought I knew your every thought and feeling but it turns out it was all deceit for your amusement. I won't make the same mistake again of believing I know you or letting you know me."

His thumbs don't move closer to where I want them but keep circling and tormenting me until I stand and move away from his addictive touch.

"Is that why you won't live at Kennedy? You think it's all lies, that everything that happened back then was an illusion?"

I spin away not standing to look at him any longer. "Yes. It has nothing but bad memories for me."

I feel his heat as he stands behind me, not touching me but dominating me anyway as if him merely being close controls my thoughts and feelings.

"I'm sorry you feel that way because Kennedy has all my best memories and most of them involve you."

I spin to face him as I step back, putting some space between us again so I can think. "Don't, Linc. I don't want to talk about the past or what happy memories you have or anything that happened before. In fact, I want it added to the contract."

"Don't be ridiculous."

His disdain and the curl of his lip make me angrier than a wet cat. "Oh, so I'm ridiculous, but you paying three million for a fuck, when you can probably get any woman you want is perfectly acceptable behavior?"

"Firstly, don't cuss."

"Why not?" I challenge as I step up to him.

He grabs me by the upper arms and hauls me closer to him, so our bodies are touching.

"Because your dirty mouth makes me want to strip you down right this second and fuck you until you scream."

For some reason his admission and the evidence of his erection pressed against me makes me squirm against him.

Linc shakes me gently. "Stop, Lottie, or I swear to God I'm going to spread you on that table and fuck some sense into you."

I still before wrenching out of his arms, my heart pounding a staccato in my chest.

"Secondly, I'm not paying three million for a fuck. I'm paying it to get the job that should rightly be mine. So don't flatter yourself. You're just the icing on the cake, not the actual cake."

For the second time at the hands of this man, humiliation warms my cheeks, tears stinging the back of my throat at the reminder that I mean less than nothing to him. This is just business with perks for him. That's all I am and all I ever will be, and I need to remember why I'm doing this and not let the past mess with my head, and I can't do that at Kennedy. "I won't live there, Lincoln."

"Oh, we're back to Lincoln now?"

I ignore him and keep my silence, not trusting myself to speak right now. He shakes his head, grabs a pen, and goes to the door of the conference room. His strides are angry and predatory as he snatches the door open and comes face to face with Hudson's angry face.

"So, you're a voyeur now, Carmichael?"

"Fuck off, Coldwell, and if I was, I'd know where to come wouldn't I? That seedy little club you own."

"Still bitter I blocked your membership?"

"Still bitter the others overruled you?"

"Can we just sign these contracts and stop squabbling like children? I need to go pick Eric up from school."

Both men look at me as if remembering why they are here.

With both lawyers back in the room the contracts are amended and signed, and it's now legal.

I'll marry Lincoln Coldwell on Saturday afternoon and my life will never be the same. I just hope this time around my entanglement with him will leave me better off and not broken.

13: Linc

"I NOW PRONOUNCE YOU HUSBAND AND WIFE."

I turn to Lottie who offers me a small smile and feel a heaviness in my chest. She looks absolutely beautiful. She was determined not to get married in a big white dress and although I always dreamed of that for her, for us, I know this isn't what this is between us. We have a deal; this isn't real. At least not for her, but for me it is. I wouldn't say I love her, but it's as real as it can be for me.

Lottie was always meant to be mine and now she's legally my wife. I have a year to convince her that we belong together, but I have to stop letting my emotions get the better of me.

Her simple lace pencil skirt is cream, and she's wearing a pale pink cami with a gold belt around her tiny waist. Three pink peonies in her hand serve as a bouquet and her hair is in soft curls pulled away from her face. She's exquisite and she doesn't have a clue that every man between puberty and retirement is in awe of her, including me.

"You may kiss your bride."

I cup her neck in my hand and pull her close, dipping my head and slanting my lips over hers. She tastes sweet, like honey, and I feel myself drown in her as she opens for me. It's new and familiar at the same time. She's my Lottie but also not and it makes me want her more.

A giggle beside us has me breaking the kiss and looking into her eyes, heady and dilated with arousal. I'm breathing fast and her chest is heaving against my arms as we fight the primal desire we have between us.

Finally, I look at Eric who's handsome in a navy suit that matches mine. Behind him is my mother, beaming wide, my brother Clark, and his boyfriend Gaspard all looking delighted for me. Clark has always loved Lottie and when he heard we were getting married this Saturday, he and Gaspard hopped on a flight straight away. It was my mother, Clark, and Gaspard who made Lottie go shopping for an outfit. If it had been up to her, she would've worn a bin bag to make a point and she still would've been the most stunning woman in the world.

After the papers are signed, we all head to the courthouse steps for a picture. My mother is snapping away like she's the paparazzi. After a few shots, I call time, and Lottie and I head to the car I have waiting. We're not having a reception, but we're having dinner with my family back at the penthouse.

Lottie frowns as she watches Eric head off with his hand in my mother's. "Where is Eric going?"

"Eric will travel with my mother and Clark to the house so we can have a few minutes alone."

"I don't want a few minutes alone."

That cuts and I snap. "Fine then how about we cancel lunch and I head back to the office for the afternoon, would that be better?"

"Yes. This isn't a real wedding, Lincoln. I don't want this confusion muddying the waters."

"May I remind you that you agreed to play the role of doting wife around my family?"

I see her bite her lip, as she hesitates, and a flood of anger hits me. "Forget it."

"No, no you're right. I did agree. I'm just not comfortable being away from him with people he doesn't know."

I'm slightly mollified by her admission and realize we both have some adjustments to make. "I understand. Would you prefer he ride with us?"

"No, it's fine."

Lottie steps into the car and I follow, sitting close beside her on the seat. The ride is quiet, filled with tension that never used to be there, reminding me that I have a steep hill to climb if I'm ever going to earn back her trust.

I glance at the huge diamond ring and the diamond band I slid onto her finger a few minutes ago and can't help thinking how right it feels, although the diamond wouldn't have been my choice for her, but I had my mother pick it out for me.

Lunch is lively with Eric entertaining my mother and Clark and enchanting everyone with his boyish excitement.

"And then I won the prize, but I couldn't have it." His face falls as he tells the story of how he and Lottie went to Pizza Parlor a few years back and they'd had a coloring competition, and he'd won the fishbowl ice cream for his picture.

"Why ever not?" my mother asks before I can.

Eric looks sad and I glance at Lottie to see guilt and regret in her eyes. "Lottie?"

I see her straighten her spine and force a smile onto her face. "Eric is diabetic."

I'm stunned speechless by the news and my mother looks at me with a question I can't answer. How did I not know this already?

"I see, well that sucks for you, little man." Clark breaks the tension, but I'm a simmering ball of fury. She should've told me.

"It's okay. Lottie bought me the spiderman hoodie and skateboard I wanted instead, so it was fine." He shrugs as if it's nothing, but it isn't. No child should have to deal with illness, and it sickens me that Eric does.

"Well, Lottie is the best." Clark kicks me under the table, and I jump and glare at him, but I do snap out of my stupor.

My hand finds Lottie's much smaller one under the table and I bring her fingertips to my lips and kiss them. "She's the best."

She's watching me as if she's waiting for me to strike her and it tightens the knot in my gut. She doesn't trust me, and she has every right to feel the way she does. I've humiliated her and shown her nothing but contempt, but that's going to change.

"Eric, would you like to see your new room before you leave?"

I'd wanted a honeymoon, but Lottie nixed that idea, and only agreed to one night alone. I'd thought it was because she couldn't bear to be alone with me and I still believe there's some truth to that but now I wonder if it has to do with her being overprotective of Eric. Diabetes is no joke, and she's been dealing with this all alone for the last three years. I make a mental note to have my lawyer settle all her medical bills. She shouldn't be made to pay that out of her payment for our deal. I won't tell her, she'll only argue with me. Lottie is much more argumentative now than she was, or perhaps it's me who's different.

"Yes, please."

I snap from my reverie and push back the chair as Lottie follows, leaving my family in the dining room to their own devices.

I'm nervous as we head to the second floor. I'd had an interior designer working night and day to get this room ready for Eric. In part to please Lottie and show her I'm not the ogre she wants to believe I am, but also because this sweet boy deserves it.

"Wow, this is so cool." Etic takes in the superhero theme of the room, with wall climbing grips and ropes on one side and a suspended den above the bed for him to do whatever it is he wants to up there. His smile transforms my mood, and I can't help the joy I feel as I watch him racing from one discovery to another with utter happiness on his face.

I turn, wanting to share it with Lottie but instead of pleasure, I see unhappiness and annoyance on her face.

"Can I have a second with you alone, Lincoln?"

I hate my name on her lips and I know she's using it as a shield. I was always Linc to her even when I didn't like it, but it was us, and I hate that she's holding that back from me.

Out in the hallway I face her, and she feels so fragile as I look down at her until I see the fire in her eyes.

"What the hell are you doing, Lincoln?"

I frown, perplexed by where this could be coming from. "I don't understand?"

She crosses her arms and my eyes dip to the swell of cleavage that has been teasing me all afternoon. It's modest, but anything on this woman drives my sexual need to preposterous heights.

"The room. What the hell, Linc? You can't do this without checking with me first."

I swallow the smile at her slip of the tongue. "I just had his room decorated, where's the harm?"

"Of course you wouldn't see it. Damn silver spoon in your mouth, but when we leave it will be hard enough on him without you filling his head with every boy's dream bedroom. He needs stability not luxury."

"Everyone deserves luxury, Lottie."

"Yes, well, not everyone can afford it."

I'm angry now, she's pissing me off with her constant battle of wills. "Stop being a bitch for just one second, Lottie, and consider Eric in this. He thinks we're in love and that I'm the big brother he always wanted, and I'm going to do what little this cost me to make him happy."

She seems to pale before me. "Consider Eric? Are you fucking kidding me? He's all I consider."

I know I'm being harsh on her, but she's driving me crazy with these walls of hers. "Then stop trying to deprive him, just because you're still nursing wounded pride over a silly prom date. It's selfish, Lottie."

I see the blow land as she draws in a harsh breath and want to snatch the words back, but I don't. Pride won't let me beg, not yet at least.

"I see."

The wounded wobble of her voice almost makes me relent, but we're interrupted by my mother and Lottie takes the chance to escape into the bathroom down the hall.

"I'm sorry to interrupt, sweetling, but I need to head out. Is Eric ready?"

"It's fine, Mom. Lottie is just feeling a little overwhelmed."

"I'm sure she is. This has been pretty quick, Lincoln."

She cups my cheek, and I'm the little lost boy again. My mother and I are close. She lives for her two sons, and we adore her. The fact our father is a lying, cheating prick only made me and Clark all the more protective of her.

Heather Kennedy is where all my father's money and privilege comes from. He was nothing until he met my mother and he charmed her into marriage and then bled her dry and continues to do so. But when I get control of Kennedy Enterprises, I'm going to change that and convince my mother to leave his sorry ass once and for all.

"It's not quick for me, Mom."

"Oh, my boy, you never stopped loving her, did you?"

"No."

She's the only person apart from Audrey who knows the truth of what happened the night I lost Lottie. I confessed everything to her the night I told her we were getting married. She knows me too well and managed to wheedle it all out of me.

"Does she know?"

"No, and I don't want her to. It serves no purpose."

"I disagree, but this is your life and I hope it works out for you. I always loved that girl and who you were around her. You lost the sweetness when she left, and I feared you were becoming someone cold and hard. I see the light in your eyes again and hope for all your sakes this doesn't backfire."

Heather Coldwell isn't wrong. I was cold and hard and I still am. Some things can never go back to what they were. I'll never be a naive boy again who believes in chance. Now I know the only way to make the things I want happen is to take them and orchestrate them.

Lottie comes out of the bathroom looking pale, and she ignores me as she says goodbye to Eric, fussing over his medication and promising to call him later. She goes over the details of what to do if he has a hypo, and it makes me see what she's been dealing with and I regret being so hard on her.

I should apologize.

When the door closes, and it's just us, I move toward her but she backs away. "I have a headache."

Lottie rushes to the spare room beside my own, or should I say our room, and slams the door locking it with a flick of the switch.

She's angry with me and Lottie in a temper isn't something to be handled. She needs to be left to calm down on her own, that much I can remember from our past, even if it does make me want to fuck her raw.

I head to my home office and pour myself a brandy. As I sit and watch the lights of Manhattan light up the sky, I let my memories sweep through me. Happy times, perfect summer nights, with sweet words, gentle caresses, promises made, and I threw it away. I wish I'd taken a different path than I did but I didn't, and now here I am, alone on my wedding night with only a brandy as company.

Jumping to my feet I head toward the bedroom and bang on the door. "Lottie, open up." Silence greets me and I pound on the door again. "Don't make me break this fucking door down. We have a contract and it's time for you to fulfill your end." Nice didn't work, so maybe reminding her of why she said yes to me is the better route. "Or would you like me to call Hudson and tell him you voided the contract and have my lawyer sue for damages?"

The door swings open and I find a fuming Lottie facing me down. She's tiny even in her heels, and I loom over her, crowding her as I back her up against the bed.

"I hate you."

Her anger makes me so fucking hard, I can feel pre-cum spill from my rock-hard cock. "Yeah, I hate you too, but I still can't wait to see my cock down that pretty little throat."

With that, I reach for the pink cami that has tortured me all day and tear it straight down the middle.

14: Lottie

MY BREATH CATCHES IN MY THROAT AS LINC PINS ME WITH HIS INTENSE gaze. Silence, but for the sound of our heavy erratic breathing, fills the air as my top hangs off me in shreds. It's seconds but it feels like a lifetime as a million different thoughts run through my head, but the only one I can grasp hold of is that I want him.

His anger and aggression shouldn't turn me on, but I feel myself getting wet, my body heavy with desire. I can't deny the sprinkling of nerves, but they only seem to heighten everything I'm feeling. Linc is a magnificent man to behold, he's so intense and demanding and yet I find myself becoming addicted to it.

The next second his lips crash into mine as he kisses me, his mouth dominating and hard, and I don't resist. No, I want this. His anger and need for me are a heady combination as he nips his teeth at my lips, forcing his tongue in my mouth and taking what he wants.

Linc grips my hips and walks me backward until my knees hit the back of the bed. His teeth graze my neck and I moan, my hands landing on his chest and fighting with the buttons there. I want to feel his warm skin beneath my fingers.

Suddenly he pulls back and the heat in his gaze as it moves over me makes me shiver.

"Undress for me, Lottie."

God that rasp in his voice makes me shiver with arousal. With shaky fingers, I undo the belt at my waist, letting it drop to the floor. My skirt follows, pooling in a cloud of lace at my feet. I shrug one shoulder and the remains of my pink cami falls to the floor. I'm standing in my cream lace underwear, a purchase I made because I wanted to feel beautiful and desirable on my wedding day, despite none of it being real and watch him devour me with his hungry gaze.

Goosebumps race over my skin as I move to kick the designer heels off my tortured feet.

"Leave them on."

My eyes shoot to Linc as he pinches his bottom lip and walks around me like I'm a prize purchase at an auction, which I almost was. I shiver when I feel his breath on my neck, the rough texture of his suit against the back of my thighs.

"Do you have any idea how much I want you?"

His voice is gravelly and deep, as he moves to stand in front of me again and I peek up at him through my lashes. "No."

"Then I need to remedy that."

He drops to his knees in front of me and bends his head to my belly, dropping a soft kiss there and my hands, as if having a mind of their own, lift to his hair. He groans as I run my fingers through the thick silky waves. His kisses grow bolder as he nips at my hip bones and then he's using his broad shoulders to push my thighs apart. He's eye level with my pussy and nerves make my stomach somersault. I've never been touched like this, not by anyone. Linc was the first and last man to touch me there, but he never put his mouth on me, only his fingers.

As if reading my mind he asks, "Has anyone touched this pussy but me?"

I want to lie, but I've never been able to lie to him, and now seems like the wrong time to start. "No."

A growl leaves his throat as he presses his nose into my panties and inhales like his life depends on it. A blush steals over me as shyness explodes on my skin, but when he kisses my clit through my panties, I shudder in pleasure.

"This pussy is mine, Lottie. Do you understand?"

I can't get the words past my dry throat, and he continues his assault on my senses. A sharp smack to my left butt cheek makes me squeal from shock and pain but then his hand is caressing me, and it feels warm.

"I said, do you understand?"

"Yes." My voice doesn't even sound like me, it's breathy and low.

"That's my good girl."

God, why does that make my body throb with need for him? I shouldn't want his praise so badly. I wish I meant the words I threw at him, but I don't hate him. I'm not sure I could, even after what he did to me.

Before I have a chance to go down the rabbit hole of lost memories, he's drawing my panties down my legs. His hungry gaze latches on to my bare pussy before he looks up at me.

"I fucking love this pussy."

Then he's licking and kissing me, his tongue swiping through my folds from my opening to my clit and I hang on as waves of pleasure wash over me. Like everything else in life, Linc is phenomenal with his mouth. He laps at me, drinking me in, tasting me and I fear my legs won't hold me if he keeps this up.

Lifting his head, he seems to sense I'm teetering on the edge. "Lose the bra, show me those pretty nipples."

I reach behind me and unhook the clasp before I let the straps fall down my arms. His eyes darken as I stand naked in front of him, vulnerable and shy and yet he makes me feel safe. It's a crazy thought considering why and how we got here and everything that has passed between us, but it's the only thing that feels real.

With a push of his big hand, I land with a bounce on the bed. As I sit up on my elbows, he dips his head between my legs and sucks on my clit hard. My back arches as I moan loudly and my hands scrabble for purchase, landing on his head.

Linc fucks me with his tongue before sucking on my clit and I moan as my body surrenders to his touch.

"Look at me, watch me make you mine."

His husky words have me sitting up on my elbows and I meet his heated stare as he thrusts two fingers inside me as he sucks again. It burns a little and I wonder how I'll handle taking his cock, but then the sensations he's causing overwhelm my thoughts.

"Fuck, you're so tight. I can feel you crushing my fingers with this gorgeous cunt."

His dirty mouth makes a rush of wetness hit my pussy and he groans with pleasure.

"You like that, don't you? You like my dirty mouth."

He thrusts inside me, and I feel full, stretched, but when he curls his fingers, I see stars. My body seizes as an electric current pulses through me and I cry out his name, begging him for what, I have no clue. I just know that if he stops I'll die. My vision goes black as pleasure detonates through me and I know if I died right now it would be with a smile.

As the pleasure ebbs and I get some sense of time and space again, I look down and see he's gently lapping up the evidence of my climax. His chin is wet from my orgasm, and it's the hottest thing I've ever seen.

"Fuck, you taste good."

I blush but don't have time to be shy as he looms over me and takes my mouth in a hot wet kiss. I taste myself on him as he explores me with his tongue and I grow bold, twisting mine against his and holding onto him, letting my hands wander all over him. This might be my first time, but I'm not innocent and Linc's body is familiar to me and yet so different.

He's broader, more muscular than before, everything is bigger, and I feel smaller somehow. He kisses his way down my throat and I arch my neck so he can have better access as shivers rush over my skin.

"Linc."

"Yes?"

"I, I..." I don't know what I want or need, just that I need something.

"Tell me."

He nibbles my breasts before drawing one tight peak into his mouth and suckling. My toes curl and my breathing becomes fast. Linc rocks his hips into my pussy and I feel the hard ridge of his cock brush my sensitive clit. Oh God, I'm going to come again. My body takes over as I grind against him and he toys with my nipples, pinching and rolling them and then I come again, softer this time but no less devastating.

As I melt into the bed I feel his lips against my neck, his arms come around me as he holds me, close and I can feel his heart pounding against me. He's still fully clothed, and I'm as naked as the day I was born and yet I don't feel weak, I feel powerful.

With a squeeze of my ass, he stands and begins to undress, but I jump up on wobbly legs and stop him. "Let me."

His hand stills on his tie and I knock it away. He stands silently as I undress him, pushing the jacket from his broad shoulders and letting it fall to the floor. My fingers fumble with nerves on the buttons of his shirt.

"Relax, sweetheart."

His deep voice rumbles through me and I glance up to see want and desire burning in his blue eyes. Linc was a gorgeous boy, but the man is something else. As I expose his warm skin to my eyes and touch, the shirt falls to the floor beside his jacket and I can't help the hitch in my breath. His tanned skin is smooth, except for a smattering of dark hair on his chest. Linc's biceps flex as he lifts his hand to my hair, stroking it away from my face and I close my eyes for a second, reveling in his gentle touch. When I open them, he's lowering his arm and I spot a small tattoo on the inside of his bicep. I can't make it out as he lowers his hand, but it intrigues me as it's the only one I can see on his body.

His pecs are toned and lead down to a ripped eight-pack that's defined and delicious. His slacks are hanging loose on his hips, show-casing the gorgeous V of muscle that makes me want to take a bite out of him.

"Like what you see, my Lottie?"

I hate that I love him calling me that. "Don't call me that."

His hand caresses my face and forces me to look him in the eye. "Why not? It's true. You are mine."

"For now."

I see him frown and then the softness is gone from his eyes replaced by determination. For what I don't know, but I'm afraid to find out because one thing I do remember about Linc is that he hates to lose.

"Are you on the pill like we agreed?"

Linc had demanded I be on birth control as part of our contract. I agreed because the last thing I need is a baby thrown into the mix right now, even his, or maybe that should be especially his. "I had the IUD fitted." It was pure luck that I was at the right time in my cycle for it to provide immediate protection, not that Lincoln need to know that.

He nods and his hands go to his belt and the clink of the metal is heavy with anticipation. "Lie on the bed, Lottie."

I do as he says and watch him remove his slacks and boxers in one move. His heavy cock bobs free and then lies hard and proud against his belly. He's big, magnificent, and terrifying. I have no idea how he'll fit without tearing me apart, but I know he will. It's what our bodies were made to do. That doesn't offer me any comfort as he fists his hand around his cock and strokes.

I'm mesmerized by the sight of him. It's the most erotic thing I've ever witnessed and my fingers itch to touch him. I've had him in my mouth, I know the silky-smooth feel of him against my tongue, but I'm like an addict and I want more.

"Touch yourself, Lottie. Show me how you make yourself come."

I hesitate, my cheeks flaming with heat, but I let my hand move over my breasts, rolling my nipple between my fingers, as the other hand circles my clit.

"Fuck me. Do you know how sexy that is? How much I want you?"

My eyes move to his cock and the head is leaking as he strokes lazily, the tip wet with his arousal.

"Open your legs."

I do as he says and Linc settles his body between my thighs, his heavy cock resting against my sensitive pussy. His head bends and he kisses me slowly this time like he's drugging me. My senses and body feel languid and heavy with desire, yet I can feel the restraint in his body, the compact power he's trying to leash. I know that one day I want him to lose that control, to show me the man underneath, but for tonight I'm grateful for his restraint.

Our tongues dance as I feel the tip of his cock edge my opening and I tense, drawing in a breath.

"Relax, Lottie. I'll make this good, I promise, but it will sting."

"Okay."

He continues to kiss me, making me forget about anything else but how I feel as he pushes in a little more. I try not to tense as his forehead rests against my chest.

"Fuck, you're so tight."

"Just do it, Linc."

He thrusts home and I yelp and move up the bed, but he holds me tight, his arms bandied around my waist, his head buried against my neck now as he kisses me softly on the wildly beating pulse there.

"Just be still, Lottie. Let your body adjust for a second."

Linc pulls my nipple between his lips and my body melts as pleasure consumes me. I give a little rock of my hips and hear him hiss when I do it again.

"You okay?"

I nod. "Yes."

Linc starts to move, his body slowly rocking into mine, filling me and the pain turns to pleasure, his pelvis brushing against my clit every time he thrusts into me. Taking my calf in his hand he wraps it around his back as he leans up on his elbows so he can see me. His palms caress my breasts and rib cage as I let out a whimper.

"Look how well you're taking my cock, Lottie."

I look down to where we're joined and the sight is erotic and beautiful.

Linc begins to slam into me harder now as I try to pull every thought and feeling into some kind of sense, but I'm awash with emotions. His jaw is hard and unflinching, and he's so beautiful it makes my throat clog with tears. It was always meant to be him and even given the circumstances, I'm glad it's him for my first time. I hate the way my brain tries to invade this moment by wishing he could be my last too, so I block out the thoughts and just ride the feelings pumping through my body.

Everything I'm feeling is mirrored on his handsome face. So captivating, so real.

"Come, Lottie, I need you to come all over my cock with that sweet cunt."

His words trigger a spasm inside me as he arches his hips, hitting a new place inside me and I scream his name, panting it like a prayer as I climax, my body pulsing around him. I feel him shudder as he stills inside me, his hot seed coating my insides before he collapses against me and rolls us so I'm lying across his chest.

As we pant, the sweat on my skin cools, the wetness of our joined pleasure chills my skin and he kisses my head before standing.

I panic that he's leaving and want to weep for being so pathetic and needy. He comes back moments later with a warm washcloth and pushes my legs apart.

Embarrassed I reach for the cloth. "I can do it."

He brushes my hand away. "I made the mess. I'll clean it up."

Tenderness for this man, makes me wish for things I know I can't have. Sex with this man is wreaking havoc on my emotions already. How the hell will I last a year with my heart intact?

I see the tint of pink on the white cloth and he catches my eye as if he's thinking the same as me, before vocalizing his thoughts. "This was always mine."

I remain silent not knowing how to react now. Will he cuddle? Does he want his space? I've never shared a bed with a man before and have no idea of the protocol. As he uses the bathroom, I curl into my side, pulling the sheet over me, and close my eyes. I keep them closed as I feel the bed dip behind me and the light extinguish, bathing the room in darkness.

A hand comes around me, and Linc pulls me so I'm lying across his body, his arm around me as I use his chest like a pillow. I'd fallen asleep like this a hundred times in the past, but it's never felt more different.

Then I'd had his love and now I don't know what we are. The void between us is littered with emotional land mines.

15: Linc

Leaving Lottie in bed this morning was the hardest thing I've ever done, but I knew if I didn't, I'd fuck her again and her body needed the rest. I'd woken in the night and turned in a panic thinking it was a dream but seeing her hair spread out on the pillow, need had gotten the better of me.

I'd woken her with my mouth on her pussy, loving the sweet taste of her arousal on my tongue. Even in sleep she responded to me, arching against my touch, riding my face until she came down my chin. I was addicted and I'd fucked her hard and fast, my need for her like a wild animal straining at a leash.

It's now eleven, and I have a meeting with the board to announce my marriage. My father will be furious he hadn't been consulted but he's nothing to me. The only people I give a shit about had been there and that's all I cared about.

Picking up my phone I call my brother, who picks up on the second ring.

"Linc, I was just going to call you."

"Oh?"

"I wanted to say again how happy we are that you finally got your head out of your ass and married our girl."

A possessive jealousy rips through me when he calls her ours. "My girl, Clark, not yours."

His rich laugh makes me smile despite myself. Clark has always been the light to my dark and we're close, I'd do anything for him and have.

"Yes, Lincoln, I know. She was always yours, but she's my friend and I'm glad she's back in our lives."

"Me too. Listen I have to work today but is there any chance you can take her shopping? Get her some stuff. You know clothes, dresses, essentials, and the same for Eric."

"You're at work?" He sounds like he was being strangled.

"Well, yeah. I had an urgent meeting with the board."

"But it's Sunday and you just got married yesterday."

"I know, but this can't wait."

"Really, Linc? Please don't fuck this up with her. She doesn't deserve you treating her like all those other women you've paraded around in the past."

I know what he means. Those women were entertaining but I was an asshole and never gave their feelings a second thought, but Lottie is different. She matters. "I'm not going to. I married her, didn't I?"

"True, but that doesn't mean you stop trying now. Lottie is special and she should be treated that way."

"Fuck, I know that, which is why I'm asking you to help me out."

"Fine, but you know I'm shit with fashion. Lucky for you I have a secret weapon in Gaspard. He'll be overjoyed to help with this."

"Thank you."

"You're welcome. No, go do your meeting and I'll handle things on this end."

I hang up and consider my brother's words as I gaze out over Manhattan.

I don't want to fuck it up, I already did that once and he doesn't have a clue. When we broke up the first time everyone thought it was because of her mother moving away, but that wasn't the truth, at least not the whole truth. I'd broken us before she ran from me, and I can't say that I wouldn't do the same thing again given the choices I had. That doesn't mean I don't regret it. The truth is I never got over Lottie, not really. I told myself I had, and I led my life for fun, never stopping to consider the people I hurt or caring much. Then she came back into my life like a tornado, and I have this urge to keep her, to make her mine, to make her love me again. Yet I'm terrified of allowing my feelings for her to take flight. If I let myself love her again and she leaves I'll be nothing but a shell, so I have to be smart and make her love me without letting myself fall for her or at least letting her know how deeply she's under my skin.

That's the real reason I left her in our bed this morning and it's the reason I'll keep my distance from her apart from when we fuck or make love.

No, that's not right. I can't make love to her, or can I? Perhaps that's the one time I can show her what we are without the risk of letting my heart get trampled into dust.

My watch beeps an alarm and I stand, switching it off. It's time I took my place as head of this company and watch my father burn.

The muttering inside the conference room dies down as I step inside. My eyes wander around the room, immediately catching the gaze of my father. He's tall like me and fit, with salt and pepper hair, but I have my mother's eyes and mouth and both me and Clark follow our grandfather on my mom's side for looks.

His lips twist into a sneer as he sits at the head of the table. My grandfather insisted this clause be added to my father's last contract and he'd been so sure I'd never marry he'd allowed it.

Charles Coldwell was so sure that I had no interest in the business that he'd gotten lazy and I'd capitalized on it.

"Son, this is a surprise. Can you tell us why you called us all here on a Sunday morning?"

More mutterings came from the other members of the board, but I suspected some of them had seen this coming. While he was playing golf, I'd been working hard and making sure I had the support I'd need to make this move.

109

Unbuttoning my jacket, I sit beside him to his left and turn to address the board, keeping his face in my eye line. "I'm sorry for the inconvenience, everyone." I catch Audrey's eye and she lifts a perfectly arched brow. My cousin was the first person I added to the board and my grandfather had been thrilled about it. Audrey was a savvy businesswoman and a formidable one too. She's the only person I wouldn't want to face down in the boardroom.

"Well, get on with it."

My father's impatience only makes me want to draw it out longer, but I have no desire to spend more time with him than necessary. "Of course. I have some news. Yesterday afternoon I married my childhood sweetheart."

Shocked gasps ring out around the room, but Audrey laughs loudly making me smirk. It's overshadowed by my father shoving his chair back and banging the table.

"What nonsense is this? Why was I not privy to this?"

His face is almost puce red, and I take a perverse satisfaction in the fact. "Not nonsense father. I married Violet Miller yesterday afternoon. Mother and Clark were there as our witnesses."

He blusters as if he can't find the right words and I'm sure if I looked hard enough steam would shoot from his ears.

"This is an outrage. You marry that cheap little slut, and I'm not even invited?"

My chair hits the floor as I lunge at him, and he scampers back, away from my fury. "Call her that one more time and I'll fucking end you."

I feel a hand on my arm and look to see Audrey beside me.

"Sit down, Lincoln. Getting arrested won't help."

I glare at the man who sired me one more time, making sure he's going to keep his trap shut about Lottie before I sit. "Now that is clear. I'd like to take my position as CEO of Kennedy Enterprises. The board is clear on the terms of my father's last contract, and they state that if I marry, the board would vote between us for the position of CEO. I'm calling that vote today."

"Let's take a vote."

Audrey sits beside me as the CFO and calls the vote. One by one the hands go up in my favor. Only two people vote for my father, and I know they're his golfing buddies and the men who go on the same trips as he does to cheat on their wives. One is also a member of Ruin, or should I say about to be a former member.

"That's eight two in favor of Lincoln taking over as CEO effective immediately."

I can hear the enjoyment in Audrey's voice and fight the twitch of my lips.

My father storms for the door before turning and pointing at me. "This will not stand. Do you hear me, boy?"

"See yourself out, father, I'll have someone clear your desk for you."

"This isn't over."

He fights to slam the air pressure door and I grin at my cousin then. When the room is filled with a tense silence, I move to take my father's position. "Thank you for giving up your Sunday for me and for trusting me to lead this company into the future. I won't let you down."

The meeting breaks up shortly afterward and I'm surrounded by men and women I've known half my life as they offer genuine congratulations.

Honey Blandford, who was my grandfather's first secretary and valued member of the original board, hugs me. Her weathered hands were the only thing that gave away her eighty-year age.

"Congratulations, Lincoln. Your grandfather would be so proud of you."

"Thank you, Aunt Honey." I feel emotion thicken my voice at her words. My grandfather was always the man I looked up to, the man I wanted to be one day, so her words have an impact I wasn't expecting.

"Now, tell me about this bride of yours?"

"Yes, Lincoln, tell us."

Audrey punches my arm and frowns, but I can tell she's pleased for me. Audrey is the only person, apart from my mom, who knows what happened between Lottie and I and why I broke her heart, and she's kept my secret all this time. I wish she could've known Lottie but up until my senior year, Audrey had lived in Italy with my aunt, my mother's sister, before coming home to the US when my grandmother died.

"I've known Lottie since she was six years old and I was nine. She was my first kiss and my first love."

Honey holds her hand over her chest. "And you found each other again."

"Yes, we did."

"Oh, that is so beautiful, but we're keeping you from her. You must go and spend your day with your new wife. Tell your mother I'll call her in the week."

Honey kisses my cheek, and her perfume is like nostalgia in a bottle. "I will."

Soon it's just Audrey and I, and I move to the console at the back and find the whiskey I'd hidden there last week.

I hold the bottle to her. "Drink?"

"Hell yes."

She watches me as I pour, remaining silent until we both have a glass in our hands.

Raising her glass, she toasts. "To putting out the rubbish and to new beginnings."

"I'll drink to that." I sip the smooth Japanese whiskey and let the burn coat my throat.

"Well, you sure surprised a few people today."

I sit opposite her leaning on the glass table. "Including you?"

"Well, yes and no. I obviously knew her because of Ruin and the auction but I had no idea you still loved her or were going to marry her. I thought it was just an obsession about the past, although I hoped for more when I realized who she was."

"I don't love her." The denial is sharp on my tongue.

Audrey raises her eyebrow. "Really, Lincoln? I know how torn up you were when you split up and I saw that same look in your eyes when your father spoke about her like he did."

"That doesn't mean I love her."

"Of course not, but you do."

"Drop it, Audrey. I don't love her. Lottie is just a means to an end. A convenience to me and nothing more."

"If you say so."

I can see she isn't convinced and when Audrey is being stubborn there's no talking to her. "I do."

"Fine. When can I see her and welcome her to the family?"

I frown. Do I want Audrey and Lottie to be friends? Will that complicate things even more if I can't convince Lottie she loves me? Will I have to contend with her friendship with my cousin to rub salt in the wound? Yet Lottie doesn't seem to have anyone else, and I hate that she's so alone. "I'll arrange something."

"You do that."

"I'll have to wait a few weeks. She doesn't like leaving Eric."

"Her brother?"

"Yes, he's diabetic and she's a bit overprotective."

"Oh, wow, I had no idea."

She's lying to me and I want to know why, but now isn't the time. I swirl my drink. "Me either until yesterday after the wedding."

"That must have been tough for her handling that alone."

"It's why she was drowning in debt."

"Life can be such a bitch sometimes."

"It has to her, for sure."

"Well not anymore, she has you now to help her out."

"Ha, if she'll let me. Lottie is fiercely independent and has walls up that would rival Everest they're so high."

Audrey purses her lips. "That's not really a surprise after everything she's been through."

I'm not one to dwell on regret, if I was I'd be toast, but I feel it now. Mine were too many and too great.

Suddenly I have the overwhelming urge to get home to see her. To kiss her and touch her like she's mine, which is why when Audrey leaves, I stay exactly where I am. If I give in and go running every time I think about her, I might as well just never leave her side. I read through some emails, send instructions to the security team to change the access for my father, and compose an email to be sent to all staff.

I'll meet with the press and media team to announce my posting as CEO at the end of the week. It will also include my marriage announcement.

Around six pm I close the computer down, gather my stuff, and head home. I'm surprised I lasted this long, but I'm nothing if not determined.

16: Lottie

WAKING UP ALONE HAD LEFT ME FEELING OFF ALL MORNING. IT ISN'T that I want Linc to cuddle me or hover over me and treat me like a real wife by giving me attention. It's just letting go of that last part of me that wants the fairy tale ending is harder than I thought it would be. I know I don't want that. I can't allow myself to want that. It's a dangerous illusion and I see that now.

The sex was better than I'd ever dreamed. Linc played my body like it was a symphony orchestra and he was the conductor. He knew every sensitive place on my body guaranteed to give me pleasure and even showed me new ones. I can't suppress the shiver at the memory of his hands and mouth on me, inside me. I wonder if some of that talent is perhaps a memory of long-forgotten summer nights learning each other's bodies, but I suspect most of it's just another damn thing he's magnificent at.

Moving through to the room we'd shared last night, I smoothed the blue cover as I sit on the huge bed. I'd imagined the many ways in which I'd lose my virginity, God knows at twenty-five it was about time, but it had always been sweet and gentle. What we'd done last night was neither and yet it was more spectacular than all the sweet talking in the world. The way he'd dominated me and the dirty things he'd said had the power to make me weak and complicit. No not complicit, needy and desperate. Even now I crave his touch, despite the ache down below from our night together.

Linc leaving me to wake alone wasn't something my Linc would have done, but this isn't my Linc. He isn't really mine and that's for the best. I have to put Eric first and not allow Lincoln to get in my head and make me fall in love with him again.

His absence this morning was actually better for my mental health, allowing me the time to rebuild the walls around my heart which last night had chipped away at. At least that's the mantra I'm reciting over and over in my head as I move back into Eric's room feeling a little lost. I need my brother home so I can focus on something other than my thoughts so I finish unpacking Eric's clothes and put them away in his new room.

Looking around at the vision-board-worthy boy's bedroom, a lump comes to my throat. I'm so grateful that Linc has done this for him. I'd been angry, but also incredibly touched that he'd gone to this much trouble and expense. But I'd meant what I said to him yesterday, giving my baby brother all this luxury and attention would only make it harder when we left.

Three-hundred and sixty-four days to go before we were nothing but a blip on each other's radar. Would Linc look back in twenty years and remember our year together or would it be so inconsequential in his life that he'd forget us?

A noise in the main living room makes me tense as I drop the clothes I'm folding and rush to the mezzanine to see what it is. Looking down, I see two men who make me smile.

Clark and Gaspard are grinning up at me with warmth.

"Hey, what are you guys doing here?"

Clark meets me as I reach the bottom of the stairs and grasps my hands, twirling me around.

"A little birdy told me you were all alone, so we're taking you shopping."

"What? No, that's not necessary. I have what I need and Eric is due home any minute now."

"I know. Mother and Eric are coming too. We're going to have lunch and spend lots of Lincoln's money."

I feel myself tense and pull away. "Oh, no. I'm not doing that."

Clark wraps me in his warm hug, and I close my eyes realizing how much I've missed my friend. He was the only person other than Linc who knew my secrets. At least he had been; now I keep the biggest one I have locked up inside me.

"Violet Coldwell, you *will* come shopping, you *will* spend Lincoln's money and you *will* enjoy it." He kisses my temple as Gaspard smiles at me. "Anyway, it was Lincoln's idea. He feels bad for working today so he called and sent the cavalry."

"He did?"

"Yes, of course. He might be a workaholic but he cares for you, Vi."

I wished I could correct him and tell him that this is strictly business, but I can't so I just smile. Did Linc do this or is this Clark saving his brother's ass because he feels bad for me? I don't know so I push it out of my head. "Okay. Let me get changed."

"You're perfect as you are."

I glance at my old jeans that are worn and comfortable and the cream sweater I threw on this morning and grimace. Comfortable they might be, but stylish they are not.

"Vi, seriously, we're going now so stop stressing."

"I forgot how bossy you were, Clark Coldwell."

Gaspard holds out my coat for me and I shrug into it. "He's très bossy."

I laugh as Clark ushers me to the door, explaining that Heather, his and Linc's mom, and Eric are meeting us there. Knowing there's no fighting this, I settle in the car and endeavor to enjoy the day.

Hours later I'm tipsy, giggly, and have spent more money in one day than I have in the last ten years.

"Oh my lord, your face when that woman thought you were my husband."

I'm holding on to Clark as he helps me into the foyer of the apartment that is my home for the next twelve months. Eric has gone for a second night's sleepover with Heather. His request this time and I feel a little guilty, but she's doting on him like he's truly the grandson her boys haven't given her yet. But watching Eric light up under her attention was like a balm to my soul, convincing me that whatever happened and whatever the cost to me personally, this arrangement is worth it. Yet seeing Eric and Heather together made me ache for my mother. The loss is never far away, like a wound that won't quite heal and will break open at the oddest times. I'm pulled from my thoughts as Clark laughs.

"I love you to bits, my darling, but the thought of that." He waves at my girlie parts with a disgusted look on his face. "No, just no."

"What's going on?"

Instantly I feel my good mood disappear, replaced by wariness. Lincoln looks handsome but tired as he emerges from the area of his office into the open-plan living area.

"Well, as instructed, brother, we took Violet out shopping, spent a ridiculous amount of your money, had lunch, pedicures, and your darling wife even had her hair done."

Linc cocks his head and I feel heat ripple through me at his gaze. "I see that. You look very beautiful, Lottie, but then you always do."

He moves into me, slipping his arm around my waist and pulling me close to his body, before dropping his lips to mine. It's not merely a touch of the lips, it's a deep kiss that leaves me shaken when he lifts his head and winks at me before releasing me.

Despite knowing his words and the kiss are more than likely for the audience we have, I preen at the compliment, my cheeks flushing pink. My dark hair now hangs in soft waves around my face, sleek and shining with health. It's truly amazing what a good cut and blowout can do for a person's sense of self-esteem.

"Thank you, husband."

"She does look beautiful, which is why you should take her out dancing tonight."

Suddenly feeling as sober as a judge, my shocked stare turns to Clark. He has no idea he's stepping into things that he shouldn't. Clark, my warm wonderful friend, is trying to infuse this marriage with something that doesn't exist. As do the others, he thinks we're in love. A sudden weight on my chest makes me wish that my life was different, that I could truly hate my now husband, that I didn't still want him. After what we shared last night, the golden chains he's wrapped around my heart are only tightening until I fear they'll strangle my will to fight him.

"Oh, no, Linc is busy. I'll just head upstairs for a bath and an early night."

Clark tilts his head at me and then Linc, and I follow his gaze to the man who hasn't taken his eyes off me once since we walked into the room.

"No, Clark is right. We should go to the club. I want you to meet my friends and we can have some fun."

"Really?"

Linc moves closer again and slides his arm around my waist, pulling me close and looking to all the world as if he can't keep himself from touching me. I know it's only because Clark and Gaspard are here but that doesn't stop my breath from catching in my throat when he lowers his head and takes my mouth in another mind-numbing kiss. When he lifts his head, his eyes are dark with desire, mirroring the way I feel.

"Wonderful, you should wear that white dress we bought today with those gold sandals."

Linc is still holding me, his fingers caressing the slope of my back and I want to purr like a kitten from his touch.

"How long do you need to get ready?"

"Oh, um, twenty minutes."

"Nonsense. Give her an hour, Lincoln. You can have a drink with us while she goes and beautifies herself some more."

Linc's eyes on my lips make me swallow remembering the feel of them on other parts of my body. "Does an hour work for you?"

"Yes, that's fine."

An intensity is building between us, stealing the air from the room and nobody but me and Linc are party to it.

"Come on, neanderthal, let her go. You can ravish her later when my eyes don't have to watch."

Linc tears his gaze from me and gives his brother a withering look. "Why are you still here, Clark?"

"I need to talk to you about a call Mom received from Father today."

It's infinitesimal but I feel Linc tense ever so slightly at the mention of his father. There was never any love lost between them and it seems that hasn't changed.

"Go, upstairs and get yourself ready, Lottie. Take as long as you need. I'll wait for you."

As Linc drops a final quick kiss on my lips, I nod and he releases me. As I rush to our room, only stopping to grab some of the bags of clothes, I wonder at his words.

"I'll wait for you."

A deep recessed part of me wishes he meant those words, that he wanted me so badly he'd wait forever but I know he doesn't. Linc doesn't love me, he never did. While I was whispering my heart's desire and giving him all my dreams, he was giving me nothing but lies. That doesn't mean I can't enjoy the time I have with him now and take the pleasure he offers so freely with no demands from me. Sex with Linc is nothing like I imagined, it's raw and brutal, dirty and base, and I love it. I crave it now I've had a taste and I want to grab onto it and treasure it because all too soon it will be gone and I'll go back to my lonely existence. All I have to do is keep him from taking what is left of my heart. I can do that, can't I?

17: Linc

THE CONVERSATION WITH CLARK HAD GONE MUCH AS I EXPECTED. HE hated our father as much as I did and was happy for me to be taking my rightful place as CEO of Kennedy Enterprises. The lecture about giving my wife more attention hadn't gone so well. I got that he was trying in his own way to help, but I wouldn't tolerate him micro-managing my marriage for me.

Thankfully, Gaspard had stepped in and reminded Clark that he was overstepping before I had to, and he'd done it in a much nicer way. I liked him for Clark, he balanced my brother's over-excitable side with a mature calm.

Tossing back the whiskey I'd poured, I turned at the sound from the top of the stairs and the air left my lungs. Lottie was standing at the top in a short white dress that cut to the middle of her toned creamy thighs. It clung to her every curve, hugging her hips and stomach before molding over the lush mounds of her breasts. My hands itched to touch her as I stared, struck still by her beauty.

She descended like a queen, head high, shoulders back, her long lush hair hanging down her back in thick waves. I had the over-whelming sense of pride that she was mine, no matter how temporary, and it struck me again the desperation I felt to keep her in my life by any means necessary. But the sharp claws of fear of letting her see the power she had over me dug in, embedding themselves in my chest.

I almost hadn't survived losing my heart to the girl she'd once been, I'd never survive losing it to the woman she was now. So, I reined my emotions into check, pushing aside the pride I felt, the tenderness she conjured in me, and shoved it into a vault. I'd win her heart and keep mine safe, I just needed to be clever about it.

"You look stunning."

The blush that crept along her cheeks made my cock thicken and harden in my pants. Knowing how she looked spread out on my bed, her skin the same blush pink after the fourth climax I'd wrung from her body left her spent, played on a loop in my brain.

"Thank you."

Taking her hand, I kissed it before leading her to the lift that would take us down to the lobby. She held herself stiff beside me in the car, as if she was nervous or scared in some way. My irritation with the gap between us made me reach out and clasp the top of her thigh with my hand in a proprietary manner.

Her indrawn breath seemed to freeze in her chest before she forced it out. My seduction of my wife continued as I caressed the silky soft skin of her inner thigh with my thumb, inching closer and closer to her heat each time, but never touching her where I knew she craved it.

What started out as a game to make her weaken for me was fast backfiring as my dick ached in my pants with the need for her touch. As the car stopped, I leaned in and took her chin in my grasp, forcing her eyes to mine. "You will have the eyes of every straight man there on you tonight, my Lottie. Do you know how that makes me feel?"

Lottie shook her head as if she didn't trust her voice not to betray her. Satisfaction wove through me at the knowledge that I could render her as unhinged as she made me feel. Taking her hand from her lap, I pressed it against the hard ridge of my cock. A pulse jumped in her neck and then she tightened her hold on my cock. I hissed as pleasure stole over me, making me feel savage and desperate. "When those men look at you, I want you to think about my cock inside you. In your hungry cunt, down that greedy throat."

"And what will you think about?"

Her voice whispered over me like a lyrical caress, soft and unsure and sexy as fuck. "How I'm going to ruin you for any of them but me."

Her eyes flashed with fire before I bent, ghosting my lips over her mouth. It wasn't a kiss, more of a promise, a tease of what was to come.

Inside the club I kept her hand in mine as I guided her up the stairs to the second floor, my demeanor warning off any man that I caught looking at the woman that was mine. I wasn't the type to get possessive, it wasn't my nature. I'd never cared if other men coveted the women I fucked. Fuck, I'd even shared some of them with Beck on occasion. With Lottie though, the men lusting after her made me feel feral as they looked at what belonged to me.

As soon as I hit the second floor Monica was there, her flirty smile gliding over me before her glance took in Lottie, before seemingly dismissing her as competition for my attention, despite the fact she had her hand in mine and we were clearly together. It amused me that she'd be so foolish.

"Mr. Coldwell, I didn't know you were coming in tonight."

There was no reason why she would either and I could tell she was trying to stake her claim by appearing as if she knew me as more than a casual fuck. I stay silent, watching Lottie regard the woman who wasn't a threat to her as if evaluating her. Monica works the second floor exclusively so may not have met Lottie before and I wonder how this is going to go down.

"Would you like your usual?"

I don't know how but Monica managed to make the words sound like more than an offer of a drink, and maybe they were, but I was distracted by the tightening of jealousy streaking over Lottie as she leaned her body into me.

"Aren't you going to introduce us, Linc?"

A smirk twitched on my lips as she glared up at me like she'd like to take a carving knife to my balls, but her words were sickly sweet. I loved this side of her, the sparky fiery side which hadn't shown itself nearly enough since our reunion.

"Yes, of course. Monica, this is Lottie. Lottie, this is Monica, my favorite waitress." I knew I was pushing it but her ire turned me on and made me want to wind her up so I could subdue it, subdue her. It was sick and slightly twisted but I'd long ago accepted I was who I was, and I liked it.

Monica batted her eyes at me before glancing at Lottie. "Nice to meet you. I haven't seen you around before."

Lottie glanced up at me with an adoring look on her face, filled with love and so much feeling it momentarily stopped my heart in my chest.

"Linc and I recently re-connected and then with planning the wedding and everything I was busy."

Monica frowned. "Wedding?"

Lottie grinned, a friendly sight, but I knew her better than anyone and I could tell she was enjoying this.

"Oh yes, Linc and I were married yesterday." Lottie flashed the huge extravagant ring I'd given her when we exchanged vows at the woman who was now giving me a withering glare.

"A scotch on the rocks, please, Monica, and a strawberry daiquiri for my wife." As Monica hustled away from us, I turned my eyes to my wife. "You enjoyed that?"

Her head cocked to the side, and I could sense the smile she wanted to give me and held back. "Not as much as you did. It won't work, Linc, so forget it."

I turned, taking her in my arms and pinning her against the railing. My still hard cock pressed against her belly as a hiss fell from her lips. "What won't work, wife?"

The word wife from my lips felt right as I stared down at Lottie.

"Making me jealous."

"Is that what I was doing? Are you jealous, my little one?"

"Of course not. I don't care what you did before or after we're over, but while we're married our contract stands. You're my husband and the only person who has any right to flirt with you is me."

My body felt like it was throbbing with liquid fire as she announced I was hers in such a strong forthright manner. I was hers, body and soul, but I'd never admit that to her. It held too much power. "Liar."

I dipped my head and kissed her, tasting her sweetness, and wishing I could just take her now, here against this balcony with every man here watching, so they'd know who she belonged to, but I wouldn't let anyone but me see her come for me again. That night on the third floor was a one-time thing. That doesn't mean I can't play around and have some fun with her.

As she softened against me, her body melding to mine, I caressed her peaked nipple through the fabric of her dress. She was turned on and I'd bet she was soaking for me. Not able to resist, I slipped my hand up her silky thigh until I was touching the drenched slip of her G-string. A growl rumbled through my chest as she whimpered, and I thrust the scrap of lace aside and speared her with my middle finger. Her tight pussy seemed to ripple around me as I teased her, swallowing the moans and whimpers. I knew the people below couldn't see anything, the glass a dark, tinted color to give the illusion of privacy but Lottie was so lost in seeking her pleasure as she rode my hand with men and women mere steps from us, so caught up in their own enjoyment that they didn't notice.

As the familiar flutters of her pussy tightened around my finger, I pulled it away, fighting the urge to make her come. I wanted to, but I wanted her on edge more. Hungry for me and aching with need the way she's had me feeling since the second I locked eyes on her weeks ago.

"Linc, please."

I smiled as I kissed her upturned lips. "I love it when you beg, but I won't ease the ache inside you yet. I want you walking around this club tonight as desperate for my cock as I am for your pussy." My voice sounded dark and husky, even to my own ears.

I pulled away and saw the drugged look of desire in her eyes before taking her hand, grabbing the drinks that had been left beside us, and walking towards the table in the back corner where I knew my friends would be waiting for us.

The table went quiet as we approached, and I could sense the querying glances at Lottie were making her uneasy. Without thought I pull her closer, wrapping my arm around her waist, giving her comfort as if it's the most natural thing in the world.

Making the introductions, I give each man a warning look that dares them to step over the line with her and I'm met by curious, almost questioning looks.

"Guys, you all know Lottie but let me be the first to introduce her as my wife."

Shock ripples around the table and I almost laugh. They never expected this from me at all.

Harrison is the first to recover. "Well, now it all makes sense. Congratulations, Linc, and you too, Violet. Or should that be good luck, Violet?"

He drags my wife in for a hug and my arms feel empty without her in them as she's passed around my friends as they offer her a heartfelt welcome. It's clear they like her and as I pull her out of Ryker's arms with a growl, I know she's just gained four more overprotective males in her life.

"Okay, enough. Give her back."

I lock my arms around Lottie as Audrey approaches last with a smile on her face and I let Lottie go again with a sigh as Audrey envelopes her in a hug.

"Welcome to the family."

"Thank you."

Audrey laughs as she pulls Lottie to sit beside her with me edging Ryker out of the way so I can sit beside my wife in the large booth. Before long, Lottie and Audrey are chatting like old friends and I relax against the back of the leather booth and turn my attention to Beck and Ryker.

The drinks keep coming and the easiness of the night begins to soothe my earlier tension, although my need for her still simmers like a viper waiting to strike when I least expect it.

"How are things at the hospital?"

Beck nods. "Good. I have a ground-breaking surgery coming up next week so won't be around much. I have to fly to Switzerland to meet with the patient."

"Will you do the surgery in Switzerland?"

Beck purses his lips and nods. "Yes, it's an eleven-year-old boy and I'm the only person who's successfully performed this particular technique."

Beck isn't just a good cardiac surgeon, he's the best and I admire him more than anyone for what he does. His competitive arrogance and drive make him the best, it's also why we clash sometimes. We're too alike.

"That's a lot of pressure."

"It is, but it's his only chance."

I lift my glass to him. "Well, here's to a successful outcome."

"I'll drink to that." Beck downs the amber liquid and then stands. "If you'll excuse me, I have a prior engagement on the third floor."

I watch him go and wonder if he too will ever get bored by the constant stream of meaningless sex as I had.

"Come on, I love this song. Let's go dance."

Startled out of my musings, I move as Audrey pushes past me dragging a smiling Lottie with her.

"Where are you taking her?"

Audrey laughs and pats my cheek in an annoyingly familiar way that she has when she's drunk. "Relax, cousin, I won't let anything happen to her."

Lottie looks at me and I see doubt has crept its way onto her pretty face. I hate that she thinks I'm displeased. I want her to be happy, to sink so far into this marriage that she'll never want to leave.

"Go, have fun. I'll be waiting here."

Her returning smile and the way she tentatively bends to press a kiss to my lips, her hand cupping my chin, makes me suck in a breath, filling my nostrils with the scent of her until I'm drowning in it. She's gone before I can react, pulled away by a different member of my family this time.

A hand claps me on my shoulder and I turn to see a grinning Harrison. "How's married life, buddy? You sure shocked the shit out of us."

I shake my head as he and the others laugh at my expense, but I don't feel anger, only a tentative contentment. "Fuck off."

"Well, was the virgin pussy worth the shackles of marriage?"

My gaze slashes to Ryker and I feel an overwhelming anger at his words. He hasn't said anything untoward as such. We talk like this frequently, but Lottie is different. She's my wife. "Watch your fucking mouth when you're talking about my wife."

My hardened stare seems to cut into him, the warning evident as he freezes, placing his drink slowly back on the table. The others remain silent as if sensing a shift in me and wary of how it might play out.

I can't explain it, nor do I even want to try when I barely understand it myself. I just know that however this started between me and Lottie, she's now my wife and deserves the respect that comes with that title from all of them.

"I meant no harm, Lincoln."

"I'm aware, but from now on you'll all treat her with the respect she deserves and keep your fucking hands, dicks, and eyes away from her."

"Or?" Harrison asks as if testing me.

A coldness sweeps over me as I consider the question. "Or I'll make the person who tests that warning cease to breathe."

Ryker smirks at me. "Easy, brother, it was only a joke. Now we know Lottie is off limits, none of us will touch her. You have our word, and she'll be treated and thought of as if she's an adopted sister."

"I'd prefer it if you didn't think of her at all."

A deep laugh blooms around the table the tension lifting as fast as it had settled.

"Fuck, man, you have it bad."

I shake my head. "Don't talk shit, I have nothing. I just want Lottie to be untouched by you animals and treated with the same courtesy you treat Audrey."

None of these men would go near my cousin and treat her less than an equal. They know better than to disrespect her like that and I'm just adding my wife to that mix.

"Message received." Ryker holds his drink aloft. "To Violet and Lincoln, long may she hold the key to his dick."

I laugh and clink my glass with the others.

A little while later I'm feeling edgy, wondering how long Audrey is going to keep my wife away from me. I head to the balcony railing, ignoring the withering look Monica sends me as I pass her. She was nobody to me and the sooner she works that out the better.

Resting my arms on the edge I looked down at the crowd and my gut clenches when I see my wife. Sudden blinding rage fills me, tempered with a sense of ownership and lust as I spy the woman who'd said vows to me dancing in the middle of a throng of men who look as dazed by her addictive beauty as I am.

My feet are moving before I realize my intent, my body pulled like a magnet to hers. The people on the dance floor separate as I shove through the throng to get to her. Capturing her around the waist from behind, I feel her stiffen and then relax as if she senses it's me without even turning her head. I dip my head low, biting her earlobe and whispering a soft warning. "I warned you not to dance with other men, Lottie."

She goes to speak, but I stop her, spinning her around and hauling her close to my body as people undulate around us like an erotic dance of foreplay. My mouth seizes hers in an angry kiss, meant to punish her for her temptation, but quickly I realize I'm the one being punished as her tongue winds into my mouth, desperate and wanting.

Dragging my mouth from hers, I see the half-lidded desire in her eyes and my restraint snaps. Turning on my heel, I drag her from the dance floor and up the stairs.

"Linc, wait."

I slow my pace slightly but keep my focus on my destination. When we reach the hallway leading to the offices where we'd started this, I shove her against the wall, pinning her with my hips.

"See, Lottie? Can you feel what you do to me with your teasing?"

"I wasn't…."

"Shut up."

Her gasp of outrage is short-lived as I bend, kissing her, swallowing the anger and letting my hands move over her thighs until her fire goes from angry indignation to pure white-hot lust. I take every whimper from her mouth into me as my hands find her breasts, pulling the top of her dress down and teasing her nipples until she's arching against me.

My cock is aching, pre-cum spilling out from me until I can't hold on any longer. "Unzip me."

"But someone will see."

"I thought you liked everyone watching if the spectacle you made of yourself is any indication."

I bite her nipple, my fingers tearing the thong from her body and then I touch her, her wet desire coating my fingers and dripping down my hand.

A growl escapes my throat as I thrust two fingers inside her tight aching cunt. Her moan is music to my ears. "Un-fucking-zip me."

Her hands fumbled at my zipper until my cock springs free.

I spin her, my vision full of the way she'd looked on the dance floor, like a siren, surrounded by hungry men.

Pressing her face to the wall, I guide my cock between her soaked thighs before thrusting into her warm heat. Her body bounces and she cries out at the intrusion but her ass pushes back into me, wanting more.

"You feel that, Lottie? You see how crazy you make me?"

A cry of pleasure breaks from her lips as I rasp in her ear and I fuck her harder, taking my pleasure from her as much as she's demanding it with her whimpers.

"Answer me."

"Yes."

My fingers tighten on her hips before I move my hand to cup her sex, feeling myself fucking into her sweet pussy. Stroking her clit, I feel her shift her ass toward me again, seeking more as I thrust into her almost violently. "That greedy little cunt just loves my cock, doesn't it?"

The only reply is her whimper so sweet it makes my balls tighten as her pussy gets wetter. My Lottie loves dirty talk it seems. "You like being my little whore, Lottie? You like earning your three million with that pussy?"

I felt her stiffen, her body going still until I pinch her nipple, dragging a moan from her and she relaxes into the pleasure I'm giving her. "You want to come, Lottie?"

"Yes."

"Do you think you deserve it after defying me?"

"I didn't."

A growl rumbles in my throat before I grasp her chin and turn her head, silencing her with my mouth.

I toy with her clit, feeling her begin to pulse and flutter around me, her breathy moans sliding down my throat like nectar. As she comes, her body seizes, squeezing me like a vice until I see stars and then I come on a roar that's drowned out by the sounds of the music below us.

Sagging against her back, I drop my head to her shoulder, feeling some of my anger being replaced by shame that I'd let her get to me like this.

Withdrawing from her body, I tuck my still semi-hard cock in my pants and pull her dress down, leaving her destroyed thong hanging from her body.

I can hardly look at Lottie, so ashamed of how I've treated her, the names I'd thrown at her, when deep down I know it's my own insecurity that has caused me to react the way I have.

I feel her eyes on me but don't meet them or speak to her as I lead her to the exit of the club, down the back stairs.

Opening the door, I see my driver Boris waiting at the curb.

"Take Mrs. Coldwell home."

Lottie grips her bag as she puts her arms around herself and she looks at me. "Aren't you coming with me?"

Her voice shakes slightly, sounding vulnerable and I have to fight not to fall to my knees and beg for her forgiveness, but I harden my heart. Tonight proved why I couldn't let myself get attached, she has too much power over me.

"Go home, Lottie. I've no further use for you tonight."

Her sharp indrawn breath shows I've hit my mark.

"I hate you."

Lifting my head, I see the devastation in her eyes coupled with a simmering anger. Stepping closer until she's backed against the door of the limo, I take her chin in my hand and force her eyes to me. "No, you don't, but you wish you did."

Lottie yanks her head away from me and I let her go, slamming the door when she's safely inside the car.

Watching the limo pull away, I realize that by hurting her to stop myself from falling for her, I was also fucking up my plan to make her love me again.

I needed a drink and to regroup. I needed a new plan.

18: Lottie

"HURRY, ERIC, YOU'LL BE LATE FOR SCHOOL."

It's been two nights since the incident at the club, and I've hardly seen Linc. He comes home late at night after I'm in bed, crawling in beside me and settling his body around me so I'm cocooned by him. Then he's gone before I wake, leaving me to think I've almost imagined the way he holds me as we sleep. I fake sleep when he comes to bed, not wanting to speak to him. In truth, I don't know what to say. We're at an unhealthy stalemate, and I hate the way it makes me feel. I yearn for the way he looks at me as if I'm the only person in the room, the way he holds me after we have sex, but I won't allow him to treat me as he did that night.

The sex at the club has confused me. He made me feel dirty and cheap but so turned on and the orgasm had almost robbed me of the ability to stand, it had been so powerful. I'm certainly no expert but that didn't seem right. Perhaps he was right and the fact I like that kind of treatment did make me a cheap whore? Yet it isn't the sex that hurt me or his words, it's the way he sent me away afterward as if I'd fulfilled his wishes and was no longer of use to him.

Rejection is something I've had to deal with all my life and for the most part, I'm immune to it, but Linc is the chink in my armor. He was always the one in my corner and it feels like a betrayal to have him treat me like all the others in my past have done.

I jump a mile when Eric speaks right next to me.

"I can't find my baseball bag."

"For goodness sake, Eric. We haven't got time for this. Have you checked the bottom of your closet?"

His face lights up and he runs off to find it while I clear the breakfast things away to keep myself busy. Mrs. Jenkins will be in later to handle the cleaning and daily tasks of the house, but I can't help being who I am, and I don't let people pick up after me when I'm perfectly capable of doing it myself.

"Found it."

"Good, now let's go."

I grabbed my bag, and we head to meet Boris who takes Eric to school every day. Linc had tried to convince me to change Eric's school during the contract negotiations, but I'd been adamant he stay where he was. He's happy there and doing well and he loves his teachers. Plus, I remember what private school was like for someone with no money and it sucked—hard.

The teachers look down on you, the kids tease you, and it's not what I want for my brother. If I hadn't had Clark and Linc, I'd have been so lonely there.

"Are you coming to my game tonight?"

I glance at Eric, raising a brow. "Have I missed one yet?"

"No, but I wanted to check. Everything's different now."

"I know, but I won't ever stop being there for you. That won't ever change. You understand?"

Eric shrugs trying to look older than his nine years. "I guess."

"No guessing. I promise you, Eric. I'll always be here for you."

"What if you get sick like Momma did?"

My heart aches that he knows such loss at his age, and I wish I could promise him that it will never happen. But the truth is none of us can promise that, no matter how much we want to.

"I look after myself so I can be as healthy as possible."

"If you died, would Linc look after me or Aunt Heather?"

Heather had asked if it was okay for Eric to call her Aunt Heather and I'd agreed. I want to keep Eric protected from future events but denying them both that connection is cruel, and I won't do it. "I don't know."

I should figure this stuff out. I'm already failing as his guardian. God knows I haven't been much up 'till now and I vow to do better. "I'll figure it out if it makes you feel better, though. Have a plan in place just in case."

"Yeah, it would."

"Then that's what I'll do."

I have no idea what I'll plan but I'll figure it out, although my first plan is not to die until I'm old and gray.

As the car pulls up around the corner from the school, Eric and I jump out so I can walk him the last little bit. Pulling up to school in a limo isn't a good look with his friends so we walk together and I kind of like this part of my day. It feels normal and helps me center myself for the day to come.

"Can you remind Linc what time the game is later?"

"I don't think Linc will be able to come, Eric."

"He is. He promised."

I frown, confusion making me stop and face him on the sidewalk. "When did you speak to Lincoln?" As far as I knew he hadn't been home when Eric was awake.

"Last night. We face-timed."

"You did?"

"Yeah, he said he'd be here."

I see his little lip wobble as doubt and disappointment crash into him. "He's a very busy man, Eric."

"I know but he said we're family now, and he wouldn't miss it."

I crouch and smooth his hair from his face. "Well, then I'm sure he will be."

His face splits into a wide grin. "You think?"

"Of course."

And he'll be there because I'll damn well make sure he is.

After seeing Eric into school, I ask Boris to take me to Lincoln's office building. We park outside the intimidating glass high rise with the Kennedy name on it and I feel a shiver of apprehension like I don't belong here. I walk inside with my head held high, trying to fake it like I did when I was young, imagining I'm a queen and not the peasant girl who cleans for the rich family. My heels click on the marble floor and I hide my shaking hands under my huge designer bag which Gaspard insisted went with everything. I'm wearing sleek black pants, a cream blouse, with black lace at the V-neckline, and nude stiletto pumps. My coat is a warm neutral cream with a hint of pink. I look good, chic, and classy even if I do say so myself, and yet I feel out of place, like an imposter. Perhaps it was because I know I don't belong. I never really have.

"I'm here to see Mr. Coldwell."

My voice, even to my own ears, sounds shrill and nervous as if I'm about to be thrown out on my ear at any second. The woman with dark hair in a stylish chignon and white blouse smiles. She's beautifully put together in a natural way, making her look like she's born for this life.

"Of course, Mrs. Coldwell. Here's a card for the lift. Go right to the top and Melissa will show you from there."

I was stunned that she could possibly know who I was and couldn't help the question that sprung from my mouth. "You know who I am?"

"Of course. Mr. Coldwell sent an email to all personnel informing us of his marriage and making security aware you were to be allowed in whenever you wish."

"Oh. Well, okay."

Could I sound like any more of an idiot right now? I take the card and, as I walk toward the lift, a smile spreads across my face. The same thing happens when I reach the top floor. Melissa, Linc's PA, is waiting to take me to his office with a huge smile on her face.

"It's a pleasure to meet you, Mrs. Coldwell, and may I offer my congratulations on your marriage."

"Oh, thank you so much."

Her smile is genuine, and I guess her to be around fifty years old with a warm demeanor, but I also know if she's Lincoln's PA, that means she's incredibly efficient and skilled at her job because he's nothing if not exacting

She walks us down a thickly carpeted corridor. The walls are a sleek gray with glass and dark accents giving the place a modern feel with just the undercurrent of the original founder, Linc's grandfather, who he'd adored.

We reach a set of double oak doors, and Melissa knocks and glances at me.

"He doesn't know you're here. He was on a call so this will be a nice surprise for him."

It will be a surprise, no doubt but I'm unsure it will be a nice one.

I keep my thoughts to myself as the voice from within calls out to enter.

Melissa pops her head around the door, blocking me from seeing him with her body. "I have a visitor for you, Mr. Coldwell."

"Not now, Melissa. I have a mountain of work to get done and not enough time."

"I have a feeling you'll want to see this one." She grins at me and pushes the door wider.

Linc is sitting behind a huge glass desk, with a view of Manhattan behind him. His jacket is off and he looks devastatingly handsome. His jaw drops as he pushes his chair back and strides around his desk toward me, the shock turning into what looks like a genuine smile.

"Lottie, this is a nice surprise."

He takes my hand and leans in to kiss my cheek as Melissa backs from the room. I expect him to drop my hand when she leaves but he keeps a hold of it as he leads me to a brown leather couch along the left wall.

His office is like the rest of the building, sleek and modern with touches of the old world, of a time gone by and it works. It feels like Linc in here.

"This is a lovely surprise."

I look at him warily, trying to ascertain if he means his words or if he's acting for an audience I can't see. Pulling my hands away, I put some distance between us as I walk to the window taking in the

137

magnificent view. He's a king up here, a powerful man with the world at his feet. Lincoln was always meant for greatness and, putting aside my bitterness, I know he's a fair man too. He proved that during his negotiations over the contract, making sure I was looked after and had legal representation when he could've left me to fend for myself.

The wound he'd dealt me the other night however still bleeds, the pain of his words and indifference as he fucked me is like a cut that refuses to heal. I look at him in the glass as he watches me warily as if I was the one to strike out with hateful indifference. His face falters and the smile he greeted me with falls away and I wait for the cool, cold man to emerge, to lash out and hurt me again.

"Would you like some coffee or tea?"

I blink, shaking my head. This isn't a social call, I'm here to make sure my brother is not hurt by promises this man will not keep. "No, thank you." I hold my bag in front of me like a shield as if to ward him away from coming closer. It's so difficult to stay angry with Linc, when a part of me wants to smooth the furrows from his brow, to ease the shadows from his tired eyes. I wonder if he's finding this as difficult as I am. Does he regret the bargain we made?

Thrusting the thoughts from my mind, I turn to face him. "I haven't come for a visit, Lincoln." I blow out a breath suddenly feeling exhausted from holding on to so much anger. "I think we both know that our relationship isn't one that invites intimate visits in the middle of the morning."

I see his eyes darken, jaw going tight as his lips purse in thought. "What *do* we have, Lottie?"

I huff out a humorless laugh. "I have no idea, but it isn't the kind of marriage where I drop by for a visit unannounced."

"A shame. I'd welcome it."

"What?"

He moves to lean against his desk, facing me at the window, his ankles and arms folded, making him look powerful and sexy in a way that's impossible to fake. Why did it have to be this man who can stoke such an inferno in my blood?

"I'm happy to see you. I've missed you these last few days."

The admission shocks me. "Pardon me?"

His smirk is soft and sexy, and my belly flutters at the sight, a million butterflies taking flight inside me.

"You heard me, Lottie."

"Yes, it's not my hearing I have a problem with, it's the words out of your mouth."

"You don't believe me?"

His statement makes my mouth gape as irritation works its way up my spine. "I'm not playing this game with you, Linc. I just came here to make sure you'd be at Eric's Little League game tonight. He has it in his head that you will be. I tried to tell him he was mistaken and that you're a very busy man, but he was adamant you said you'd be there."

"Yes, I will. It's at six, right? At the sports field behind his school?"

I pause momentarily stunned that he knows all this information, then I'm angry as I try to understand the game he's playing. "Yes, but I'd prefer it if you didn't come."

Linc frowns and pushes off the desk moving towards me, stopping when he's just inches from my body. Like a magnet, I feel sucked toward him and fight the need to just lean in and rest my head on his chest. To let him take the reins from me for just a little while. Stiffening my spine, I tilt my head to meet his gaze.

"And why is that, Lottie? Just a second ago you were here to demand I be there and not let Eric down. Now you want me to break that promise to him."

I folded my arms across my chest to hide the way my nipples respond to the deep timbre of his voice. "I won't have him dragged into whatever game you're playing. He's a child and he's been through enough."

Linc flinches like I've struck him in some way, but I know I'm mistaken. He's heartless, and men like him can't be hurt.

"You think I'd toy with a child's emotions?"

"I don't know, Linc. I don't know you."

"Bullshit, you know me." His words are harsh and short, and he seems angry, but he tamps it down.

I blow out a short breath. "I knew you once, but that was a long time ago and the boy I knew would never treat someone like you've treated me."

His hand lifts quickly and I flinch away, not wanting his touch on me, because I know I'll crumble. I'm helpless when he touches me, and my emotions are too close to the surface today. His hand drops and he sighs as he moves to the other side of the desk.

"You're angry with me."

I'm so much more than angry, I'm hurt, I'm humiliated, and yes, furious but not with him so much as myself for allowing him the means to cause me pain with my stupid hope.

"No, I'm not angry, Linc."

"You are and you have a right to be. I was an asshole the other night and I should never have spoken to you the way I did. I apologize."

My chest seems to tighten at his words and the sincerity in them. I didn't expect his apologies or want them. My anger keeps me safe from falling in love with him all over again. Of thinking this is more when we're just pawns in each other's games. Truthfully it hadn't been the words he'd spoken when we fucked, it had been the cold way he'd rejected me straight after and the doubt he'd made me feel about myself.

I'm far from experienced. He was the first man to kiss me, to touch me, to fuck me, and even in between that I'd only had a few boyfriends that had never gotten past second base. Not because I hadn't wanted it, I had but because I'd constantly looked for the way Linc had made me feel when we were together the first time, and never found that rush of excitement and nerves he'd given me.

I didn't say any of that though, I'll never tell him how weak he makes me, and never allow him that power again. "It's fine, Linc."

"No, it's not and despite the rocky start we've had, I'd like us to be friends."

"Friends?"

I walk toward him, wanting to understand how one man could be such a different person from one day to the next. He keeps showing me glimpses, albeit small, of the boy I'd worshiped and then the next moment, he's the asshole who demands I bow to his needs.

Linc closes the distance between us and I can't seem to find it in me to move away. His pull is so strong, and as he takes my hand in his and runs his fingers over my wrists, stroking the delicate skin, I soften.

"I'd like us to start again. To be friends so that this year isn't fraught with fighting and resentment. We were friends once and I think we could be again. It will make life easier for all of us living under one roof if we're at least amenable to one another."

"Friends who have sex?" I question, wondering if he'll let that part go and not knowing if I want him to give in and release me from the yearlong pleasure he's shown me or not.

His lips quirk as he lifts my wrist to his lips, placing a kiss on the pulse point that makes my pussy flood with heat.

"We've both agreed to this contract, Lottie, and if you think for one second I'm going to give up that sweet pussy for even a second, then you're sadly mistaken."

I shiver as Linc nips his way up my arm, pulling me closer as he does, and I go willingly. When I'm within the bounds of his arms, his hands resting on my lower back, my front pressed against his heat, he drops a light kiss on my lips.

"I'm sorry for the way I spoke to you the other day. I was an asshole."

An unexpected laugh burst from me, pushing my breasts against the hard wall of his chest. "Yes, you were." I sober as I give him a small nugget of truth and I don't even know why I do it. "Honestly, Linc, it wasn't what you called me. It was the way you were after. It made me feel like a cheap whore and no woman wants to feel that way, at least none I know."

"It won't happen again. I'm truly sorry."

"Fine, then we can try married friends with benefits, but don't mess with Eric's feelings. That is a hard no for me, and I'll cut off your balls if you hurt him."

His face spreads into a smile that makes my legs turn to jello, he's too handsome for words sometimes. "Deal."

"Well, I should go. I have an entire day of getting in Mrs. Jenkins' way ahead of me."

I pull out of his arms, and he lets me go.

"Shall I pick you up or meet you at the game?"

The fact he's asking shows me he's listened and is attempting to be a good person. "We'll meet you there."

His expression remains the same, but I see a slight line mar his brow before he hides it with a smile. "I'll see you later then, wife."

I shake my head and laugh. "See you later, Linc."

I'd come here looking for a fight and had gotten something else entirely. It would remain to be seen if that was a good or a bad thing.

19: Linc

"Is he asleep?" I ask as Lottie walks into the kitchen and puts Eric's medication back in the fridge. I hadn't known a lot about childhood diabetes, or diabetes in general, until him. But having read up on it extensively in the last few days, I'm now aware more than ever of what Lottie had been facing alone.

"He was exhausted."

Her small smile is like a feather over my spine, seductive and gentle, making me want to touch her. Instead, I pour us both a glass of the red wine I've found she likes and hand her one. As she leans her hip against the counter, I watch her throat move as she swallows admiring the delicate arch of her neck.

"I'm not surprised. He worked his butt off tonight."

"Eric is small for his age so he works twice as hard to make up for it."

"He's a great kid. You should be proud."

"I'm incredibly proud of him."

"As you should be, but I meant you, Lottie."

Her head tilts and she looks at me with such confusion, that I can't control the impulse to pull her into my arms. The wine sloshes against the glass as she places it on the island, and I know she must be able to feel my dick pressing into her hip.

All week I've been filled with guilt and shame for the way I behaved at the club. I might be that person with other women, but never with Lottie. Yes, I'm controlling and possessive and I like sex a certain way but being cruel to her had left me cold. Too many memories and too much history between us eradicated my ability to switch off my feelings for her.

So, in the early hours of Sunday morning when I'd been holding her stiff body in my arms as she feigned sleep, I'd come up with a plan. I'd rekindle our friendship. She'd fallen in love with me once when we started as friends and perhaps she could do so again.

Getting to know Eric had been a separate decision, despite what she'd thought. I saw a boy who craved a male influence, and I wanted to be the one to give him that, a positive one, not the one I'd had from my father. Eric was a good kid, funny and smart, and he didn't deserve the hand he'd been dealt. Losing his mother and his own diagnosis must have been incredibly hard, but he had Lottie and that also made him lucky.

"Me?"

"Yes, you should be proud of yourself. I don't know how you coped as long as you did. You're amazing."

She snorts, placing her hands on my chest to try and put some space between us, but I only tighten my hold on her. "Stop buttering me up, Linc. I'm a sure thing, remember? We have a contract."

Her words irritate me. I hadn't been thinking of the contract or softening her up when I spoke, I'd just been thinking about her. "Still awful at taking a compliment, I see."

The blush starts on her cheeks and spreads over her neck when she realizes I mean every word.

"Thank you. Eric makes it easy. He's a good kid."

He was but even a good kid can be a handful and she makes it look easy. I drop the subject not wanting to embarrass her further. "What are your plans this evening?"

Her head tilts at my question. "I thought I'd go swim in the pool downstairs if that's okay with you. Eric won't wake and I'll only be an hour."

"Take your time. I have some work to do in the office." I think I see disappointment flitter across her face but it's gone before I can be sure.

"Aren't you going to the club tonight? You were there every night before."

My lips quirk as I stroke a finger down her neck, feeling the pulse in her throat beat faster. "The draw isn't quite the same now a certain barmaid is missing."

"Can I ask you a question?"

"You can ask. I don't promise to answer."

"Did you play in the club a lot before we were married?"

My dick seems to throb as the image of Lottie on the third-floor flashes through my mind. "Why do you want to know?"

"I heard rumors."

"Oh? And what were they?" Someone was getting fired if I found out anyone was breaking the NDA they'd signed.

"That you and Beck liked to share."

God, I could feel my cock leaking like I was a damn teenager as she said the words. "Is my past relevant?"

"No, I just… Do you miss it?"

"No."

It was a quick response, but it was the truth. I don't miss any of it. Lottie has consumed my every thought since I'd laid eyes on her again. I've missed her more than I ever realized.

"Will you use the club once we're divorced?"

I didn't want to think about that because if I had my way, we wouldn't be getting a divorce, but I needed to be careful how I handled that answer or I'd give myself away. "Would that bother you?"

Lottie bites her lip, her eyes falling away as she tries to get away from me. I turn her so her back is to the island and place my hands on either side of her body, trapping her. "Eyes on me, Lottie." I deliberately deepen my voice, seeing if she'll respond to it. When she does, her eyes finding mine, a growl rumbles from my chest. "Good girl."

Her cheeks pinken even more, and I know my little Lottie is wet for me. I can almost smell the scent of her arousal.

"Do you like the idea of a sex club?" I lean in so my lips skim her neck, the pulse beating wildly. "Does it turn you on?"

"No."

I chuckle. She's so stubborn. I remembered that about her and I'm pleased to know that the sassy side of her is still alive. "Liar."

My hands slide from the island and grasp her behind her knees, lifting her easily onto the counter as I take the space between her legs. She looks flushed, sexy, beautiful, and like she was made for this life. Lottie is classy, not because of money or birth, she just has it. A certain look, a way about her that can't be learned or faked.

My eyes scan their way down her face, her neck, catching on the pebbled nipples the t-shirt she'd changed into from earlier can't hide from me. Lifting my hand, I thumb the hardened peak, relishing the sigh that escapes her throat as her head falls back, revealing the long line of her throat. Lottie is so responsive to my touch and so eager to please. I trail my lips over her neck, sucking lightly on her pulse. "Do you want me to show you what the third floor has to offer from a personal level, not as an employee?"

Her head snaps up, her eyes dark and half-lidded with desire. God, I wanted to kiss her, to consume her. She's so perfect for me. She was made for me and every second with her proves I'm right.

I pinch her nipple, making her gasp, before I bend my head to suckle on it through the fabric. Her hand threads into my hair at the nape and, as I pull pleasure from her, the fingers at my scalp tighten. A delicious pain prickles through me and I groan around her tit.

Her hips are rocking into me, seeking the hard ridge of my cock, and I'm not even sure she's aware how much she wants this. As her movements became frantic, I lift her in my arms and stride toward the couch.

Sitting heavily, I settle her so she's straddling my hips, her core pressed against my cock. Just a few layers of fabric lie between me and what I need. Two days without the feel of my cock inside her cunt feels like forever. She's like a drug seeping into me, destroying my control.

"Take my cock out."

Her breath hitches at my words but she does as she's told. Her soft fingers wrap around my length, causing me to hiss. My eyes fall to her hand where she's stroking me a little tentatively, reminding me that she's inexperienced and yet I've never been so turned on before. Folding my hand over hers, I tighten my grip, showing her how I like to be touched and, before long, she has me on the edge. I push her hand away and see the way her face falls as if she's done something wrong.

"Did I hurt you?"

"Fuck, no. You were gonna make me come all over myself like a fucking teenager."

Her eyes dilate and her lips fall open, her tongue touching her dry lips. *Fuck, she wants to watch me jerk myself off.* "You like that idea, Lottie?"

Her short nod has my balls tightening up. Standing abruptly, I keep her straddled around me, her heels digging into my ass as I walk us to our room. Her lips find my neck as I walk, and I think my legs will give out when she bites my neck, her teeth grazing my skin and making my dick jerk against her heat.

Kicking our bedroom door closed, I thank God for the thick insulation in this apartment knowing it won't wake Eric. I love the kid but if he cock blocks me now, I'm gonna hang him upside down by his feet from the roof.

Dropping Lottie on the bed, I stop to look at her, my skin prickling with desire at the sharp look of need and excitement on her beautiful face. Lottie has always been pretty, even as a child, and as she got older that has only blossomed until the woman panting before me with need is beyond stunning. I'm not sure if a word has been invented to describe how beautiful she is and if there is, I certainly don't have it at my disposal.

Dropping to my knees, I drag her to the edge of the bed by her ankles as she keeps her eyes on me watchfully. "Do you want me to teach you about pleasure, my Lottie?"

"Yes."

147

"Then you must do as I say without question. Can you do that for me?"

"Yes." Her head bobs wildly, eagerly.

"If I do something you don't like, tell me and I'll stop."

"Do I need a safe word?"

My fingers, which had been smoothing up and down her toned thighs, still. "A safe word?" I wonder what she's heard at the club.

A pretty blush spreads over her neck and down her chest and I want to trail it with my tongue, to follow that delicious, tempting path.

"I read some books and heard it on the third floor when I was working."

"Ah, I see."

"Well, for now, you don't need a safe word. A simple no or stop will suffice."

"Okay."

"Good girl."

She almost preens at my praising her and I smile inwardly. Quickly I divested her of her pants, her smooth skin warm against my touch before I lift the tee over her head, leaving her in just her bra and panties. I take a second to admire her as she leans back on her elbows, hair tumbling over her shoulders, lips red from my kiss, and my cock jerks as if seeking her out.

As she watches, I give it a few hard strokes to ease the ache but I know nothing will be enough, not until I'm inside her again and until then I have to exercise restraint. My Lottie has so much to learn and I know I have to start at the beginning, not go in all guns blazing and fuck her like an animal without teaching her a damn thing. Our wedding night had been fucking phenomenal, and I know she'd enjoyed it, but I should have eased her into this and not rushed it.

Bending my head, I kiss her calves, moving up until I'm kissing her creamy thighs. I reach for her hand as she watches, her eyes eager and bright with excitement.

Placing her fingers at her pussy, I show her what I want. "Make yourself come while I watch."

Her fingers began to move, circling her clit as I stroke my cock slowly. Her low moan of pleasure as she slides her fingers into her wet pussy make me clench my fist tight around my cock to stop me from coming all over her stomach. I don't want that, at least not yet.

"Keep going, Lottie. Show me how you touch yourself."

Her hands travel over her body, knowing every place that makes her squirm and I watch, paying attention to how responsive she is to nipple play. I'll get some pretty clamps for them, and she'll be stunning as she screams her release.

As her fingers begin to move quickly, her pants became louder and the sound of me fucking my fist keeps her eyes glued to my dick.

"You like watching me, don't you, Lottie?"

Her answer is a gasp as her back bows and she comes, her eyes closing before popping open as if she's worried she'll miss something.

"Don't worry, pet. I won't come without your eyes on me."

As her climax ebbs, I jerk my hand faster, moving so I'm closer as she sits up on her elbows.

"Where do you want it, Lottie?"

"On my stomach."

On a growl I come hard, my seed hitting her belly in rapid jerks and it's like a fantasy playing out before me as she places her palm over my release and smooths it into her skin.

"Fuck me, you're perfect."

The rest of the night is spent showing my wife how much my cock likes being inside her.

20: Lottie

"WOULD YOU LIKE TO HAVE LUNCH WITH ME TODAY? THERE ARE A FEW things I'd like to discuss with you."

Linc walks out of our bathroom with just a towel around his hips, his bronze body on display, making it difficult to form a coherent thought. The man I married is magnificent. The dark smattering of hair on his chest forms an arrow pointing down to the impressive V leading to where the towel is now straining with his erection.

"Lottie."

I glance up at the way he growls my name to see him watching me. "What? Sorry?"

He moves toward me with a chuckle that fills my chest with warmth. Looping his arms around my hips, he pulls me close so I can feel every inch of that hard body against me.

"I asked if you'd like to have lunch with me today."

"Why?"

"Can't a man take his wife with benefits for lunch?"

I smile at the term we've coined to describe this relationship we have. The last month has been perfect and I'm half waiting for the other shoe to drop and for something to rip it all away again. "I guess."

My hands trace the lines of his chest distractedly. I've turned into a sex addict since our wedding night. Linc has unleashed a side of me I didn't know existed and I find myself wanting him all the time.

Linc still doesn't wake up in bed beside me, and I haven't asked him why, but he often comes in once he's woken Eric for school with a cup of coffee for me and then takes his shower. It's our routine and I like it, maybe a little too much.

I catch a glimpse of the tattoo on his arm again and still. I haven't seen it properly and haven't asked about it either but now it intrigues me. I pull back with my hand on his bicep, tilting his arm so I can get a better look. I feel his eyes on me as I study the tiny flower, my breath hissing out on a rasp as I make out what it is.

My eyes shoot up and lock with the bright blue of his gaze. "You have a violet tattooed on your arm. Why?"

"Why do you think?"

He looks unsure of himself and it's not a look I'm used to Linc wearing. I shake my head. My thoughts are swimming and I can't seem to grasp one of them. "I don't know. That's why I asked."

"After you left, I was…." He pauses as if he can't find the word or doesn't want to admit to something. "Adrift. I missed you so I had that done one night when I was blind drunk."

"You weren't old enough to drink."

Linc quirks a brow at me as I trace the tiny delicate flower.

"I wasn't worried about that at the time."

I have a feeling there's more to the story, but if I ask he might ask about why we left, and I don't want to open that can of worms. I can't tell him and I'm not sure I ever will. "Why didn't you remove it when you got older?"

"It's a reminder of a time in my life when I was truly happy, and I like it."

I have no words, so I push him toward our bed. Eric is with Linc's mother this morning, so I can be brave and make the first move, which isn't something I've done so far in this relationship.

The tattoo has loosened something in my chest, and I feel another inch of the frost around my heart melt for this man. He hurt me, but perhaps there's more to it than what a fifteen-year-old girl believed to be true.

Linc lets me push him onto the bed on his back and watches me with a grin as I sink to my knees. The towel has fallen from his body and all that's left are a few droplets of water on his chest. His eyes flash with desire as I take his cock in my hand and stroke him just how he likes.

"Fuck, Lottie. If I'd known the tattoo would get this reaction, I'd have shown you on the first night we met up again."

I chuckle as I wrap my lips around his thick cock and hum. His head falls back as he rests on his elbows, and I marvel at the sight he makes. Even like this, he's powerful and in control, even though he lets me think I have the power.

"Jesus, Lottie, that fucking mouth of yours is heaven."

I never knew giving a blow job would be such a turn-on for me, but it is, and I snake a hand down the front of my sleep shorts to touch myself and find that I'm dripping wet with need.

"That's it, work that sweet pussy as you suck my cock."

His words only add fuel to the already out-of-control fire inside me.

I remove my hand, wanting to concentrate on his pleasure, not my own, but find myself shoved forcefully off his cock as he stands.

"Bend over and put your hands on the bed. I want to fuck this hungry pussy."

Linc moves behind me, yanking my shorts down as I do as he says and then I feel the blunt head of his cock at my entrance.

"Hold on."

That's all the warning I get before he slams into me. My body rocks forward on my hands and I cry out from the feeling of him inside me, but Linc doesn't give me a second. He grips my tits in his hands, fingering the tight buds of my nipples and continues to pound into me fast and hard.

I love it, my senses are being assaulted from every angle and all I can feel is the pleasure building at a rapid pace.

"I wish you could see how beautiful you look taking my cock." His hand leaves my breast and I feel it skim down my spine before he caresses the soft skin of my ass. "Gonna fuck this too."

His thumb grazes my tight puckered hole and I tense when he breaches me with just the tip of his thumb.

"Relax, sweetheart, I won't fuck you there yet. You're not ready. I'm just playing."

I relax and enjoy the new sensation as he mirrors the movements of his thumb with those of his hips and I feel a flood of desire move through me like a wave.

"You like that don't you? I can feel you squeezing my cock."

God, his dirty talk is my kryptonite. "Yes."

"Who does this pussy belong to, Lottie?"

"You."

"Yes, it fucking does. You're mine. You've always been mine."

I don't respond because he moves the angle of his hips and suddenly I see stars as he hits that spot inside me that I was sure was a myth. A keening cry fills the room and I barely recognize it as my own as he continues to fuck me through my release.

"One."

He does this, he makes me count the orgasms he gives me and won't come until I've had at least two. It's exhausting but oh so good.

"One."

His thumb pops free of my ass and he pushes me down so my face is in the bed.

I hear a phone ring and turn my head to see his phone on the bed where he dropped it before his shower.

I think he'll ignore it until I see him reach for it.

"Coldwell."

Oh my God, he answered the damn phone while he was still inside me. He slows his pace as he talks but he doesn't stop what he's doing. I wriggle to try and get free and feel the sting of his palm on my ass as he spanks me. I turn to glare at him and see the sexy smirk on his face before his fingers find my clit and then I moan into the bed, trying to muffle the sound of my pleasure.

"I don't care what the board says, I won't be making a statement about my marriage."

His finger circling my clit and the slow deep thrust of his cock are making my body hum and I know I'm moments away from coming again. My walls flutter around his cock and he rewards me with more pressure on my clit.

It's all I need and I'm coming again as my screams disappear into the bed, and all I can do is hold on as wave after wave hits me and white sparks shoot behind my closed eyelids.

When I become aware again, Linc is throwing the phone on the bed beside me, the call ended.

His hands grip my hips tight, and I know they'll leave marks and I don't care. I like carrying his mark on me throughout the day. It makes me feel closer to him and I know he likes to see it too.

I clench my inner muscles knowing that it drives Linc crazy and feel his fingers flex.

"Fuck me, could you be any more perfect?"

I don't answer because it's a rhetorical question.

As I feel him swell inside me, euphoria comes over me. This right here is perfection, the way he makes me feel, the way he touches me, all of it.

As he comes inside me, I wonder what it would be like to have a lifetime of this with him. Even knowing it's a fruitless hope, I still cherish it as he wraps his arms around me and pulls me up to him so he can kiss me.

"You good? I didn't hurt you, did I?"

Linc is a beast in bed, but outside of it, I'm finding he's a man who's sweet and attentive, the man I always thought he'd be, only now he has a dirty side which I love just as much.

"Not at all. Although I can't believe you answered that call."

His lips quirk and I'm floored by how handsome he is when he smiles, which is happening more and more of late.

"It was important."

"And I'm not?" I ask the question with a grin but deep inside I wonder what I am to him now. I go to turn away. I need some space to clear my head from the sex fog and think clearly, but he holds me tighter and grips my chin in his fingers, making me look at him.

"You are the most important thing to me. Do you have any idea how much you consume my every thought?"

"No."

He kisses my lips, my cheek, my eyelids, and even as he softens inside me, I can feel my body wanting him again.

"You do, I've missed you, Lottie, far more than I ever thought I had."

My heart squeezes at his sweet admission and I know it's happening all over again. Linc is showing me the side of himself nobody else gets to have and it makes it impossible not to love him.

He drops a kiss on my neck as he pushes off me. "And now I get to go to work knowing my come is inside you all day."

I laugh as he moves away and heads for the bathroom, the dirty side is new though and I not so secretly love it.

"I don't think so, mister. I'm taking a shower."

He smirks. "That's okay, I'll just give you another load when you visit me at the office later."

"I never said yes to that."

"You will. You can't resist this any more than I can."

He's right. I can't and I'm not even sure if I want to anymore.

21: Linc

"So, what do you think?" I'm talking with the head of legal about the fuss my father is making when I hear a knock on my door. "Come in."

I smile when the door opens to reveal my wife looking as stunning as when I left her. I stand and move to take her in my arms, kissing her deep and feeling her sink into me. A cough behind me reminds me Danny, our legal eagle, is still in the room. I pull away and Lottie blushes.

"Sorry, I didn't realize you were in the middle of something."

"It's fine, we were done." I keep my arm around her as I face Danny. "Will you get those documents filed for me today?"

"Yes of course."

Danny is the best. I poached him from the top law firm in the country when he was an associate and people thought I was crazy, but I saw the same thing in him as was in me, determination and drive.

"You should consider doing the interview the board wants though. It will go a long way to smoothing over the investors' jitters."

I frown. "I'll think about it."

Danny nods and after a polite smile at Lottie, he leaves us.

"What was that about?"

I lead her to the couch in my office and pull her down so she's sitting in my lap, the blue flowery dress she's wearing skims her thighs and I take advantage by running my hand up her silky thigh. "My father is making some noise and stirring up the investors."

Her hand skims my cheek. "You must have known he was going to do that. Your father is hardly a man who likes to lose."

"I know and I'll handle him."

"But?"

I stroke her inner thigh and she opens for me, making me smile. Lottie is so responsive and eager to learn and to say she's a quick study is an understatement. She was made for me in every way and as much as I'm fighting it, I know I'm falling head over heels for my wife. "But the board wants us to do an interview with New York Weekly about our wedding and how we got together again. They think it will settle everyone's nerves to know more about the man running the Kennedy Empire."

"Then let's do it."

My eyes flash up from where they were enjoying the expanse of her cleavage poking out from the demure neckline of her dress. Lottie is watching me with openness. "Seriously? You'd do that?"

"Of course, if it helps. The only thing that's off limits is Eric. I want him kept out of this as much as I can."

"Of course."

I shift so she's straddling me, her skirt riding up so I can see the lace of her blue panties.

"Set it up and let me know when and where you need me."

I rock my hips into her. "I need you now."

Her smile lights up my world. Her just being close lights up my life and I think she might feel the same way, but it's too early to find out

"You're insatiable."

I lean in and nibble on her neck. "I am when it comes to you."

Her giggle warms something inside me and thirty minutes later, we're walking from the building hand in hand with my come inside her.

Sitting across from her at La Galerie, my favorite restaurant, I watch the surreptitious looks men cast her way and know I'm a lucky bastard because, despite my horrendous behavior at the beginning, I'm sitting with the most beautiful, sweet, kind, and sexy woman on the planet and she's smiling at me.

I have her hand in mine as she tells me about how she's been invited to help out at Eric's school by listening to the younger children read and I can see the joy on her face.

"Do you want kids of your own, Lottie?"

"Yes, one day. I want four."

"Four? That doubled since we were kids."

"I know but back then I was different. Being around Eric and watching him grow has shown me how much I enjoy it. What about you?"

I want to say 'however many you want' but I don't. I don't want to scare her off. "Yes, one day."

We fall silent but it's not uncomfortable just contemplative. It's on the tip of my tongue to ask her why she left me. Why she never gave me a chance to explain, but we're getting on so well and I'm loath to rock the boat. Things are good right now and there'll be time for that once I've won her over and convinced her this is real.

"So, you wanted to talk to me about something?" Her fingers twist around mine mindlessly, as if she needs the contact as much as I do.

"I did. I'm not sure if you know about the charity called Love Books."

"Are you kidding, of course I do. It's helping so many kids that were in my position when I was younger. If I hadn't been lucky enough to have you to teach me, I'm not sure I'd be reading now."

Our order of sea bass and dauphinoise potatoes is set down by our waiter and we wait for him to leave before we continue.

"You would have. You were determined and smart and you'd have figured it out somehow."

I love that she gifts me with helping her, but the truth is, Lottie would have succeeded anyway. She's one of the smartest people I know, and dyslexia doesn't take away from that one bit.

"Thank you."

A blush steals across her cheeks and my heart tightens in my chest. I thought I was falling for her but now I know I'm madly in love with my wife. I always was it seems and maybe, just maybe, things will end differently this time, or God willing, not at all.

"Love Books is my charity and I want you to be the Ambassador for it."

Lottie is stunned silent, her fork mid-air as she looks at me.

"Say something."

"Something."

I laugh as I take her fork and lower it to the plate.

"Are you serious? Love Books is yours?"

"Well, mine and Audrey's. She had a friend who struggled in school too, so we set it up to help other kids get the help they needed."

"Oh my God, that's amazing."

I'm relieved. When I set it up. I convinced myself I was doing it to help my cousin out, but I know the real reason was Lottie. Looking back over the last ten years, I can see her influence in the things I did, even the small things.

"They do wonderful work, and we need a new front person and I thought you'd be perfect. That's if you're interested of course. You don't have to. I just wanted to put it out there into the world and see what you thought."

"Yes, I'm interested. Tell me more."

Over lunch, I give her the details of what we do and how she'd be involved. I want her to be as involved as much as she wants, and I respect that Eric comes first for her.

"You can meet with Dana, our operations manager, and discuss it more and go from there."

"And Audrey is okay with this?"

"It was her idea." I blush at the admission, wishing it had been mine, but it seems my cousin knows the way to my wife's heart better than I do.

"Oh wow, that's really kind of her. I must admit I'm a little in awe of her."

"Audrey?"

"Yes. She's like this powerhouse of a woman who isn't afraid to go after what she wants."

"So are you."

Lottie rolls her eyes. "Oh please. I was a broke waitress who was about to sell her body. Who *did* sell her body."

"No." My hand reaches for hers as I bark out my denial. "Listen to me, Lottie. You're a woman who put her brother first and did her absolute best with the shit hand she was dealt. None of what happened was in any way in your control. I hate the thought of you thinking about yourself that way."

"But the truth is our contract states it."

Her voice is softer as if she's trying to make me feel better and it only makes me feel worse. I wish we could go back and I could woo her and make her fall in love with me and then I could have married her and rid her of her debt without the stupid contract between us. Now it will always be there, and I hate it.

"Hey, it's okay. I'm happy with my decision. I've secured a future without debt for me and Eric, and I feel like I got my friend back and with orgasms to go with it. I'm not ashamed, Linc."

"Good because you have nothing to be ashamed of. You're amazing."

"Thank you."

I get the bill and take her hand, but as we walk toward the exit, I meet the eyes of the last two people on earth I want to see right now.

"Son, how lovely to see you."

My grip tightens on Lottie as she moves closer to me. "Father."

"Aren't you going to introduce me to your new wife?"

I have no desire to do so, so I counter. "Aren't you going to tell me why you're having a cozy lunch with a woman more than half your age who isn't your wife?"

I see his lip curl and know I landed a hit.

"Don't be silly, son. You remember Arabella. She was your date to the prom if I'm not mistaken. We were just doing a little business."

I sense Lottie stiffen beside me as she's reminded of the night I left her standing waiting for me at the door to her little house as I drove past her with Arabella as my prom date instead. He knows what he's doing. After all, he was the one who instigated it but as I feel her hand shake in mine and turn to see the color has drained from her face, I wonder if there is more to it.

"Since my son is so rude and has forgotten the manners his mother and I taught him, I'll introduce myself."

He tries to step around me to Lottie, but she only leans in closer and I block his attempt.

"Violet, it's lovely to see you again. All grown up and looking as delightful as the last time I saw you."

If it's possible, she seems to pale even further, and I know I need to get her out of there.

"Mr. Coldwell."

Her voice is a whisper and I curse as I pull her closer to my side. "It seems Lottie is feeling unwell. We need to leave." I glance at Arabella who was never a bad person, just the pawn in my father's games the same as I was. "Arabella."

"Lincoln. Violet, I hope you feel better soon."

She manages to rush out a cursory thanks before I drag her out of there. The second she's in the car, I reach for her, and she lets me hold her as she shakes.

"Tell me what to do, Lottie."

"Just take me home."

I give the instruction to my driver and for the hundredth time this week, curse the man who gave me life.

The closer we get to home the more the tension in her body eases and the shakes finally subside but as we step into the elevator for the penthouse, she's still incredibly pale. I keep her tucked into my body and she holds on to me as if her life depends on it.

Sweeping her into my arms, I head straight for our bedroom when the doors swish open. Ignoring the questioning look from Mrs. Jenkins, my housekeeper, I place her on the bed and pull off her shoes, kicking mine off as I go and then I settle myself on the bed beside her, hauling her into my arms as I do.

Lottie huddles close as if she's trying to burrow inside me and I hold her tighter, pressing my lips to her head. "Talk to me, Lottie."

"It's nothing. I just don't feel too good."

"Was it seeing Arabella? I know it was a shock and I promise you I never would've gone there if I had any idea they were going to be there."

"No, it's not Arabella."

"Is it my father? Has he said something? Because if he has, I'm going to kill the bastard."

"He hasn't said anything."

The tone of her voice is off, and I know she's lying but I also know how stubborn this woman can be, and pushing her will only make her pull away from me. I might be a selfish bastard, but I need to hold her right now. When she went so white, it scared the shit out of me and I'm not ready to let her go, so I stay silent.

My hands skim her body, not in a sexual way, but to try and soothe her. I don't even know who I'm offering comfort to, her or myself. We stay that way for a while, wrapped in each other's bodies but both lost in our own thoughts. Eventually, I hear the soft sound of her breathing change and know she's fallen into a light sleep.

I remain with my eyes on the ceiling of our room trying to recount the lunch we shared and at what point it went so wrong. I keep coming back to the moment we saw Arabella and my father. Seeing the woman I ditched her for to go to prom must have been hard, but was that all there was? My father was unpleasant but he's always been unpleasant, and Lottie must remember that from when we were younger. Had he been mean to her and I was unaware? It wasn't such a huge jump to think he'd warned her away from me given that he'd manipulated me to end our relationship the way he had.

Lottie stirs beside me, and I turn to see her sleepy face looking at me.

"I fell asleep."

I kiss her nose. "You did."

I watch as her face goes from relaxed to contemplative to panicked in the space of a split second. She shoots up, her hair untamed and sexy as hell around her shoulders.

"I have to pick up Eric."

I place a hand on her shoulder. "Why don't I get Eric, and take him for a burger? It will give you some time to relax, maybe have a bath, read a book, whatever."

She looks unsure and I don't know why I offered. I have a thousand things to do at the office and I know for a fact I missed an important meeting from the emails flashing on my phone by the bed. Yet I know I want to do this for her. Lottie has spent the last three years at least, working like a dog with no time for herself to keep her head above water and give her brother the life he needs, and she's done it on her own.

It's about time someone stepped up and gave her a hand.

"Don't you have work?"

"Nothing that can't wait."

"Are you sure?"

I can see her wavering and want more than anything to give her this small thing. I stroke her cheek, cupping it with my palm. "I'm sure. Let me help you, Lottie."

She turns her face and kisses my palm, sending a spark straight to my cock, but not only that, she lodged a giant crack in the wall around my heart. Lottie was breaking down every barrier I'd erected after our split and she wasn't even trying.

"Thank you, Linc. A bath does sound nice."

I kissed her lightly, or at least it starts that way, but the fire between us is always so hot and we end up panting by the time I pulled away.

"As much as I'd love nothing more than to kiss every inch of you, I need to go. I don't want to be late for Eric."

"Thanks again, Linc."

"My pleasure. You're not alone anymore, Lottie."

A sadness comes over her face which makes my stomach ache but she pushes it away with a smile that is genuine.

"What's your favorite cookie?"

"You mean apart from yours?"

163

Her head shakes as she rolls her eyes at my lame joke. "Yes, apart from mine."

"White chocolate chip and hazelnut."

"Nice."

I don't ask why she wants to know but pull my shoes on, and with a final kiss head out to pick up Eric.

22: Lottie

I HEAR THE LIFT TO THE PENTHOUSE OPEN AND CAN'T STOP THE SMILE at the familiar sight of my handsome husband walking toward me. True to his word, Linc had been nothing but wonderful since our discussion in his office. We spent our evenings when he wasn't working with Eric, either at ball practice or doing something, like playing video games or watching movies. I sucked at video games, but Linc was a natural and Eric was blossoming under his attention.

I'd tried to put the encounter with Charles Coldwell and Arabella Miles behind me. I was annoyed that I'd let it rattle me so much, but it was something I hadn't been able to control. I know Linc had been scared by my reaction, and for a few days after he'd hovered a little, and I knew he hadn't been convinced by my excuse of a headache.

Lincoln knew me too well and ten years apart seemed to have fallen away as if it had never happened. Linc was amazing with Eric. He listened and made time for him, and I could see my brother relished having Linc in his life. A male influence was the one thing I'd never been able to give him and neither had our mother, so Eric had missed out. I'd worried Lincoln would let him down, but he'd bonded with Eric as if it was natural, and deep down I knew why, although I could never tell him.

The nights were my favorite, though. Linc fucked or made love to me every night and far from finding it a burden, I craved his touch. I couldn't get enough of him and the things he was showing me about myself. He opened me to a world of pleasure I'd never experienced and knew, once this was over, I never would again. Far from the eager way I'd counted down the days of our yearlong marriage to begin with, I now found myself wishing I could hit pause.

"Hey, something smells good in here."

He moves to me and kisses my cheek, as his hands slide around my belly pulling my back to his front. I shiver at the feel of him and wish I could bottle it so I can take it with me when this is over.

Every day is a war between me and the hope I battle with daily. Things are so good between Linc and I, so easy, and I fight to remember it isn't real or I'll find myself in love with my husband and nursing a broken heart when it ends. Which it will, Linc has made no suggestion that this is real and why would he? It serves a purpose, and I'll do well to remember that.

Sliding my hair back, he kisses the space between my neck and shoulder, and I feel desire shoot between my legs.

Pulling from his hold, I busy myself stirring the pasta. "It's penne alla vodka."

"Is something wrong?"

I look back to see him studying me. Linc is perceptive and, since that encounter a few weeks ago, he's been watchful. "Not at all. Everything is fine but I do have a surprise for you."

"You do?"

"Yes, go check under the lid of that container."

His eyes light up and he looks so young as he grins and heads toward the box where two dozen of his favorite cookies are sitting.

He lifts the lid and grins before taking a bite and groaning with delight. "If I hadn't already married you, I'd be on my knees begging you to right now."

I laugh and shake my head. "You paid me three million dollars, Linc. The least I can do is make you cookies now and again."

"Lottie?" I glance around at him from where I'm adding more salt to the sauce and see his frown. He hates it when I bring up the contract and it's why I do it. I need to remind both of us what this is before we fall down a rabbit hole and get lost.

"Yes?"

I feel his hands on me as he spins me to face him. His hair is tousled like he's been pulling at it and I see for the first time how tired he looks. Running my fingers up his lapels, I go up on tip toes to kiss him. He kisses me back, tasting of sweet cookies as he loops his arms around my back and deepens the kiss.

"I don't want to hear about the contract, wife."

"Sorry, I just don't want us to get carried away and fall into a trap of thinking this is real when it's not."

Lincoln cocks his head. "It's real, Lottie."

"I know it's real but it's not really real."

Linc watches me before he nods, and he lets me go with a small smile. I immediately regret his loss and the way he pulls back emotionally, shutting me away from his thoughts.

"I have to work. I'll be in my office if Eric needs me."

"Do you want dinner first?"

He shakes his head and I know I caused this with my determination to keep my heart safe. I made him pull away when things had been perfect between us but it was that perfection I didn't trust.

"Just leave me anything you don't eat in the fridge. I'll have it later."

I watch him walk away, the slope of his shoulders heavy and weighted.

I listen as Eric talks all the way through dinner, his constant chatter only penetrating the peripherals of my mind.

"Well?"

Finally, I look up realizing I have no idea what he said. "Well, what?"

"Can I stay at Aunt Heather's again this weekend?"

I frown. Heather has been absolutely wonderful to Eric and me, throwing her affectionate arms open wide to us, but I don't want to take advantage. I already feel bad about us pulling the wool over her eyes. She'll be crushed when we get divorced.

"We'll see."

"Cool. Can I go play my new game?"

"Have you done your spelling?"

"Yes."

"Then, yes, you can."

Eric races off and I clean up the mess from dinner. Mrs. Jenkins and I have come to an understanding. She's a really sweet woman and we've worked out a rhythm to our days. I do miss working though, not the fifteen hours a day on my feet but the people, and I'm eager to get started at the Love Books charity next week.

I sit in the living room curled up on the couch, but the book in my lap doesn't hold my attention and before I know it, it's eight already and time for me to check Eric's blood sugar again.

He's good at doing it himself now and his sugars are so much more stable on these new drugs. I tuck him in and put his teddy next to him. It's one our mother gave him when he was born, and he treasures it.

"I like living here with Linc and having Heather and Clark and Gaspard in our family."

"Me too, Eric."

"Do you love Linc a lot, Vi?"

I don't want to lie, but then I wonder how much admitting to Eric that I love Linc is a lie anymore. "Yes, I love him very much."

A movement at the door makes me turn to see Lincoln watching us with a soft look on his face, his shoulder resting up against the door jamb, his hands in his pockets. He's loosened his tie and lost his jacket, the sleeves of his shirt rolled up his muscular forearms, and I want to see him looking at me like that for always. The thought brings a tightness to my throat.

Smiling I move to walk past him but he cups my bicep in his big hand. I glance up and he kisses me before bending to whisper in my ear.

"Being sweet makes me want to fuck you so hard."

I shiver at his words, wanting him with a desperation that is almost feral. "Who's stopping you?"

A growl leaves his mouth before he lets me go, and I stumble as he smirks. "Thirty minutes, my office."

I see him smile at Eric as he says goodnight to him, taking a couple of minutes to hear about his day before he ruffles his hair. I rush to our bedroom and move through the dressing room that's full of new clothes Linc insisted I get. I spot what I'm looking for in the drawer and anticipation zips through me.

On nervous legs I walk to Linc's office and see the door is ajar. I hear him speaking on the phone, so I knock quietly. The door swings open and Linc looks me over from head to foot, the phone at his ear gripped with white knuckles when he sees what I'm wearing.

Hooking me around the waist, he drags me closer so I can feel his rock-hard erection pressed to my belly. His eyes haven't left mine and I feel exposed as if just the searing look he's giving me will make me combust.

"Ryker, I need to call you back." He shakes his head. "No, this can't wait."

A thrill goes through me at his words.

Disconnecting the call, he drops the phone on the couch just inside his office door. "What do we have here?"

"A treat."

"For me?"

"You look like you had a hard day. Isn't it a wife's job to relieve her husband's stress?"

Linc's eyes twinkle. "Then don't let me stop you."

I've only taken the lead in our sexual encounters once before and my belly is filled with nervous anticipation. Yet I've had this fantasy since the first moment I saw him in this office, sitting at his desk like a king, power oozing from every pore.

I push him back a couple of steps before I take his tie in my hand and lead him toward his desk chair. His hands cup the naked skin of my ass cheeks, caressing me before I turn and, with a little shove, make him sit in the chair.

Standing between his spread, muscular thighs, I shuck off the red silk robe to reveal the red lingerie I'm wearing. A growl of appreciation echoes from his throat as his eyes move over me slowly, his hands tightening on my hips as he pulls me closer.

"Now what, my little Lottie?"

I still don't have a clue what to do next. My little scenario had never really gone past this point and when it had, the woman in my head was very different from the one I actually am in real life.

Seeing my unease, Linc trails his fingers through my hair and cups my scalp, giving a little sting as he pulls on my hair. "On your knees and open that pretty little mouth."

He kisses me hard and demanding before letting me go, the breath seesawing in and out of my lungs from just that small act is fast.

Linc pushes lightly on my hair and I lower to my knees. My hands tremble as I unzip him, stroking my hand over his cock as I free him from the confines of his pants. I lick my lips, the power beginning to ooze through my veins as I flatten my tongue and take him in my mouth. A hiss leaves his lips as I suck, taking more of him on each bob of my head. Linc is in no way small, and I have to wrap my hand around the base of his cock where my mouth can't reach.

He's bucking his hips up into me now, and it's gone from me blowing him to him fucking my mouth and I love it. The control, the way he takes without asking, the way he can make me feel so desired.

Suddenly he pulls out of my mouth and I find myself lifted onto the desk behind me, papers and pens scattering to the floor in his haste. Linc looms over me, his eyes wild and dark and on any other man they'd terrify me, but I trust Linc with everything in me, even my heart it seems.

His big hand grips my throat, lightly and I hold his gaze as his thumb gently strokes my pulse.

"Do you have any idea what you do to me?"

"Show me."

His palm flattens and he strokes down my body, in between my breasts, over my belly until he gets to the edge of the red lace thong I'm wearing.

"You're so fucking beautiful it's hard to look at you sometimes."

His fingers hook the edges of the thong, and he draws it down my legs before he drops to his knees, burying his nose against me and inhaling deeply. I blush but before I can react, he swipes his tongue through my folds and my back arches off the desk.

I'm so turned on that it doesn't take long before I'm climaxing, my body spasming as pleasure sweeps me away until all I can do is feel. It's like drowning. I can't catch my breath and a euphoria comes over me that is unparalleled.

Standing, Linc bends and grips my jaw as he kisses me and I can taste myself on him, making it all the more erotic and perfect. Feeling the nudge of his cock at my entrance, I think this will be hard and fast but as he pushes into me slowly, I know it's different. It's never the same with Linc, but he always seems to sense what I need and gives it to me, without me ever having to ask.

His eyes never leave mine as he rocks into me slowly and even though he's fully dressed and I'm all but naked, I still feel like I'm in control. This man who hurt me so badly is apologizing in the only way he seems able to.

As I come, the wave cresting slowly this time, I feel him swell inside as his cum fills me.

"Fuuuuck." He drags out the word before he slumps against me, his nose rubbing along my neck as I hold him close.

23: Linc

THE ICE IN MY GLASS TINKLES AS I SET IT DOWN ON THE TABLE IN front of me. "Harry, you're talking out of your ass. My employees love me." I squeeze Lottie's hand in mine as I shoot her a wink. "This one even married me she liked me so much."

"Yeah, I think you need to see a doctor, my friend, because that's not how I remember it."

It's a rare occasion when we all get together for dinner outside of Club Ruin, but it's one I enjoy immensely. Maybe that's because I have Lottie with me. She's the first person outside the five of us to come and it's equaled the dynamic, or maybe it's just because I'm hopelessly besotted with her.

"How are you enjoying working at Love Books, Lottie?"

I skim my hand over her shoulder, as I watch her interact with Audrey. My tough-as-nails cousin and my wife are becoming fast friends. The truth is, she'd ensnared the devotion of all my friends over the last few months. Lottie is easy to love, and I know that better than anyone. My mother adores her, and Clark and Gaspard call her more than they ever did me and I'm thrilled by it.

Life has fallen into an easy rhythm between the three of us. I wake her with my mouth on her pussy more often than not and then make her tea, which she prefers to coffee, and leave for work. She then gets Eric sorted for school and heads to Love Books, before collecting Eric after school.

Dinner is always a lively affair with Eric holding the conversation and me counting down the seconds until I can make love to my wife. We'd been to the club a few times, but if I'm honest with myself, the draw of the kink has faded. Lottie is my addiction and while I still love the control she gives to me so freely I don't need to be surrounded by others. I like to have her all to myself.

Although my sweet woman has a bit of a voyeuristic trait, which I fucking love. It gets her so wet and turned on when we watch others at the club, she goes off like a rocket the second I slip my hand into her panties.

"Oh, I love it. Everyone is so lovely, and I get such a thrill from watching the kids go from hating reading to enjoying it."

"They speak very highly of you." A blush tinges her cheeks, which makes my dick harden.

"I'm so grateful for the opportunity."

"You have a unique perspective, and the kids can relate to you in a way they can't with some of the others."

"Oh, how so?"

Harrison was studying her as he spoke and didn't catch the warning glare I sent him. Lottie never mentions her dyslexia and I'm not sure how she feels about others knowing.

"I'm dyslexic, so I know exactly how it feels to see the letters jumble in front of your eyes and the panic and shame that can bring, even though it's nothing to do with intelligence."

"Wow, I had no idea."

"Well, I was lucky I had a great teacher who was patient with me."

"School teachers can be so important to self-esteem with dyslexic children."

Her face tips to me and she gives me a shy smile which makes my heart contract. "It wasn't a teacher who taught me, it was my best friend."

I lean forward and capture her mouth in a kiss, savoring the taste of the lemon torte she'd eaten for dessert mixed with something that is uniquely her. I hold her eyes with mine as we pull back. "It was my pleasure."

Beck is looking back and forth between us as I scoot my chair closer, not even wanting a few inches between us. I hold up my glass in a salute. "No fucking way."

"Yes, way. Lottie was my best friend growing up and I taught her to read. Although it was my excuse to spend time with her so I'm not sure who the real winner was in this, her or me."

"So, you two have known each other for a long time then?"

"Almost twenty years but we haven't seen each other for the last ten."

Beck rubs his chin. "Wow, that explains the chemistry and the reason you two were shooting sparks off each other every time you were in the same room together."

Harrison was watching Lottie. "Shit, the auction. Man, I can't believe you let it get that far."

I turn to see her looking down, fiddling with her fingers. "Can we change the subject, please? How about you tell us about your latest girlfriend, Harry?"

He rolls his eyes and knocks back his scotch. "Nothing to tell. We fucked a few times, it was fine and now it's over."

"She get too clingy?"

"Something like that."

I'd been reading people since I was in middle school and I knew when my friend was lying. I also knew when to let something go.

"Who's going to the gala next Friday?"

Ryker was a typical tech nerd, in so much that he wasn't overly social outside his small group, and functions like that were his idea of hell. Which was weird to me because, inside the club, nobody could charm the women like he did.

"I'm out of town. I have a meeting with the new manager for the London office."

I glare as Audrey smirks at me. "Well played, cousin."

"Why don't you take, Lottie? Give you a chance to show off your beautiful wife, and some of the board members will be there too. She can get dressed up and you can show her how bad you are at dancing."

The board had agreed to let me out of the interview with New York Weekly if I made myself more available to our investors, and this would be a great opportunity. "Would you like that, Lottie?"

I see indecision war on her face and don't want to push her either way, but I want the world to know she's mine, at least for now.

"Who would be there?"

I list a couple of names on the board, and she seems to relax a little, the tension in her shoulders easing.

"Yes. I'd like that if I can get a sitter for Eric."

"My Mom will have him."

She bites her lip and I find myself jealous of her fucking teeth. "I don't want to take advantage."

"You won't be, she adores him."

"Okay, if you're sure."

I kiss her as my answer and shortly afterward I take her home and show her exactly how sure I am about her, even if I can't find the words to say it to her.

"HAVE I TOLD YOU HOW BEAUTIFUL YOU LOOK?"

Lottie pats my bowtie with her fingers, before running her fingers over my chest, making my blood heat up. "Yes, but I love to hear it and you don't look so bad yourself, Mr. Coldwell."

"When do you think we can leave?"

Her husky laugh does nothing to make me change my mind about wanting to blow this off and head someplace I can make her scream my name as I fuck her.

"Not yet, we haven't even finished our first drink and you promised me a dance."

"I did, didn't I?"

We're standing in the grand ballroom of the New York Performing Arts Centre. The room is decked out with a stage so that the emcee can get up and thank us all for coming and persuade us to open our bank accounts again. There must be four hundred of New York's elite in this room and I can't wait to leave.

Lottie is wearing a red dress with a thigh-high slit up the leg, the lace clinging to every curve. At first glance, it looks demure, with a high neck covering my favorite attributes, but when she turned, I almost swallowed my tongue. The back dips so low I can see the dimples at the top of her ass.

When she walked down the stairs from our room where the hairdresser and a make-up artist my cousin had hired to glam her up had been doing their thing, I'd been in two minds whether to just turn her around and demand she wear a black trash liner or take out an advert in the local news to warn every man within a hundred-mile radius not to even look at her.

I'd gone with option three and told her she looked stunning and then whispered in her ear what I was going to do to her when we got home as I made her cum with my fingers on the ride here.

Taking her glass of champagne from her hand, I place it on the tray of a passing waiter and lead my wife to the dance floor. I have no idea what song this is, but I know it's a new tune being played in a classical arrangement to fit the tone the organizers are aiming for.

I pull her close, my hand splayed on the base of her back in a possessive manner, trying to stop every pervert in here from looking at her and knowing it's a lost cause. She's just too beautiful and her light shines too bright. She's so unaware of the effect she has on people, and that only adds to the attractiveness radiating from her. Far from the models and socialites watching us with open interest who are always so aware of every facial expression and movement of their bodies. The woman dancing with me is laughing as she steps on my toe for the second time tonight.

"Oh gosh, sorry."

"It's fine, I'll let you make it up to me later."

Her eyes twinkle as she looks up at me, her fingers playing with the back of my neck, causing a zing of awareness to ripple down my spine.

"Oh, and how do you propose I do that? A foot rub?"

"I was thinking you could rub something else."

"You're insatiable."

I'm addicted to the sound of her voice, so light and silky with mirth behind her words. "I am for you."

I stroke her spine and feel the way her nipples peak and press into my chest. A shiver racks her body as I watch, hypnotized by her beauty. It's hard to believe I've been without her light in my life for the last ten years and yet that thought makes me remember that our time is limited and growing shorter by the day. That is, unless I can make her fall in love with me again. Some days I think I'm making headway when I catch her looking at me a certain way but other times, I see the doubt in her eyes and wonder if I'll ever make her love me again. I know we have our friendship back, but I don't want that from her even though it was my original aim. I want it all, I want forever as we are now.

"Want to go home?"

She hears the real question and I see the hunger in her eyes as she looks at me. "Let me just use the ladies' restroom and I'll meet you out front."

"I'll go hand over a huge check to the organizer. Be quick."

I squeeze a handful of her sexy ass before letting her go with a kiss. "Insatiable."

I am and I don't care who knows it. I want my wife, so sue me.

24: Lottie

THE LIQUID DESIRE IN MY EYES IS HARD TO MASK AS I WASH MY HANDS after quickly using the lady's room. I've freshened up as best I can, my body is on fire for the man who removed my panties on the car ride here and still has them in the pocket of his tux.

My face is flushed, my lips swollen from the kisses he keeps peppering me with and I love it. We're like two addicts and our fix is each other. I'm so absorbed with my thoughts that I don't notice the woman who comes in until she's standing beside me.

"Arabella."

She's everything I'm not. Tall and willowy with blonde hair and fair porcelain skin. Her lips tonight are a bright fire-engine red and her hair is swept to the side, exposing her delicate bone structure. She was never a mean girl in school, but she wasn't exactly welcoming either. Her father was a huge donor at the school we attended, and it was always drilled into me by the head teacher that it was only his good graces that let me attend the snobby education center in the first place.

"Violet. How nice to see you again."

She looks genuine but I'm not a fool and don't trust a word of it. I don't respond but give her a short nod as I turn to leave.

Her hand on my arm makes me flinch and she pulls back imme-diately.

"I'm sorry for what happened with Lincoln when we were younger." Her words are rushed as she studies me.

I want the world to open up and swallow me, but such is my luck it doesn't happen. "It's fine. It was a long time ago and we were just kids."

"It's not fine and it's isn't nothing. I saw you that night."

"Please, stop."

"I saw you waiting for Lincoln to collect you and I knew it was you he wanted to be with, not me."

I'm getting upset and it's making me angry now. "Clearly not."

"He hardly spoke to me all night and left early. I'd seen the way he looked at you in school and I was jealous, but I wouldn't have done anything except he asked me to go with him. I was shocked but happy about it. I liked him, all the girls did, and this was the first time he'd shown even an inkling of interest. When I saw you there, I knew why. He was in love with you."

Her hand flutters to her delicate neck and I watch, not wanting to hear her words but trapped by them.

"I don't know why he asked me to go with him when it was clear he wanted you, but I want you to know it wasn't malicious on my part."

Her words should make me feel better, but they only confuse me more. If Linc wasn't even into her, why had he shattered my young heart like it was so disposable to him? "Thank you for telling me, Arabella, but it's water under the bridge."

She smiles and I wish it would reveal crooked teeth or, at the very least, lipstick on them, but she's picture perfect as always.

"I'm so happy you found your way back to each other. It makes me believe in true love again after all."

I wished I could be a bitch, but she was being so nice to me and seems to be genuine. "Did you not believe before?"

"Being left at the altar will do that to you."

Her chuckle is dry and without humor, and I feel a wedge of

emotion stick in my throat. Reaching for her hand, I squeeze gently. "I'm sorry."

Arabella shakes it off and forces a smile, ever the socialite. "Don't be. He never looked at me the way Lincoln looks at you. You can practically feel the love he has for you spilling from him. I want that and I won't give up on it now I've seen it can happen."

I didn't have the heart to tell her that what she thinks is love spilling from him is good old-fashioned lust.

"It will. Just remember your worth."

Arabella leans and hugs me unexpectedly and I hug her back. I sense that a part of me has healed in some small way by taking the time to hear her out. "Good luck, Arabella."

"Thank you." I watch her leave giving myself a few moments to regain my equilibrium.

I walk out of the bathroom in a daze, my thoughts on the conversation I just had, which is why I don't see the snake of a man who corners me.

"Well, look who it is. The whore that spread her legs for my son a second time."

Charles Coldwell wraps his hand tightly around my arm as he drags me into an empty room. My heart is hammering like a runaway train as I smell the booze on his breath and see the wild slightly unhinged look in his eye.

I'm immediately thrown back to the past, terror clawing at my skin as the room around me falls away and I'm in my old room at Kennedy House. The walls feel like they're closing in, and I have to fight to draw breath into my lungs and keep my head. I physically shake off the memory and look at the man who was leering at me like I'm a fresh piece of meat.

"Get your fucking hands off me." I step back yanking my arm from his grasp and put some space between us and feel my back hit the door knob.

"What? You don't want to dance with me like you did Lincoln? Rubbing that body up against him in public like a little slut."

I turn to leave even as my legs feel like they'll give way after a few steps but find my face shoved against the door, Charles' pillowy body behind me, his erection pressed to my spine. Bile crawls up my throat and I swallow it back, trying to stay calm when all I want to do is scream.

"Don't worry, I don't want to fuck you. I don't want sloppy seconds and that cunt of yours is probably gaping from the dicks it's had inside it. Although your mother was pretty tight for an old girl."

My fury gives me a strength I didn't know I had, and I stamp down hard on his foot with my heel and when he releases me with a cry, I push him away. "Don't you ever talk about her like that again."

Charles looked furious as red blood vessels seemed to pop on his skin. "I'll do what the fuck I like, and you know what else." He pauses and sneers, and a dread goes through me that's bone deep. I want to run, to hide and turn back time, but I can't. "I want custody of my son."

My world implodes at his words.

"Eric needs a role model, and I'm going to show him the ways of the world."

"You stay the fuck away from him or I'll kill you myself."

"Now, now don't be dramatic, Violet. We both know I have the money to hire the best lawyers and take that boy away from you."

My shoulders sink because he's right. He can hire the best and even my three million wouldn't be enough against his unending funds.

"How do you think Linc would take it to know he's living with his own brother and you didn't tell him or my darling wife? How hurt would she be to find out you duped her?"

I want to say not as hurt by what he's done and the destruction he's caused but I know they'd both be devastated. I also know Charles doesn't want Eric. He's using him as leverage.

My shoulders sag again for a second and he sees it, smiling in triumph.

"What do you want?"

"I want my company back and if you help me, I'll forget about Eric and leave him for you to raise. If not, I'll take him and everything else you love from you."

I don't give a shit about me but losing Eric to this monster will *not* happen. It's my job to protect him when I hadn't protected my mother. And I meant what I said, I'd kill him first. "How am I supposed to do that?"

"Not my problem but find a way to make my son see reason and resign from his position and re-instate me or the world will find out about Eric."

He pushes past me and stumbles enough to show me how drunk he is, but his threats are the same. As the door closes, my knees give way and I sink to the floor. My worst nightmare has come to pass, and it's my own fault. I'd known it was a possibility, but Linc had won me over, convincing me that our marriage was the answer, that I could solve my financial worries by handing over twelve months of my life.

He'd been right, but it had opened up a bigger nightmare and I have no idea how to get out of it without sacrificing either my baby brother, who was so innocent and sweet, or my husband, the man I'm desperately in love with.

Tears sting my eyes and blink them back wishing like hell I could go back and make better choices, but I can't and now I have to find a way out of this mess.

Standing, I head quickly back to the ladies' room and thankfully find it empty. I splash cold water on my face and suck in some calming breaths that do nothing for my equilibrium. I look at the woman in the mirror and she looks like she's seen a ghost and it feels like I have. The ghost of my mother's rapist and I had to make the right choice now.

Although it wasn't a choice. Linc will recover but Eric, in the clutches of that evil man, will not. Smoothing my dress, I take several breaths and exit the bathroom running right into the man who I was going to have to deceive and the only man I want to hold me while I fall apart.

"Lottie, where have you been? I was worried sick."

I smile wide and let him haul me against his body as tears prick my eyes. Savoring his strength and the scent of his cologne and wishing I had another way. Maybe time will give me that, I need to think. I need space but selfishly I need him to hold me and bolster me more.

"Sorry, I was chatting with someone I knew from the charity, and time got away from me."

"That's okay, sweetheart. Are you ready to leave now?"

"Yes, take me home and do the things you promised me."

His grin is devilish as he leads me to the car and he makes good on his promise, making me forget everything but his touch, and I selfishly absorb it, tucking away each memory because I know it's only a matter of time before everything comes crashing down around me.

Later as Linc sleeps, I get up and slip his shirt over my naked body. I sneak out of the room and go to the large terrace that overlooks Manhattan. Tucking my legs under me, I huddle on the outdoor day bed and wish I could cry but even my tears have abandoned me. My mind goes over my options again and again, finding no alternative except one and I'm not sure I can do it. That I can trust someone with my secret. The sun is coming up, basking the sky in the orange hues of a new day when I feel him.

"Lottie."

His warm body wraps around me and the tears that had been absent want to make an appearance at the soft question in my name.

"Sorry, I couldn't sleep."

"You should have woken me. You're freezing."

He holds me tighter, wrapping his arms around my waist as he settles my back against him, tangling his legs with mine, his warmth thawing my chilled skin.

"You looked so peaceful. I didn't want to disturb you."

"You could never disturb me, Lottie."

His kiss on my shoulder makes me want to cry more, but I bite it back, not wanting him to know that something is up. He probably already suspects. Linc is too perceptive not to have noticed. "Linc?"

"Yes?"

"Do you enjoy your job at Kennedy?"

He chuckles. "That's what's keeping you awake?"

"No, I just wondered."

He settles back, laying me across his chest as we both watch the sun rise.

"Kennedy is more than a job to me. It's a legacy, a family that employs thousands of people and it's my honor to hold that legacy and nurture it to growth and health so that those people can feed their families and put roofs over their heads. It's not something I take lightly. It's in my blood and it's a privilege that I don't take for granted."

"Did your father?"

I feel him stiffen.

"Take it for granted?"

"Yes."

"My father is a piece of shit who bled as much as he could from Kennedy and my mother, and offered very little in return. He spent his time pushing his responsibilities onto others and using the time when he could be bettering Kennedy to line his pockets and play golf with his friends. That's when he wasn't fucking his floozies behind my mother's back."

I could sense the hatred rolling off him like a physical being, ugly and putrid. "You hate him."

"I'm ashamed to admit it but yes. I loathe the man and if I could have one wish it would be that he wasn't my sperm donor. He's like a cancer to everything he touches."

His words only make it that much harder for me, even though I wholeheartedly agreed. But knowing how much he loves Kennedy and what it would do to him to step away or have his father back at the helm kills me, because I know I have to find another way through this nightmare that won't impact him or Heather.

"Tell me about Club Ruin. If you love Kennedy, why did you start the Club?"

"Ruin was my salvation through a dark period in my life. We all went to college together, except Audrey and she was my best friend outside of Beck, Harry, and Ryker. We were just kicking around ideas that would be something for us, with no influence from our families. The kind of wealth we have can taint things and we were five people driven to succeed on our own merit."

"I get that, nobody wants to think they've been handed something without work unless they're an asshole."

Linc kisses my head. "I'm still an asshole, Lottie."

I hold up my hand, pinching my forefinger and thumb close. "Maybe a little."

His chuckle warms my heart, defrosting the ice Charles had put there hours earlier with his threats.

"Why a club though, and a sex club?"

"The club was simple. We could never get in anywhere when we were younger. We were all too well known so we wanted something that was ours."

"As soon as Harry was old enough, he got the license but by the time we opened it we were all legal age anyway, but we'd invested so much time and money and loved it. The rest is history."

"And the top floor?"

"That was Audrey. She saw a need for it and an opportunity to make some more money. That book that came out had opened up a world to people that enjoyed kink and promoted sexual exploration to the masses as a good thing and not something to be ashamed of and she wanted to expand on that. Audrey believes we all have a kink of some kind, which doesn't make us weird, and we should celebrate it. Celebrities and the rich and powerful can't explore that like some can for fear of it coming out in the paper. Club Ruin allows them that freedom."

"Do you have a kink?"

"I like to be in control. Not BDSM or anything but I like the power in my hands. I also like to explore my boundaries."

"Have you ever had a threesome?"

"Do you really want that answer?"

"Yes."

"Yes, and four and five."

"All women?"

I sit up shocked as he laughs.

"And men, although I don't get involved with the men in a sexual way."

"Who?"

"Beck and I have shared a few times."

"Would you share me?"

His face goes glacial. "Not a fucking chance in hell."

I kiss him and he holds my face in his hands.

"Good. I don't want that. I just want you."

"Thank fuck, because I'd hate to disappoint you."

"I do like to watch though."

Linc growls and I can feel his hardness against me. "I know. It makes you wet and needy."

I want to ask if we could explore a few things together so I can test my boundaries but I'm not sure we'll get the chance before our lives go to shit.

Linc doesn't need me to voice my needs though, he always seems to know. "I do want to show you a few things though."

"Oh?"

His hand curves around my ass, his fingers finding me wet. "So needy."

He slides a finger inside me and pumps a few times as my breathing goes jagged. When he withdraws, I think he'll tease my clit but his hand slides backward and finds my puckered hole. He massages me there and I feel my pussy clench with pleasure.

"I'm going to take this first too. I want to fuck you here while your fingers toy with that sweet swollen clit and your nipples hang low with gorgeous clamps attached."

Jesus, I'm so turned on at his words I'd have said yes right then, but he withdraws his hand.

"But not today. Today I'm taking you back to bed and fucking your sweet pussy and then I'm going to show you how much pleasure a sixty-nine can give you."

I let him, wanting him more than oxygen, and knowing I'll take what I can get from this man who owns my heart for as long as I can.

25: Linc

I STEP OUT OF MY CAR AND ROUND THE HOOD. IT'S THE MIDDLE OF THE workday, but I have things on my mind and only a mother's advice will do. Three days ago, I found Lottie on the day bed at dawn and since that morning things have been off. I can't say why exactly because she's been as loving and sexually open as ever, but something is off. She's holding back from me somehow and I don't like it.

I wonder if she's guessed my feelings for her and if they scare her as much as they do me. I never wanted to fall in love with her again, but it happened so easily that I wonder if I was ever out of love with her in the first place.

"Mom," I call out as I enter the wing my mother favors.

"In here, sweetheart."

I follow the sound of her voice and find her in the library. My mother loves to read, she's a true crime guru and I sometimes wonder if she's trying to find the perfect way to bump my old man off. She needn't bother; I'd happily pay for someone to do it to rid her of him.

She looks up as I enter and her still beautiful face crinkles into a warm smile. I instantly feel my worries ease. There's something magical about being around your mother. When everything else feels like it's going to hell, she's the constant force of love and warmth in my life.

"Darling, how lovely to see you." She offers her face for a kiss, and I oblige before sinking down into the chair opposite her.

She lays aside the new book on the life of an infamous serial killer and lifts the phone beside her. "Coffee, darling?"

I nod. "Yes, please."

"Cynthia, could we have some fresh coffee and some of those delicious blueberry scones sent into the library please?"

She hangs up and looks at me and it's difficult not to squirm. My mother has always been able to see right through me. It's what made the loss of Lottie so hard for me. I couldn't tell my mother without causing a huge row with my father and at the time I was still of the opinion he might hold some affection for my mom, and I didn't want to be the reason they fought.

"To what do I owe this pleasure?"

I shrug. "Can't a son visit his mother?"

She smiles, resting her hands in her lap. "Of course he can, and he should do it more often, but I sense this isn't that."

I'm given a small reprieve as Cynthia, the lady who replaced Lottie's mom, walks in carrying a tray loaded down with coffee and scones. I rise to take it from her, and she gives me a shy smile back.

"Thank you, Cynthia."

"Will that be all, Mrs. Coldwell?"

"Yes, thank you."

I set the silver tray down and pour the coffee, adding milk and sugar for my mother, just how she likes it and then doctor my own with just half a sugar.

"So?"

I don't know how to start this conversation without breaking her heart. She was ecstatic when I told her about the whirlwind wedding to Lottie and, since then, their relationship has blossomed, only made stronger by Eric, who my mother adores.

I sit forward, resting my elbows on my knees. "I think I'm in love with Lottie."

My mom frowns at what must seem like an obvious statement to her before she cocks her head. "And?"

"Mom, Lottie and I aren't really married."

"Don't be silly, I was there and I watched you sign the papers."

I bob my head. "Well, yes, we're legally married, but it isn't real. I paid her to marry me to get the company from Dad." She pales but doesn't react and I rush on. "It has an expiry date of a year."

"I see. So, you don't love her?"

My sigh feels like my soul leaving my body, it's that deep. "That's the problem. I do. I've fallen in love with her." I sweep my fingers through my hair. "I mean how could I not? She's kind, beautiful, and funny. She's great with Eric and so loyal. I love her, Mom."

"So, what's the problem?"

"Mom, you know what happened with Lottie and me years ago, how I promised to take her to prom but didn't."

"Yes?"

"I didn't tell you why."

"No, but I'm betting it had something to do with your father." Her lip almost curls with disdain and it's the first time I'm seeing it from her.

"It did. He said if I didn't take Arabella, he was going to send Clark to a military academy."

Her indrawn breath brings my eyes to her face, and she looks shocked but quickly I see fury replace that.

"He did what?"

"He said he was going to send him to some place his friend runs to help straighten him out unless I took Arabella. It broke my heart to do it, but I didn't have any other choice. I either broke Lottie's heart for a short time or guaranteed my brother's safety. We both know he wouldn't have come out of a place like that alive."

My mother stands and crosses to me, taking my hand in hers. She's so put together, even now wearing her pearls with the silk blouse and pants, but she looks like someone else in this moment. She reminds me of my grandmother. Her mother was a force of nature with a backbone of steel.

"But she left before you could speak to her."

"Yes. She was gone before I got back from prom. I was going to explain it all to her in person. I didn't feel I could do it over the phone."

"That's why you cut yourself off for so long."

"I loved her, Mom. Even then I knew she was it for me and when she left without a word, I was so lost."

Her arms wrap around me, and I let my head fall to her shoulder.

"Oh, my sweet boy. Trying to save the day and your brother when I should have been doing it. I'm so sorry."

"No, Mom. Don't say that. You're the best mom a man could want."

She pats my face and I see tears glitter in her eyes. "I appreciate that, but the truth is I failed you. But no more."

"What do you mean?"

"I've met with a divorce attorney. I'm divorcing your father. He's taken enough from this family, and it was seeing you and Lottie together that helped wake me up. I'm fifty-five years old and still have life in me and I'm not going to spend it being married to a man with no respect for me or our children."

I don't know why I ask but I need to know what drives her. "Why now? Why didn't you do it before?"

She looks at the fireplace where the mantel is covered with pictures of me and Clark through the years. "You know your grandfather never approved of Charles. He hated him to be truthful, but I was going through a rebellious stage and thought myself in love. I was in love. Charles wasn't always the man he is today. He was charming and attentive and driven to succeed, and he said everything I wanted to hear. He was a good man, or so I thought, but after we were married, he changed. It was slow, the first few years were magical, but over time my father chipped away at his confidence. He didn't trust him or like him and he made it clear at every turn. Eventually, the man I married didn't exist and he became cold and cruel, his infidelity became blatant and his disdain and hatred for this family became more evident.

"He became power hungry and entitled. He became the man my father knew he'd always been. For a long time, I blamed my father for it and prayed that if I was steadfast and ignored his indiscretions, the man I married would come back. Over time I realized he'd never been that man. That was the act, not this."

"I'm sorry, Mom."

"Don't be. I got the most wonderful sons from my marriage and they are the greatest blessing and gift I could ask for."

"I'm happy for you, Mom, and you know you have mine and Clark's support."

"Thank you, my angel. That means a lot, but you didn't come here to listen to my woes."

I feel as if a weight is lifting to see the fire inside my mother. She looks younger, stronger, and I want that for her.

"So, you love your fake wife."

I chuckle and rub my eyes. "I do. God, what a cliché."

"And that scares you because you don't know if she loves you?"

"Yes. I mean I think she might, but I don't know. She's dealt with so much heartache, Mom, so much loss, and she's done it alone. She's so strong. I'm in awe of the things she's handled alone. A weaker person would have crumbled."

"My darling, you're head over heels for her, and let me tell you a secret. She feels the same way. You may not see it, but I do. She watches you, and she gets this soft look on her face. That girl has always loved you."

"But what if she doesn't? What if I lose her?"

"What if you don't?"

"It's a risk."

"It is but look at the reward if you get it right."

"So I should just tell her?"

"Yes. Make a gesture. Go big. Show her how you feel about her and don't hold back over the fear of rejection. Be bold and fearless."

My blood is pumping faster with sudden energy, and I jump to my feet. "I need to go." I kiss my mother's cheek. "Thanks, Mom."

"Always, darling, and bring my little Eric next time and my gorgeous daughter-in-law."

"I will."

I rush to my car, an idea taking shape as to how I'll do this. I'm going to tell Lottie how I feel and take a leap off the cliff.

26: Lottie

I CLUTCH MY HANDBAG LIKE IT WILL PROTECT ME FROM WHAT I'M about to do. My gut is roiling with nerves as I sit in the familiar waiting room. The pretty receptionist smiles kindly as if sensing my nerves and I try and smile back but it feels like a grimace.

The last few days have been torture. I'm sure Linc knows something is up with me. I've been as jumpy as a cat on a hot tin roof and several times I've caught him watching me as if trying to work out what's wrong.

Making love with him is the only time I can allow myself to forget the nightmare dragging me into hell. I feel drained of energy, exhausted by it all. Everything was going so perfectly, and I should have known it wouldn't last, it never does. Fate hates me for some reason and won't release me from her treacherous claws.

A door swings open and I stand when Hudson walks toward me. "Violet, this is a nice surprise."

He guides me into his huge office, and I get a sense of déjà vu. It feels like a hundred years ago I was sitting in this leather chair as we hashed out the details of my contract. He sits behind his desk, the fabric of his vest pulling tight across his broad shoulders as he claps his hands together and looks at me.

"I hope you don't mind me calling you."

He smiles wide and, even in love with Linc as I hopelessly am, I feel the effect of it.

"Of course not. Friends, right?"

I smile and then promptly burst into tears.

Hudson is around the desk in a minute and offering me a tissue as he crouches in front of me. "What's wrong? Has that jackass hurt you?"

I dab my tears and shake my head. "No, Linc is perfect."

That only makes me cry harder as I think of Linc and the way he's been so kind, so loving and that I'm going to break his heart no matter what I do.

"I think perfect is a stretch, but okay."

His words force a chuckle to my lips.

"That's better, you're too pretty to cry."

Hudson moves to his office door and asks his secretary to bring in some coffee.

Once he's seated in the chair beside me and the coffee is delivered, I have a better handle on my emotions. "I'm sorry."

"Don't be. Now tell me what's going on."

I don't know where to start and the words stick in my throat, they've been buried so long that this feels like too big a step.

"You can trust me, Violet. I'm bound by client confidentiality, and I'm your friend. Whatever you say won't go any further."

"Okay." I sip the coffee, letting the bitter taste envelop me. My tears were a release and I feel my backbone hardening again. "Ten years ago, Charles Coldwell tried to rape me."

I look to Hudson, but he doesn't react, just nods for me to go on.

"My mother got in between us and he raped her instead, while I ran and hid in the closet. We left the Kennedy estate that night and ran. My mother got a job as a waitress, and we rented a tiny apartment with the money she'd saved."

"Go on."

"Eric is the result of that attack. He has no idea of course, and I never want him to find out. It was my mother's dying wish that I keep him safe, and I've failed."

"How so?"

"A few nights ago, Charles Coldwell cornered me at a gala we were attending. He said he knows about Eric and he's going to file for custody if I don't help him force Lincoln from his position as CEO of Kennedy Enterprises and help him get his job back."

"Piece of shit."

"He is. I don't know what to do. I can't let him get Eric, I just can't, and he has so much more funds and contacts at his disposal than I do. But I can't help him destroy Linc either and losing Kennedy will do that. Plus, he threatened that he'd tell Heather and Linc about Eric. I need help, Hudson."

"Well, that answers my question about whether Linc knows."

"He doesn't."

"Well, we have a few options."

"I'll spend every penny I have if we can win this, but I'd still rather it didn't go public. I don't want my brother living with the fact he's the product of rape. He's been through too much already."

"Don't worry about the money. I'd do this for free anyway."

"No, I can pay you."

"No, Violet, you won't. I hate men like Charles Coldwell and seeing that bastard get what he deserves is all the payment I need."

"We will discuss that later, but what can I do?"

"Well, we have a few options. Did your mother file a police report?"

"No, she didn't think anyone would believe her."

He frowns. "This system doesn't protect the victims like it should."

"What else?"

"Are we one hundred percent sure Eric is Charles' son?"

"Absolutely."

"Rape is always hard to prove and without the victim, he can claim it was consensual."

"What about me? I was a witness."

"A distraught teenage girl and a ten-year-old memory of an event.

Not to be brutal but any lawyer worth their name would chew you up and spit you out."

"So, he wins?"

"I didn't say that. With a man like Charles Coldwell, an attack like this won't be an isolated incident. He'll have more victims out there and we need to find them."

Bile rushes up my throat at the thought of him doing what he did to my mother to other women. But I know without a doubt what Hudson is saying is true.

"I'll get my investigator on it immediately."

"And in the meantime?"

"I suggest you talk to Linc. Tell him what is going on and about what happened."

"No, I can't do that."

Hudson gentles his voice. "Why not?"

I feel a flight or fight response biting at my heels. "He'll hate me."

"Why would he hate you?"

"Because I lied to him. I should have told him why we left, about his dad."

"He might be hurt but he'll understand."

"How can you be sure? You don't even like him."

Hudson links his fingers and leans on the desk. "I might not be his biggest fan, but I know he cares about you."

"Maybe, I just…." I sigh. "I'm so used to handling this alone and I hate the thought of anyone judging my mother or looking at Eric differently."

"Anyone worth giving a shit about won't do that."

"What about Heather? She's been so good to us. She adores Eric, and he loves her. If she found out he was the product of her husband raping my mother, it would hurt her, and she'd definitely hate me."

"It's not an easy situation, Violet. I suggest you start with Lincoln and go from there. He'll be in your corner. I'm sure of it and then he can guide you as to who, if anyone, you tell after that. In the meantime, I'll have my investigator look for other victims and see if we can build a case."

He gets up and walks toward me as I stand. "I'd also recommend some counseling for you. I bet you've never dealt with what you saw properly, and you need to."

As Hudson walks me onto the street, I turn to him. "You're a good man, Hudson Carmichael."

I lean up to hug him and kiss his cheek and he wraps his arms around me, and it feels like I found a brother, there's no sexual chemistry at all. As he releases me, he lifts his hand to swipe my cheek. "You have panda eyes."

"Well, thanks for telling me now."

His laugh is deep. "Sorry."

I wipe my cheeks and he smiles before bending to kiss my head.

"Tell him. He'll forgive you."

"I will and thanks again, Hudson."

"My pleasure, Violet."

I cross the street and hop into a cab and head home. I have a lot to think about before Linc gets home.

27: Linc

I'M PRACTICALLY FLOATING AS I ENTER THE JEWELERS. THE RING I bought Lottie for our wedding was loud and obnoxious and can be seen from the moon, but it's not the ring I would've given her. That's tucked in my pocket where I've just retrieved it from my safety deposit box at the bank.

"Good afternoon, Mr. Coldwell, how can we help you today?"

My family has used this store for generations and are the original crafters of this piece. The man worked here during the thirties when my grandfather had it crafted for my grandmother.

"I have a ring I'd like cleaned up for me please and perhaps the stones checked to ensure they are secure."

"Of course, Mr. Coldwell."

Mr. Zedner takes the ring from the box and tilts his glasses to better see before his eyes flash to mine. "This is one of my father's pieces."

"I believe so. It was my grandmother's engagement ring. My grandfather had it designed and made here."

"It's one of his earlier designs and, in my opinion, one of his finest. The sapphire is cushion cut and then set laterally with the two diamonds on either side transitionally cut. It really is a work of art."

"I agree and I know I bought my wife the other engagement ring, but I'd like her to have this one too."

"A fine choice. I'll clean it and reset the stones as the claws need tightening."

"How long will that take?"

I'm eager to tell Lottie how I feel and have the strongest desire to run toward my future with her at full speed.

"I can have it done by tomorrow afternoon."

"Fantastic, thank you."

"No, thank you. This is a treat and gives me a wonderful sense of nostalgia."

I exit the store on cloud nine and head down the street feeling almost light. I pass a pastry store and see apple fritters in the window and duck in to pick one up for Lottie. They're her favorite and I know she doesn't like to eat them in front of Eric. If I head home now, I can surprise her before my afternoon meetings start.

I pay the lady, adding a bear claw for me, and a diabetic-friendly cookie for Eric before stepping out. I glance across the street as I go to cross the busy intersection and stop still. People curse as they bump into me, and I don't care. My eyes are glued to the scene in front of me.

Lottie is the arms of my enemy.

I feel frozen in time, numb with shock as I watch in painful fascination as she reaches up to wrap her treacherous arms around him and kiss his cheek. He holds her tight before releasing her and tracing his thumb over her cheek. She laughs and then he kisses her on the head with so much tenderness I feel like I've been sucker punched. The bag of pastries falls from my hand and are crushed in seconds by the stampede of people rushing around New York and it's fitting because that's how my heart feels. Like it's been trampled into the ground by a lying, deceptive bitch.

I turn on my heel, not bearing to look at the scene in front of me for another second and walk towards the nearest bar.

"Whiskey neat and make it a double."

The bartender gives me a raised eyebrow but does as I ask. He must see this kind of thing a hundred times a week. Men coming into this bar with broken hearts, because lying sluts have sold them a dream only to rip the rug out from under them.

I toss back my drink and point to the glass indicating I want another. I can't believe she'd do this to me and with him of all people. While I was falling in love with her, she was screwing Hudson Fucking Carmichael.

I should have known better than to trust her. She broke me once and people like her don't change but God, she sold it. My heart feels like it's in smithereens, and I know that I'll never come back from this. No woman will ever get her claws into my heart again. I should have stuck to my guns and kept her at arm's length.

I should have let her suck my dick and left my heart out of it. But she suckered me in and showed me what I could have with her sweet smiles and flirty looks. The way she responded to me and gave herself to me. The cookies she baked, the way she'd listen to me as if every word out of my mouth was important to her.

I huff out a laugh as I down the next drink, feeling the buzz finally begin to numb the pain inside me. She probably wasn't even a virgin.

No, that's not a lie, but then how would I know? She managed to pull the wool over my eyes about her being such a deceitful whore. I wonder how long she's been fucking him. Was it before or after the wedding? But maybe she made him wait for her pussy until after I fucked her? Did she scream for him like she did me? Did she wrap those sweet lips around his cock and suck him so hard he saw stars?

My love, which was so bright this morning, is now a burning hatred that feels like it's a living breathing poison inside me. I want to hurt her, to make her bleed inside like I am.

Would she have welcomed me home tonight with a tilt of her lips for my kiss? Would she have let me make love to her and whispered sweet nothings all the while thinking of him?

I have no idea how long I sit at this bar until a familiar form sits beside me. "Fuck off, Ryker. I'm not in the mood for your shit today." My words are slurred, and I frown.

"I haven't said anything yet."

My friend orders a drink and sits quietly beside me, and I'm grateful for it, but I want to be alone to wallow in my fury and heartbreak.

"So, what has you day drinking?"

"Lottie is fucking her lawyer."

Ryker's eyebrows rise. "No way."

I sway. "Yes, way. I saw it with my own three eyes."

"Two eyes."

I frown and watch his lips move. "What?"

"You said three eyes, it's two."

"Whatever."

"Are you sure about what you saw, man?"

"Yup."

"Shit, man, I'm sorry. I would've bet my fortune on the fact she was head over heels for you."

"Then you'd be broke."

I go silent and close my eyes, images blurring in front of me of Lottie and me and then merging into Lottie and Hudson.

"Don't trust 'em, Ryker. I'm telling you, don't trust 'em. They're all lying, deceitful bitches who just want to break us. They're like those insects."

"Praying mantis?"

I point a finger at Ryker and squint so I can see him better. "Yes, those. They just want to have sex and then destroy us."

"That's why I'm single, man."

"Wise, very wise."

"We should get some food inside you."

"Nah, not hungry. I want to get laid. Let's find some pussy."

"Hold up, Casanova. Don't make any snap decisions until you sober up."

"I'm fine."

"You're most definitely not."

"Uh, why couldn't it be Beck who found me? He'd have helped me get laid."

"Because, dumbass, I'm the tech wizard who can hack your phone, not Beck."

"You hacked my phone?"

"You missed a meeting."

"Asshole."

"That's genius asshole to you."

"What about those two chicks over there?"

"No chicks at all."

"The blonde looks like she could suck a golf ball through a hose."

Ryker rolls his eyes. "You need to fix this with Lottie."

"No. She lied to me. She made me love her again and then threw me away."

"You don't know that."

"I do."

"I have a meeting I can't miss but Harry is on his way. Can I trust you to wait here until he arrives, or do I need to babysit you to stop you from making any bad decisions?"

"Go, I'm fine."

I feel Ryker's heavy hand on my shoulder. "Whatever happens, brother, we have your back, okay?"

"Thanks, man."

I see him walk away in the reflection of the glass and despair washes over me again. I've lost her, but then, I never really had her to begin with.

"Hey, handsome, want some company?"

I turn to the blonde who was eyeing me from the other side of the room. She's pretty in a made-up Barbie way. She isn't Lottie though. My little Lottie doesn't need artifice, she's a natural beauty. Her smile is the kind that lights up a room, no, a God damn stadium. She's the only woman I want, and it seems I'm doomed to spend my life without her love, but I don't have to let that define me. I'm certainly not going to let her ruin sex for me.

"Sure, pull up a seat."

My body rebels as she lays a hand on my arm. I don't want her touch. There's only one woman I want touching me and she's nothing but a fucking liar. Fighting my response, I turn to her, laying my charm on the line. "Want to get out of here?"

"Sure thing, sugar."

I toss a handful of Benjamins on the bar and let the woman, who's still nameless, lead me out. Manhattan is dark except for the city lights, and I realize how long I've been in the bar.

"Where to?"

I pause, wondering if I can go through with this and know it's the only way to ensure I hurt Lottie as much as she's hurt me. "My place."

28: Lottie

IT'S GONE MIDNIGHT AND I STILL CAN'T GET HOLD OF LINC. I PUT ERIC to bed and told him that Linc was working late. I hope he is because I'm getting worried. He's never been this late and certainly, he's never gone dark on me this way. I've called his friends and they said they'd look for him and if they found him, they'd call me back.

I'm about to call the hospital when my cell rings. I snatch it up seeing Ryker's name. "Ryker, did you find him?"

"Yes. He's fine."

I don't know why but I sense a hesitation in his voice and maybe a coolness that wasn't there before. "Are you sure, Ryker? I've been worried sick, and he's never not called me back."

"I'm sure. You should go to bed."

Relief is sharp and my shoulders sag. I didn't realize how much I'd grown used to him being here until he wasn't. I hang up with Ryker and head to bed knowing I won't sleep. The bed feels too big without him, and I miss the feel of his arms around me making me feel safe. Linc is my world once more and I decided while I was waiting for him to come home that I was going to take Hudson's advice and tell him everything, and that included how much I loved him.

I must doze off, the adrenalin of the day and the worry of the last few days catching up with me. I wake abruptly, my eyes going wide when I hear what sounds like someone bumping into something. I sit up, grabbing the robe off the end of the bed, and slip it on. Linc might be hurt and I want to make sure he's okay and that he doesn't wake Eric.

As I make my way into the living area, I'm sure I hear a giggle and I pause at the entry to the living room. Linc is standing beside the couch, trying to shrug his jacket off, but it's the woman who's helping him get undressed that spots me first.

A squeak pops from her lips and she jumps back from him. I fold my arms and try to hold in the waves of pain that feel like they're about to take me down. Linc sees me and straightens, and I beg him silently to give me an explanation that I can believe. That he isn't breaking us in a way that's so much more permanent than what happened before. His cheeks are covered in pink lipstick and I can smell her perfume mixed with his scent and it makes me feel nauseous.

"Ah, there she is, my beautiful, deceitful, slut of a wife."

Shock makes me step back as if he's slapped me. "Linc, what's going on?" I know the answer, but I want to deny this is happening in front of my eyes and for him to give me an explanation I can believe.

"You tell me, Lottie. You're the expert on cheating and lies, after all."

The woman looks at me as she grabs her bag. "I should go."

"No don't go, we were gonna have some fun. Lottie can watch. You like to watch, don't you, sweetheart? It makes her pussy all wet."

I never thought in my wildest dreams that he'd hurt me intentionally like this. "You disgust me."

"Yeah, well, join the club."

I always thought that when people said they could die of a broken heart that it was a figure of speech. But this feeling inside me is so bad, the hurt cutting so deep, that I'm shocked not to see my blood on the floor at my feet. "Why? Why are you doing this."

Linc looks at me and I wish I could attribute this to alcohol, but I know Lincoln would never make a mistake, especially one like this. He's doing this to hurt me, to rip me to shreds, and it's working.

"Because I can."

Tears rim my eyes as I watch the woman he was going to fuck in our home edge toward the door. I turn, pinning her with my gaze. "Stay. The damage is done anyway. You might as well get some fun out of it. I don't care anymore."

"Like you ever cared."

I shake my head sadly. "I cared, Lincoln. No, I more than cared, I loved you, and you just threw it all away. And for what? A quick fuck."

"You don't know how to love. You just lie and betray. You're nothing but a whore who sells her body for money. You just exact a higher price than most."

Nothing he could've said could have wounded me deeper and I know any love I had for this man is gone, destroyed like a fire turning wood to ash.

I have no words and I'm seconds away from falling apart. So, I turn as the door closes on the woman he'd brought into our home. No, his home. This beautiful place was never my home.

"Don't you walk away from me, Lottie. I'm your husband."

I spin on my heel and face him, the man I love with all that I am, the man who has ruined me for a second time. "We could've been happy. We could've had it all and you just threw it all away."

"I didn't throw it away, you did."

I shake my head. "You're the person who brought another woman into our home."

"You mean my home."

I look away, not able to look at his handsome face for a minute longer. "I guess I do."

"I should have known you were nothing but a whore when you got down on your knees so easily for me."

I suck in a breath and it seems to lodge in my chest like a blade. "I was never ashamed of what I did to protect my brother and the truth is, I'd do it again because I love him, and I never stopped loving you, even after everything that happened between us. But tonight you drove a stake through that love and at least now I'll be free to move on and find someone who deserves me and doesn't make me feel cheap for trying to protect someone I love."

I have nothing left in me right now and I'm teetering on the edge of what I can handle, so I rush to the bedroom and slam the door as I hear a roar. I gather my clothes and head to Eric's room as glass smashes in the main living room. I'll sleep here tonight. I can't face being in our bed with the scent of him on our sheets and the memories of what we shared all around me.

My sweet brother is sound asleep, and I thank God for it. I crawl in beside him in the big bed and listen as Lincoln stumbles around the rooms before I hear him walk past this room and pause. Even now after everything, I'd do anything for him to say it was all a mistake, but he doesn't, he just carries on to our room and the night falls silent.

I wish I knew why he'd done this. I'd been so sure we were on the same page. He'd been sweet and attentive since our wedding and nothing like the cold, cruel man I'd seen in the beginning. Maybe I should have kept my guard up and held him at arm's length. But he'd pulled me in, making me trust his every word. Just like last time he's shown me what I really meant to him and that was less than nothing.

As the dawn light comes through the drapes of Eric's room, I get up. Silently, I slip from the room and dress in the attached bathroom. I'd grabbed my old jeans and a sweater I had from when my mom was alive. I need to feel her strength around me right now.

I swipe the tears that keep trying to appear away and head out to the terrace on the other side of the penthouse. Hopefully Lincoln will sleep late, and I can get out of here before he wakes. I honestly don't think I can face him right now.

Dialing the only person I knew who would help, I waited.

"Violet?"

A sob almost chokes me at the sound of his voice. "Hudson, I need your help."

"What's wrong?"

"Eric and I need to leave."

"Did Lincoln not take the news well?"

"I didn't get a chance to tell him. He came home drunk with another woman."

"That jackass."

A laugh erupts from my throat at his indignation, but it quickly turns to a hiccupped sob as the realization of everything begins to hit me. "Will you help me?"

"Of course, Violet. I'll have a car to you in twenty minutes."

My knees sag at the words. "Thank you."

"My pleasure, Violet, and don't worry. We'll figure this out, okay."

My voice feels small and broken as I reply. "Okay."

I hang up and swipe my eyes with my sleeve. I don't want Eric to see me cry or ask questions I can't answer right now. I needed to get him to school so I can have a few hours to figure out my next move. The penthouse is quiet except for the sound of Eric in the bathroom. Since moving here he's taken it upon himself to make sure he's awake and ready for school each day.

I sense Lincoln was still here, probably passed out in our, no, his bed. I hope he'll stay that way for a few hours and give me the time I need to get away. I pack a few of my things that I can't live without into a small bag, leaving all the clothes he bought me, and slip off my wedding rings, leaving them on the counter in the kitchen.

Taking one last look around, I think my heart will sink to my toes it feels so heavy. I'd been happy here, not just content but truly happy. I'd begun to hope and that was my mistake because fairy tales aren't for people like me.

When we hit the ground floor, I usher Eric to the door and spot both Lincoln's driver, Boris and Hudson standing at the curb beside black town cars. I falter as Boris smiles and then I put my head down and rush toward Hudson.

He opens the door, seeming to know I don't want to make a scene in front of Eric and holds his hand up to Boris to warn him off.

"In you get, Eric."

"How come we aren't going to school like usual?" My brother looks at Hudson with protective wariness on his little face.

"I have a meeting with Hudson today, so this makes sense."

He accepts my answer barely, but I knew later there'll be a bombardment of questions and I'm just not ready for them. The drive is quiet but I can tell Eric is unhappy. I don't get my usual wave when he exits the car or a look back as he enters.

"He'll be okay, Violet. You both will."

"I know." But the truth was I don't know if we will be. Lincoln had given us both a glimpse of the perfect life and then snatched it away like we were nothing to him and the pain is almost more than I can bear.

29: Linc

I ROLL OVER IN BED AND REACH FOR HER AND FIND THE BED EMPTY. I open one eye and close it quickly as the drummers in my head begin a new rendition of something awful. I open my mouth and my tongue feels like it will stick to the roof of my mouth, and tastes like something died in there.

Silence in the apartment makes me sit up slowly as I try to piece together the events of the day before. I stagger to the bathroom and I'm greeted by Lottie's scent, and it sends a pang of pain to my chest.

She was with Hudson.

I look in the mirror and see bloodshot eyes, a two-day scruff, and a ton of regret. My collar is stained with pink lipstick in a shade I know Lottie would never wear and now I'm not sure I want my memories to return. I shed my wrinkled suit and turn the shower to cold. I wince as the freezing water hits my skin but tolerate the abuse as my brain finally begins to clear.

I was drinking at a bar. Ryker was there and then he was gone. I remember a woman with blonde hair and fake boobs. Oh, God, did I fuck her? Did I cheat on my wife to get back at her?

I glance at my limp dick and wish it could give me some answers, but it just hangs there as if he too feels shame for some, as yet, unknown crime. Once I've scrubbed my body, I turn off the water and wrap a towel around my hips. I brush my teeth and scrub my tongue to rid myself of the disgusting taste in my mouth. Shaving is a step too far today and I can still feel the stench of booze reeking from my pores.

God, how much did I have to drink?

I sit on the edge of the bed and notice the silence once again. Lottie must be taking Eric to school. The image of her in Hudson's arms almost makes me roll over and go back to sleep to get rid of the painful image from my brain, but I know it will just follow me into my dreams.

I down some pain relief and fill the glass from the bathroom with water and drink it back. Jumbles of conversation hit me and I begin remembering what happened. Watching it play out behind my eyelids like a car crash I want to stop but can't.

Me calling Lottie a whore, the woman from the bar kissing my neck in the elevator. Just the thought of another woman's lips on me has me heaving over the sink. Seeing Lottie had made me want to lash out and hurt her like she had me, but I knew I'd gone way too far when I'd called her hateful names and saw the pain etched on her beautiful lying face. I'd brought that woman home to hurt her, and it seemed I'd managed that. My head hangs as regret and shame fills me. I was an utter asshole. I hadn't thought about Eric and the possibility he'd witness it all. I thanked God he'd been spared that and selfishly, so had I. That boy means the world to me and I would hate for him to have seen me that way. Not that I deserve being spared that humiliation, but I want him to be proud of me.

I splash my face with more cold water before I sluggishly move to the bedroom. I dress in old jeans and a white tee and shove my feet into an old pair of boots that have seen better days.

Walking through the penthouse, I poke my head into his room and see it's clean and tidy as always. He's a good kid and deserves better than what I'd been willing to let him see last night.

I freeze as I hit the kitchen and spot the two rings sitting on the kitchen island.

No!

I rush forward and my stomach roils as I see her wedding rings sitting there. The magnitude of the situation hits me, and I race to our room, yanking open the closet doors, relief hitting me as I see it full of her clothes. Her scent clings to me and it makes me sink to my knees right there in the closet. How could she betray me like this and with him? I see her in my mind asking me why, telling me she loved me, and I wonder if I'm just making it all up in my head to soothe the pain inside me. Doubt burrows inside me like a poison and the heavy feeling that I've made the biggest mistake of my life sits on my chest, making it hard to breathe.

I spot an empty space where the bag she arrived with usually sits and I scrabble around looking for her old clothes, but they're gone. I stagger from the closet and I do the same in Eric's room, I look for his teddy and it too is gone.

She's left me. She's broken the contract we made but that feels irrelevant right now as my world feels like it's caving in on me.

"What the fuck did you do, Lincoln?"

I spin to see my cousin watching me, her hands on her hips as she takes in the room. "She left me."

Audrey blows out a breath and shakes her head. "Let's get some coffee in you and take it to the terrace. I don't think I can handle the fumes coming off you in a closed space."

I follow her, every step feels heavy like I'm being led to the gallows and I haven't got any fight left inside me.

She left me and I don't blame her.

I look out over the city I love as Audrey hands me a mug and I take a sip and feel my brain start to fire, playing out every word we exchanged last night in technicolored detail. I relive every word we exchanged and all I see in my mind is her hurting and me slinging a horrible diatribe at her.

"The things I said, Audrey. God, I wouldn't blame her if she never forgives me."

My cousin looks at me with sympathy in her eyes and I hate it because it shows me that I'm right, what I did was unforgivable. "Ryker found footage of her leaving Hudson's place of work."

My eyes shoot to her. "He did?"

"It was all very innocent. Yes, he hugged her, yes she kissed his cheek but there was no passion, and when he hacked his office cameras' there was nothing to suggest this meeting was a tryst of any kind."

"Why was she meeting him then?"

"There could be any number of reasons. A will to protect Eric. Financial advice, legal advice. All of them innocent and not a reason for you to blow your fucking top like you did."

"But she hugged him."

"So? Why didn't you come home and speak to her, ask her about it?"

I look down at my half-empty mug, the coffee suddenly souring in my stomach. "She left me."

"I know. I saw the rings on the counter. I take it you confronted her?"

"I brought a woman back here."

"For fuck's sake, Lincoln, what the hell were you thinking?"

"I didn't fuck her and I wasn't thinking. I was reacting."

"I'm not sure that makes it better at this point. What did you say to her?"

"I called her a whore, said she sold herself like a common whore only she charged more."

Audrey is glaring at me, and I can feel her anger directed at me. "Why would you be so cruel?"

"I paid her to marry me. To get my father out of Kennedy and because Lottie was drowning in debt."

"Is that the real reason?"

I should have known my cousin would see straight through me. "I never stopped loving her and I think in the back of my mind I thought if I could just get some time with her and show her what we could have, she'd love me back."

"And did it work?"

"I love her, so damn much, and last night she told me I broke us. That she loved me, and we could've had a beautiful life and I threw it away. And she was right, we did have a beautiful life. For those few short months my life was perfect. She made everything better, she made me want to come home at night. She gave me a reason, she was my reason, and I was a fucking asshole. I would kill any other man for speaking to her like I did, for hurting her and she was so dignified. She didn't scream or shout she just took the barbs I threw at her and she fucking left."

I let my head fall in my hands as a sob escapes my chest and I try to hold it back the pain of my own making. The enormity of what I've done hits me. Tears hit my cheeks and I feel like bawling like a newborn over the loss that is so huge it feels like I'll never recover.

"Oh, Lincoln. Why are men such idiots?"

I sniff and wipe my wet eyes on the edge of my shirt. "I fucked up."

Audrey smirks. "Ya think?"

"What am I going to do?"

"What do you want to do, Lincoln? Do you want her back? Because I gotta say if it was me, you'd have an uphill battle after that shit show. Or you could cut your losses and let it go and move on."

"No." The denial is out of my mouth so fast as I jump to my feet. "No. I'm not letting her go without her letting me explain. I love her, Audrey. She's everything to me. I feel like I can't breathe without her."

Audrey stands and grips my arm. "She doesn't owe you a chance to explain, Lincoln, and she may not give it either." I know she's right, and hell, I don't deserve it either but I'm selfish, and want it anyway.

"She has to, I love her."

"Shame you didn't figure this shit out before you blew up your world."

I glare at her. "Are you going to help me or are you going to keep telling me what an asshole I've been?"

"Both, dipshit. I might be your family, but I'm also a woman, and she deserves my support too."

"Fine. So, what do I do?"

"Well, do you know if she has any friends she'd go to?"

"No, she has nobody."

"That breaks my heart."

"She was always all about Eric and worked two jobs to keep her head above water."

"Well, let's start with Hudson Carmichael then."

My lip curls as I think of the man who had his arms around my wife.

I BARGE PAST HIS ASSISTANT AND THROW OPEN THE DOOR TO HUDSON'S office, half expecting to see Lottie there and my shoulders sag when she's not. Hudson jumps up from his desk as his assistant appears at my shoulder with Audrey beside her.

"You can't go in there."

Hudson looks at her as he rounds the desk. "It's fine, Claire."

"Do you want me to call security?"

"No, I can handle Mr. Coldwell."

I smirk. "Yeah, course you could, Carmichael."

"Lincoln." I feel Audrey dig me in the ribs and ignore her warning. "Where is she?"

The door closes behind us quietly and I glance around the room as if she might be hiding behind the desk. I see a door and head toward it as Hudson folds his arms and glares at me. I look in his private bathroom and find no sign of the woman I love.

"Violet isn't here."

"But she was." I step forward getting up into his personal space and see his nostrils flare. A fight is just what I need to tether my anger at myself right now and, if I push hard enough, Hudson will give it for free.

"You know, you really are a piece of shit. I have no idea what a sweetheart like her would see in a prick like you."

I shove him back and he bumps the desk but doesn't go down. "Don't fucking talk about her."

"Or what? You're going to ruin me? Going to send all your friends after me, Coldwell?"

"I don't need my friends to fight my battles."

"No, I guess not, especially when it's to hurl disgusting accusations at such a wonderful woman and to shove your sluts in her face."

"So, you have seen her."

"Yes, I have. I picked her up this morning when she rang me in tears to say she was leaving you."

"Where is she?"

"Like I'd tell you."

I shove him again and he pushes me back. So I throw a punch, landing it on his smug face and in the next second he hits me back and we're rolling around the office floor, trading punches. I can hear his assistant screaming and then ice water hits me and I gasp, jumping back.

Hudson rolls to his knees and he's as soaked as I am. I see Audrey standing with an empty water jug in her hands and murder on her face.

"Have you two fuckwits finished behaving like two boys measuring dicks in the playground?" She folds her arms and neither of us speak. "Good. Now, Hudson, would you be amenable to telling us if Violet is okay?"

He wipes the blood from his nose, and I get a sick satisfaction in seeing him bleed.

"No, she fucking isn't. He," his finger points accusingly at me, "broke her fucking heart."

"I made a mistake."

"No, a mistake is forgetting your anniversary or a birthday. You went home with some cheap trollop to hurt her deliberately and it worked."

"I saw you two hugging yesterday and jumped to the wrong conclusion."

"What you saw was me consoling a friend and her thanking me for being one to her. Violet loved you. She came to me to try and protect you and this is how you react? You devastated her, Coldwell. I've never seen someone so heartbroken."

His words land like knives in my gut and I deserve them. "Protect me from what?" I have to concentrate on that because the alternative is him using the word love in the past tense.

"I can't tell you. Client confidentiality."

"Then tell me where she is."

"I can't. I promised her, and she's had enough people break promises to her and let her down. I won't be joining those ranks."

"I love her."

"Well, you have a fucking funny way of showing it."

"I fucked up, but I need to fix it. Please give me something. I'll do anything." I hate to beg this man but I'll do anything to put this right.

"Just give her some time. I'll tell her you want to speak to her, and she can reach out when she's ready. In the meantime, I suggest you speak to your father or better yet, have that tech expert you're friends with do a deep dive into him and maybe see if you can look at the cameras from the gala the other night."

I feel unease inch up my spine and want to ask more, but I can see by the way he stands that Hudson won't be helping me anymore.

"Now get the fuck out of my office before I call the police, and take your little guard dog with you." He casts a hot look at Audrey, and I pause, wondering at the look of hatred that crosses between them.

"Fuck you, Hudson."

"Not even if you paid me, Ms. Kennedy."

I'm now the one grabbing a furious Audrey and hauling her from the office. Hudson stands in the doorway with his hands on his hips watching us leave and I stop. "Can you give Lottie a message for me?"

"For fuck's sake, I'm not your personal fucking assistant."

"Just tell her I never meant what I said and I'm sorry."

"I'll tell her, but I have to say after seeing her this morning, I don't think that will make a difference. You took something sweet and pure and you broke her, and you might just have to live with that."

I shake my head as his words hit their mark. "I can't."

"You might not have a choice. You played your hand, and it was the wrong one. Only she can decide how the rest of this plays out now and I have to tell you, I'll be advising her to seek an immediate divorce under breach of contract."

"I didn't breach the contract."

Hudson cocks his head. "Didn't you? Because I'm pretty sure I could get a judge to believe you did from the images I found on the internet already this morning."

I don't respond because he walks back into his office and closes the door.

"So, genius, what now?"

We stand in the exact spot I saw Lottie hugging Hudson and Audrey looks up at me. I must look like a drowned rat, and I don't give a damn. My only focus is finding Lottie and getting her back. "We speak to Ryker."

30: Lottie

IT'S BEEN ONE HUNDRED AND EIGHT HOURS SINCE I LEFT LINCOLN AND my heart feels like it's been put in the shredder and it might as well be for all the use it is to me now. I've run the gamut from numb, to angry, and now I'm just downright sad. Every foot in front of the other as I try and rebuild what is left of my life feels like climbing a mountain.

Eric is hardly speaking to me, not understanding why we left and why I won't let him speak to Lincoln. Yet how can I explain the complexities of adulthood to this young boy without exposing him to the hurt we, the grown-ups, cause each other?

The apartment Hudson found us is small, exactly what I wanted but in a lovely part of the city and away from Lincoln, which is what I needed. He said we could stay with him, but that felt like a betrayal somehow, living with another man so he let me choose out of the four apartments he owns.

It's only for a short time. I've refused to touch the money Lincoln put in my account and I have a meeting later for a job at an Irish bar not far from here. They have an opening for the day shifts and although it will mean the tips aren't as good, I can work it around Eric better.

The last four days have been busy with me moving and getting set up. Hudson has helped so much and given me lots of good advice. The papers he drew up to apply for a divorce from Lincoln on breach of contract sit in the drawer by my bed.

It was my idea to get the ball rolling and get this done. I just want away from him and his father. Hudson's investigator has found a woman willing to meet with him who worked for Charles, and we're hopeful that she'll tell us her story.

I curl up in my bed and hate that I miss him, that the loneliness that was once only a blip on my radar is now front and center, showing me how alone I really am. I miss him, I miss Audrey and Heather. I miss Clark and I've avoided all the efforts from anyone to reach out to me. I eventually changed my number and now the silence hurts as much as the voicemails they left me begging me to call them.

Most of all I miss Linc. His arms around me in bed, his smile when he walked in the door at night and the way he made me feel so special. I got the messages he sent through Hudson, but I dismissed them. I can't allow myself to fall for his lies again. Fool me once shame on you, fool me twice shame on me. My mother would always say that when someone shows you who they really are, then listen.

I'm listening finally and it hurts. My body aches and I feel nauseous. I haven't washed my hair in days and I only bathe so as not to embarrass Eric when I walk him to school. I've taken Lincoln off the approved list for speaking to or collecting Eric and every time I approach the gates, I'm worried he'll try and speak to me there.

I fall asleep around two am and wake around five. My brain doesn't seem to want to let me have any peace. I make a cooked breakfast for Eric of bacon and eggs with brown toast and his favorite pan-fried tomatoes. I need to try and fix the void that is between us. I can't lose my brother over this and the thought sends a sting of choked tears to my throat.

He sees it the second he walks from his room into the kitchen diner.

"You made breakfast?"

"Yes, I thought we could eat together."

"Why?"

He takes a seat and I sit opposite him at the little table nook. "Well, I miss you and I know things have been rough the last few days."

"Why did we leave?"

He shovels eggs into his mouth, and I smile around my mug of tea, pleased that at least his appetite hasn't suffered the same way mine has. I've dropped seven pounds in four days, most of the weight I'd gained living with Linc. "Well, sometimes things don't work out."

"Don't you love him anymore?"

God, this kid. "It's not that simple. Sometimes we can love someone, and they can still hurt us."

"Did Linc hurt you?"

I see his fist tighten on the fork and place my hand over his. "Not like that. But he said some things that hurt my feelings."

"Doesn't he love you anymore?"

"I'm not sure Lincoln ever loved me, Eric, but I know he loved you."

"He told me he loved you. Did he lie?"

My breath hitches at his words and it takes everything in me not to break down. "I think he just got mixed up and confused."

"Will we see him or Heather again?"

I wish more than anything I could say yes. But with Charles' threat still hanging over me and the safety net of Linc's protection gone now, I just won't take the risk. "I don't think so."

Eric pushes his food around his plate, and I know I've killed his hope and hate that I'm once again the bad one.

A hand lands on my shoulder and I look to see him so grown up watching me. "It's okay, Vi. Don't be sad. You have me and I love you to the moon."

I choke as I try and force back a sob and wrap his hand with mine. "I love you too, buddy, so much."

"And if Linc doesn't love you then I don't want to see his stupid face."

I know I should correct him and tell him it's wrong to call anyone stupid, but it feels so good to have him in my corner that I let it go.

He heads to school with a smile this time and I have hope that I might get some remnants of my life back one day. Not my heart, that will forever belong to Lincoln. I head to the park for some fresh air as I've done every morning after school drop-off. I can't stand being in my apartment alone and people-watching allows me to weave happy stories around the people I see here.

It's the end of summer, and the fall is starting to push its way in, but the summer isn't quite done and it's a beautiful day as I sit and watch the dogs play and little kids giggle with the excitement of youth.

I feel her before I see her, and I tense, wanting to run away but also wanting to cry and beg her to tell me how Linc is doing.

"Can I sit?"

I shrug at Audrey who takes it as my assent. Silence fills the air for a few minutes until I can't take it a second longer. "What do you want?"

"How are you?"

I turn to look at this formidable woman who runs an empire and goes toe to toe with the biggest hitters in the city without flinching and see unease in her expression. "I'm fine."

"You're not."

I look away, shaking my head. "Why did you ask if you knew the answer?"

"I wanted to see if you'd lie to me."

"What does it matter?"

"It doesn't but I thought we were friends."

I sigh and cross my arms over my midsection. "We were, but you're Lincoln's cousin."

"I know and that's the only reason that asshole still has balls."

A laugh escapes me, and I look at her with a tilt of my head. "Don't stop on my account."

"Nah, it feels too much like kicking a puppy right now. He has no defenses."

My mood sobers at the thought, and I have to harden my heart not to ask if he's okay.

"He misses you."

"No, he misses easy sex."

"He made a mistake. He saw you with Hudson and instead of talking to you like a normal human being, he went off the deep end."

"Yeah, I heard. That doesn't excuse what he did. But it's not even that, although that hurt like a bitch. It was the way he spoke to me and the things he said."

"He regrets it."

"I'm sure he does, but I can't forgive him. I won't give him the chance to do it to me again."

"He loves you."

I shake my head, my hair flying around my face as tears prick my eyes and clog my nose. "No, he doesn't get to use that as a way out of this. You don't hurt the people you love. You protect them at all costs."

"True, but you left him before and it almost broke him."

"That wasn't my fault, I had no choice and anyway, he had Arabella."

"His father made him take her or he was going to send Clark to military school. Lincoln was trying to protect his brother. It was an untenable position for him. He'd end up hurting someone either way he went."

"Wow, poor Clark. Charles is such a bastard." My venom must have shown as Audrey cocks her head.

"Did he threaten you? We saw footage from the gala and he seemed to be threatening you but there was no audio."

My stomach feels like it's in my mouth as I stand abruptly. "I need to go."

Audrey catches my arm. "Please, tell me."

"I can't. Just leave it alone. Tell Lincoln to grant me a divorce and forget he ever knew me."

"He isn't going to do that, he loves you."

"No, he doesn't." I stamp my foot to get my point across.

Audrey stands slowly and squeezes my arm. "He does. He always has, but he's a stupid male and let pride and fear control him. He hurt you when he should've talked to you and believe me, he regrets it. If you want nothing more to do with him, I understand, but don't shut me out. I might be his cousin, but I thought we were friends. Believe me, when you're as rich, gorgeous, and as successful as I am, true friends are rare, and you're that to me."

Her words are said with a hint of a smile, but I see the truth in her eyes. "Just give me some time."

"Can I have your number so I can call you?"

"Contact me through Hudson. He can get hold of me anytime."

Her lips curls. "Urgh, that jackass."

"He might be, but he's been the only person in my corner in all of this and dropped everything to help me."

"Perhaps Linc was right about you and him having a connection?"

"Not at all. I see him as a friend, and he sees me the same way. Apparently, I remind him of his mother." I laugh and so does Audrey as we walk to the edge of the park side by side.

"Well, I guess not then."

At the gated entrance we stop, about to go in different directions.

"The truth is I wish I could see a man like Hudson that way, but I've only ever loved Lincoln and fear he was my one shot at happiness, and look where that got me."

"Don't give up on him."

"I have no choice, Audrey. It's the only way I can keep my family and my heart safe."

She kisses my cheek as she hugs me and I wish things were different, that I could've had the life I glimpsed so briefly forever.

"Take care."

"You too and please don't tell Linc you saw me."

Audrey purses her lips, and I can tell she's considering it. "Okay, I promise."

THE REST OF THE DAY I'M PLAGUED BY HER WORDS. NO MATTER HOW much I want to hate him I can't, and it kills me.

I thought the night he spewed such hatred at me that I was done, that I was finally free, but as the days have worn on, I see that his words, while painful and unforgivable, didn't kill my love for him. They merely anesthetized it and now they're wearing off and the feelings are as strong as ever and more redundant too. I know what I need to do.

I make the call and wait for Hudson to call me back.

"Hey, you okay?"

"Yes, fine. I just wanted to let you know I've signed the papers and want you to file the action for a divorce."

"What made you change your mind? I know you were unsure."

"I can't risk him talking me around. I'm weak around Lincoln and I can't afford to be with what Charles is holding over my head."

"But we might have a case now."

"I know but look at the mess it will cause. Linc will hate me for lying about Eric. Heather won't be able to look at us and it will blow up in my face. Maybe not now, but one day he'll get angry with me about something like he did this time, and he'll use it against me and I can't take that chance. I just can't."

"Okay. You know my feelings on this so, I'll support you."

"I know and I appreciate it more than you know."

31: *Linc*

THE FIRST TWO DAYS WITHOUT LOTTIE I'D BEEN ANGRY STILL, WITH myself, with her, with the world, intent on finding her and demanding answers. Indignant that she'd leave me but now, almost two weeks later, I'm sick with missing her. Nothing matters without her in my life. Not the company I'd spent my whole life wanting. Not my apartment that had reminders of her at every single turn, not food, nothing, and I couldn't seem to snap myself out of this funk.

Time and reflection had held a mirror up to my actions and how I'd treated her. A part of me knew she was better off without a man who could be so cruel, but a bigger part missed her so much he was willing to forget his abhorrent behavior.

I was wearing sweats and a t-shirt with a stain, which I thought might be pizza sauce on it when I was alerted that I had a visitor. Personal hygiene, food, and anything not related to getting Lottie back have gone out the window. I've lived on a diet of cola and pizza since the night I got so blind drunk I imploded my marriage.

I groan, not wanting to see anyone. My friends had stepped up, even Beck had been by and called to check on me, but he didn't get it. He'd never been in love and didn't understand the deep grief losing her had thrown me into.

Ryker walked through my door a few minutes later with a hard look on his face and I felt my body tense. He'd been trying to find out what Hudson had meant about my father and so far he'd had no luck.

His nose wrinkled as he got closer to me.

"Fucking hell, when was the last time you showered?"

I shrugged. "Dunno."

He walked past me on the couch and moved to my kitchen. "Get in the fucking shower while I make you some coffee and real food. We have serious shit to discuss and I'm not doing it while you look and smell like a sewer rat."

I stand and prowl toward him suddenly my heart beating faster, as hope fills my belly. "Did you find her?"

Ryker cuts me a look that would freeze vodka. "Get in the shower, then we'll talk."

I knew arguing with him would be fruitless so I stalk off to my room to shower and change, feeling alive for the first time in days. Twenty minutes later, I'm showered and clean in jeans and a blue tee when I walked back into my living space and smell bacon. My stomach rumbles like I haven't been fed in years, and I honestly can't remember the last time I'd eaten.

"You eat, then I'll talk."

I shovel bacon and eggs in my mouth, swilling it down with hot coffee which seems to rejuvenate my body instead of dulling it like the endless junk food the last two weeks had done. "Talk."

"You're not going to like this."

I sit forward, a feeling of dread moving over me. "Tell me anyway."

"Your dad is a nasty piece of work."

I snort. "Tell me something I don't know."

"No, I mean he's bad. I couldn't find anything for a while and then I found two buried NDAs from women he'd paid half a million dollars to each."

"What?"

"It gets worse. The NDA didn't tell me a lot so I hacked Hudson's files."

I didn't ask how, or if it was illegal because I suspected I knew the answers to that.

"I found something."

I threw up my hands. "Enough with the theatrics, Ryk, just spit it out."

Ryker was seated beside me and he hung his head before looking up at me.

"It looks like your dad attacked Mary Miller ten years ago and Eric is the result. He's the reason they ran like they did and now he's blackmailing Lottie that if she doesn't help him get re-instated as CEO of Kennedy, he's going to file for custody of Eric."

It feels like all the air has been sucked out of the room; a buzzing sounds in my ears, and nausea swirls violently in my belly. I can see Ryker's lips moving but the sound is muffled. He moves and grasps my neck, shoving my head between my knees and I suck in large gulps of oxygen until the buzzing recedes and I can focus on what he said, not what my body was doing.

His hand shoved a glass with amber liquid at me and I shake my head. "No." I sit up, my shock still holding me captive but my brain knows I need air, not more booze.

I get up and move to the terrace, sucking in the fresh, cool evening air. How had I not known that the man who sired me was so evil? Why hadn't Lottie told me any of this? I thought back to how I'd been at the start. How cold and closed off, how I'd treated her, and I had my answer.

My beautiful Lottie was alone against the world with my brother. The thought almost takes the wind out of my sails and I have to brace my hands against my knees. To think I had a baby brother. A sweet innocent boy who's done nothing in this world except exist and the only person fighting for him was the woman who had my heart, body, and soul.

I felt a presence at my side and turned to see Ryker looking out over the city we'd made our own. "Did it say anything else?"

"It looks like Mary wasn't the only one. The NDAs suggest there were similar things and Hudson has his guy chasing leads too. It also mentioned he'd advised his client to talk to you about it."

"When was this?" Ryker looked uncomfortable and I knew. "The night I fucked it up."

His nod was short.

"Fuck." I banged my palm against my head. "So, she was preparing to bare her soul and tell me everything to try and protect me, and I was ripping her heart to shreds because I was a pathetic schoolboy with jealousy issues."

Ryker stayed silent and I don't blame him.

"I need to see her, to apologize."

"I didn't find out where she was living. Hudson keeps meticulous case notes but her whereabouts isn't one of them."

He pauses and I can sense he was hiding something.

"Audrey saw her."

I round on him, my voice a growl. "What?"

Ryker held his hands up. "Don't come at me. She saw her in a park downtown near the school Eric goes to."

"And nobody thought to tell me?"

"What would you have done apart from flying over there and making shit worse? Plus, Audrey promised her she wouldn't tell you."

I respected that my cousin hadn't broken Lottie's confidence, God knew she needed people she could trust, and I wasn't in that camp right now, but God, I wanted to be. I needed to make this right. "Call Audrey and get her over here."

I wait on the terrace as Ryker makes the call. It isn't long before my phone alerts me I have another visitor.

I accost Audrey the second she walks into my apartment. "What did she say?"

Audrey throws her bag on the couch and walks to the bar area and pours herself a drink. That can't be a good sign. I run my hand through my hair, catching a glare pass between her and Ryker.

"You broke her, Lincoln."

My belly clenches at her words and the accusing look. Audrey is angry with me and rightly so. "How did she look?"

"She's lost weight, her hair was a mess, she was pale and gaunt." She took a gulp of her drink and shook her head. "And sad, so very sad, and convinced you never loved her. And I have to say she makes a good argument."

I sink into the couch, my legs heavy. "Did you ask her about what my father said to her?"

"No, but when I mentioned him she clammed up and pretty much brought the conversation to a close."

Anger unfurls in my belly when I think about what he did and what he's still doing.

Audrey looks between me and Ryker as I spin on my heel and plant my fist in the wall. Pain blooms on my knuckles but I don't care, I want blood and only my father's will do.

"Tell her," I grit out to Ryker because I don't have the bandwidth to explain it and keep my shit together. Just hearing it a second time is like drinking poison and I know what I have to do.

"Oh, God. Poor Lottie. And, Linc, your mom."

I hadn't even considered how this would affect my mother until now. She'll be devastated, and she adores Eric, the product of her husband raping a woman under her roof.

I grab my keys from the side near the elevator and press to open the doors. Ryker and Audrey rush to catch up with me.

"Where are we going?"

"I'm going to see my father and drag a fucking confession from that piece of shit."

"Not on your own you're not."

I glance at Audrey who looks a little pale and a thought strikes me. "He never?"

"Oh God, no. Never."

"Thank God."

"We should call Hudson first."

"What the fuck, Ryker?"

"No, he's right. We should in case this is going to fuck up any plans he has."

I don't like the idea of calling him for anything. He's the man hiding my wife from me after all, but I know they're right.

Audrey is dialing as we hit the lobby, and we head to the front where my car is always waiting. The bonus of being filthy rich is you never have to wait for anything.

"Hudson, it's Audrey."

I hear her explain what we know and where we're going and the sound of his voice rising on the other end of the phone.

I snatch it from her and put it to my ear. "Look, asshole, you can hide my wife from me, but you won't stop me from confronting my father, so any words of advice before I hang up?"

"I'm not hiding her. You fucked up and I'm helping her."

"I'm hanging up."

"Record the conversation if you can. New York is a one-party consent state, so if you can get a confession we can use it in court."

"Fine."

I hang up and hand Audrey her phone back. "He says to record the convo if possible."

"Oh, cool. I have this new bit of tech I want to try out. Let's stop by my office first."

"Now isn't the time to try out your new toys, Ryker."

"It's not a toy, it's a million-dollar piece of equipment my company is making for the military and it works perfectly."

"Fine."

I'm itching to get to my father and drag the answers I need from him.

32: Linc

AFTER RINGING AROUND, I'M DISMAYED TO FIND MY FATHER IS AT Kennedy Estate, the scene of the crime and now Lottie's refusal to live here makes perfect sense to me. My mother's car is in the drive when we roll up and I grimace. I don't want her to find out like this, so I turn to Audrey and she nods as if reading my mind.

"I'll handle Aunt Heather."

I fiddle with the recorder Ryker gave me and he swats my hand. "Leave it alone. I don't want you breaking it with your big paws."

Taking a breath, I exit the car and walk inside with Audrey and Ryker at my side. I haven't said it, but it means the world to have them here in my corner with me.

Audrey veers off to find my mother.

"Aunt Heather?"

"In the library, my darling."

Audrey nods as she walks off in the opposite direction. I know my father will be in his study on the opposite side of the house and Ryker follows me. He'll wait outside in case I need him. Not because I'm worried my dad will get violent but because I'm worried I might not be able to hold myself back from killing the sick bastard.

He looks up as I walk inside his study, his ruddy complexion from years of alcohol abuse making him look old and tired. "You finally come to your senses?"

I remain standing as he glares at me and I realize that to him I've always been the enemy. "Yes."

His face lights up and he leans forward. "You're going to hand over the CEO position to me?"

"Tell me something, were you always a piece of shit, or have you just got worse as the years went on?"

His eager expression morphs into outrage. "How dare you come into my home and speak to me in such a way."

"But that's just it, this isn't your home, is it? Grandfather left it to me and Clark. This is my home, and you're here at my good grace."

"We'll see about that."

"Oh, you have something up your sleeve, old man. Maybe black-mailing an innocent woman?"

His eyes flash and he huffs, lifting his head. "I have no idea what that little tramp told you, but I did not blackmail her."

I lunge forward, grabbing him by his collar and hauling him up until he's face to face with me. The calm exterior I was showing him dissipates at his vile words directed at the woman I love. "What did you just say?"

"Lincoln, what are you doing, son?"

I release him like he's a venomous snake, and he sags back into his chair.

"I'm no son of yours. I don't have to force myself on women to prove how powerful I am."

"Is that what she told you happened?"

He was patting his shirt to remove the wrinkles from it and I step back, trying to find my cool in the face of this man's inhumanity.

"The truth, son, is she wanted it. Your little Lottie as you called her, was a fucking tease. She paraded around in these little skirts and tops to tempt me and when I made my move, she cried wolf."

I had to swallow the bile in my throat hearing his words. I was across the desk before I could process what he was saying fully. My vision blurred at the edges, my entire body tensing as I breathed through the words he had spoken. My fist clenched as I hauled back and let my rage have an outlet.

I felt the crunch of bone under my knuckles, the warmth of his blood, his voice rambling in my ears like it was coming through a tunnel. The vision of her at the mercy of this man, at the idea I was at a god damn prom while she was facing this filled me with fury and shame. I hadn't been there when she needed me. The thought was enough for me to leash my anger. Killing him as much as I wanted to right now would mean I was leaving her alone once again. I wouldn't do it. Even if she never spoke a word to me again I would always be there for her and I couldn't do that from prison.

Shoving him away, I peered down at him with all the hatred I felt for him and knew I needed to finish this.

"She was fifteen years old."

He wiped the blood from his nose with the back of his hand, which shook and still he had the audacity to try and defend himself, to justify his sick perversions.

"Old enough to bleed, old enough to breed. Luckily for me, her mother stepped up and gave me what I needed instead."

I wasn't sure if I had the physical ability to hate him more than I did right now but every word he spoke proved me wrong. I just wanted him to admit his guilt so it was clear and then I would never have to look at him again.

"And what was that?"

"A tight pussy. Mary Miller lay there and let me fuck her while her little princess watched from the closet like a whore."

"You raped her."

"I like to think of it as her finding a way to keep her job. These sewer rats think they can live like us when they don't belong. Sometimes we have to teach them a few lessons."

"And have you taught other women these lessons over the years?"

"A few, yes, but it's the way of the world, son. You wouldn't understand. Your mother made you and Clark soft."

"She made us into men, not animals. You're nothing but a vile, disgusting rapist."

"That's how you see it, but I view it differently. I'm a man who takes an opportunity when it comes, however it comes. Let's be honest, these sluts fight me but they want it really. They all do."

"So you admit Mary fought you?"

I need him to make it clear. I don't want this bastard getting away on a technicality.

"Oh, she fought me like a wild cat. I wanted Violet, so young and innocent. Her pussy would have been so tight but her mother fought me, so I took her instead. I had to get a little rough and mark her up a bit too. You know, to show her who was in charge."

I want to hurt him, to destroy him so badly that my hands shake with the effort it takes to keep from punching him. The thought that I have his blood running through my veins almost makes me vomit on the thick rug beneath my feet.

"Now this is out in the open, I'll extend my offer to you. Give me back my position as CEO or I'll file for custody of that little bastard under Violet's care. It might be nice to have another son to mold into my own image."

Over my dead body would I let that happen. "Did you get all that?"

Ryker steps into the room followed by two uniformed officers, a detective, and Hudson fucking Carmichael. The cops had been planned but Carmichael was not.

I looked at my shocked father who had ruined so many lives and felt nothing but hatred and disgust. "You're fucking finished, old man."

I turn on my heel and stride from the room. I need some air. I run as my feet hit the outside and head for the one place that has always given me peace. I slow as the old shed and the rose garden come into view. A million memories swim into my mind as I sank to the cool ground. All of them centered around the woman I'd hurt so badly.

Lottie was the first girl I ever loved, and she'll be my last no matter what happens between us. I take my phone from my pocket and begin to scroll through the images of us from the last few months. Seeing the changes from the start when she'd been wary and unsure to the last few weeks when she was alive and unguarded, giving me a gift I never knew I had until I threw it away.

I settled on an image from the night we'd had dinner with my friends. She was talking to Audrey and laughing, and I'd captured her as she turned to give me a soft look. I saw it now, the love, the trust she had in me. I saw it all and I prayed harder than I ever had before that I'd find a way to make her forgive me because I was nothing without her. More than that though, I prayed she'd be happy. Whether that was with me or someone else.

Lottie deserved a man who knew her worth and, while I thought I was that man, now I knew she may never trust me again and that was something I'd have to live with.

"Hey."

I looked up to see Audrey sinking down beside me. "Hey, is he gone?"

"Yes. Ryker went with them to make sure the recording equipment was handled properly."

"How's my mother?" I should go to her but I needed this time to piece myself back together first.

"She's doing okay, actually. She's in the living room with my mother."

"Aunt Ruth is here?"

"Yes, she flew in yesterday. Apparently, your mother was already speaking to a lawyer about divorcing your father."

"She was."

"How are you doing? I heard some of his verbal vomit."

"Honestly, a little numb. I had no idea what Lottie had been through, and it makes me feel like I don't know her or deserve her."

"Well, I have to say when all this first went down, I would've agreed. You behaved horribly and while I still don't condone it, I do see how much you love her."

"I do. I really do."

"So what's the plan?"

"I don't have one. Maybe sort my shit out and deal with making myself a man worthy of her before I grovel in the dirt until she takes pity on me."

"Lincoln Coldwell, billionaire sex symbol, groveling on the floor. Now that I must see."

I let out a chuckle and know I'll have an uphill battle but for the first time, I'm ready to make the change and open myself up to everything that comes my way, good and bad.

Two weeks later, I'm back in my office after my second session with my new therapist and trying to read through a statement the company is putting out about my father's arrest. With my mother's and the board's support, we're going to come clean about everything and wipe the slate clean.

Secrets got us into this mess, and I want no more skeletons in my closet just waiting to jump out and derail me or Kennedy Enterprises. The shares will tank initially but after speaking to Harrison, who made all his money on the stock markets, we're certain that it will just be a blip and, with my leadership and plans for taking Kennedy forward, things will right themselves quickly. My work life will recover, I wish I could say the same for the dumpster fire that is my relationship with Lottie.

To say it had been an emotional few weeks, is an understatement. My mother was distraught to find out that the man she'd shared a bed with could do such heinous things to a woman in our home and not just once, but over and over again. She'd sobbed on my shoulder over what Lottie had been through, feeling in some way responsible. We both knew she wasn't, but I understand how she feels. How could we not have seen? But the truth was, he'd pulled the wool over all our eyes. Yes, we'd known he wasn't a good man or father, but we hadn't known how bad he was.

My mother planned to reach out to Lottie and offer her support and love in any way she could. Her love for Lottie and Eric hadn't waned and neither had mine. If anything, it grew with each second and revelation. I found my evenings empty and desolate, wandering around my penthouse with so much wealth and opulence. It might has well have been a shack for all I cared. Outside of my company I cared about very little now. Food was tasteless, color seemed less vibrant than before, music felt like it was meant to torment me, as the last time we'd been happy she'd been in my arms.

At least my father would rot in prison for the rest of his miserable life. Hudson had spoken to the District Attorney, who was a friend, and assured me the full weight of the law would be thrown at my father and they were building a case that would ensure he went behind bars for the rest of his life.

I wanted to reach out to Lottie, my fingers itched with the urge to call her, to beg her to forgive me, but my therapist had advised I write her a letter instead. It had been the single hardest thing I had ever done, and the most cathartic. I'd poured my heart into it, and pages and pages of truth, both the good and the bad, had bled from me. The pain of losing her when we were young, the constant battle to seek acceptance from my father, when in reality he didn't deserve me. The battle I waged inside to protect my brother from my father's wrath. To fight to be the me I was with her when he always sought the brute that I ended up becoming. I had grieved so many losses on those pages and I hoped that even if she never forgave me, for the things I'd said and done that she'd see them for the bullshit they'd been. She was everything good in this world and she deserved a man who would cherish that, even if it ended up not being me. A thought that brought me to my knees when I let it fester.

Hudson had promised he'd deliver the letter to her and that had been two days ago. Now I just had to wait and see if she was willing to talk. I continued to fight though. I would never give up believing that we were meant to be. She was my soulmate, and you didn't give up on them. I sent flowers and limited edition signed books from authors I knew she loved. I had cupcakes sent to the office of Love Books where she'd thankfully agreed to go back to work. Thanks in a big part to Audrey, who I adored for caring for the woman I loved.

What I didn't do was turn up there and cause a scene. Lottie would hate that, and it would prove I hadn't learned from my mistakes. I needed to show her respect and staying away and letting her decide when she was ready to speak to me was my way. The gifts just made sure she didn't forget or think I'd stopped caring.

My phone buzzes and I sigh. "Yes?"

"You have a visitor, Mr. Coldwell."

I don't have time for this right now. I've spent the last two days answering questions from the board and I need to focus. "Who is it?"

"It's Mrs. Coldwell."

I sigh, because I won't turn my mother away ever and I know she needs me and Clark now more than ever. "Send her in."

I look back down at the papers in front of me as the door opens. "Give me a second, Mom. I just want to finalize this press release."

I'm met with silence and suddenly the air around me feels charged as I look up and see Lottie, looking more beautiful than I've ever seen her and yet I spot the nervous way she twists her hands, looking unsure and like she might bolt.

"Lottie!" I jump from my chair and rush toward her, having to physically stop myself from wrapping her in my arms and never letting go.

"Hi, Linc."

She's lost weight, her eyes seem bigger, and she's pale and anxious. I did that to her and I hate myself for it. Yet she still looks stunning to me.

"Please sit. Do you want some tea?"

I usher her toward the couches where we sat the last time she was here, when she loved me. Just having her close has my body responding and I want to feel her soft skin beneath my fingers. More than that, I just want her to smile at me the way she used to before I fucked it all up.

"No, nothing for me. I can't stay long. I got your letter and I just wanted to say thank you. I heard what you did, and I can't tell you how much it means to me to finally get justice."

"God, Lottie, you shouldn't be thanking me. I should've known, should've seen it."

Her ponytail moves as she shakes her head. "How could you? I never let you see and until that night, I had no real idea either, just a

239

feeling when I was around him."

I look at my hands, which are clenched in my lap to hide the shake, the knuckles white. "I'm so fucking sorry." My voice is thick with tears that I can't hide and I blink to clear my vision. She glances up at my eyes and I let her see it all. My shame, my regret, my weakness. I owe her that.

"I know and I'm sorry for not telling you about Eric before. I won't keep you two apart, but I beg you not to tell him who you are. I don't want him to know how he came into this world until he's old enough to understand that it in no way reflects on him."

I nod, wishing I could touch her, hold her but I gave that right up when I let another woman into my apartment and was cruel to my wife out of spite. She is talking like it's over and I feel panic take hold. I respond because she expects it but my heart feels crushed. "Thank you, and I won't say a word. I know a little of how he might feel and don't want that for him either."

"How is Heather?"

"She's okay. She filed for divorce from Charles. She wants to reach out to you but isn't sure you'd be open to it."

"I know. Hudson contacted me and we're going to arrange something when things settle."

I grit my jaw at his name, but I've come to realize over the last few days that I owe him my gratitude, not my hatred. He stepped up and helped the woman I love, and while I hate that it wasn't me, I'm grateful she had him.

I can't stand it a second longer and reach for her hand and she lets me take it, and suddenly everything feels right with the world again. "Did you read my letter?"

She nods and a tear slips down her cheek.

"I meant every word. I'm not trying to make excuses. I just want you to know everything about me." I pause running my thumb over her wrist. "Can you ever forgive me?"

"I don't know. You hurt me, Linc."

Her voice is strong despite the wobble in it.

"That's not a no and I promise I'll never hurt you again. Not as long as I live. You make me whole, Lottie, and losing you this time was my own fault. I have nobody to blame but myself."

"Is the great Linc Coldwell admitting he's wrong?"

I feel a kernel of hope flicker at her teasing. "Don't tell anyone."

A warm laugh escapes her throat and despite the tension, my dick hardens at the sexy sound.

"It's not about forgiveness, not really, Linc. I understand you were hurt and jealous. I may have even reacted the same way."

A growl leaves my throat at her words, the thought to horrible to consider.

"It's about trust and I don't know if I can trust you not to reject me again when you get mad or angry. To lash out because you perceive something that isn't true."

I fall to my knees in front of her and hold both of her hands. "I won't, Lottie. I promise you I've learned my lessons. I've lived without you and it's an awful, cold, barren place, and I'd never risk that purgatory again. I hate that I hurt you. I love you so much and I was such a bastard and said the most awful things to you, and I'll regret that until the day I die."

"You're confusing me. Are you sorry you're a bastard or are you sorry for the words you said?"

I still until I see the teasing smile on her face and my world rights itself. Hope unfurls like the first bloom of spring, tentative and shy. "I'm sorry for both. I don't deserve you. You are a thousand times the human I'll ever be and I love and adore every single inch of you. I promise you if you give me another chance, I'll never give you a reason to doubt my love for you again."

"That's the first time you've said you love me."

I freeze and watch her as I lift my hands to cup her cheeks, running my thumbs over her full bottom lip. "I love you so much I think my heart might burst from it. I'd give up everything I own for just one day with you, Lottie. You own me, heart and soul, and no matter whether you decide you can forgive me or not, that won't change. I've loved you since I was nine years old and didn't have a clue what it was, and even in the ten years we spent apart, I loved you. I never stopped and I never will."

"I love you too."

"I know and I'll treasure that love and hold it safe if you let me."

"So cocky."

My lips brush hers as our foreheads touch and I feel the mingled wetness of our tears on my hands. "Give me a chance to make this right. Be my wife forever and I promise you'll never regret it for even a second."

"How about we agree to date for six months and see how it goes?"

I pull away with a frown. "No. I can't be without you that long. I need to have you with me in our home."

"Your home. I can't go back there, Linc."

"Fine. I'll sell it and we can buy a new place."

"Really?"

"Yes, I told you I'd give it all up for you."

"Yeah, well, don't do that just yet. I kind of like having money to pay the bills."

"Does that mean you'll take me back?"

"How about a compromise?"

I groan and drop my head into her neck, inhaling her scent. "Go on?"

"How about we rip up the contract and you live with me at my new apartment until we find a new place?"

"Yes."

"Really?"

"Yes, really. Now give me that mouth, woman."

I capture her lips in a hungry kiss that cements the deal of a lifetime. Finally, it feels like I'm right where I'm meant to be and with the woman who was always meant to be mine.

"Fuck, I've missed that mouth."

"Oh yeah, what else have you missed?"

"Why don't I lock the door and show you?"

Epilogue: Lottie

IT HAD TAKEN SIX MONTHS FOR US TO FIND THE PERFECT HOME BUT THE second we'd seen this one in the waterside development of Sandy Hills both Linc and I had fallen in love. Set on four acres, it had its own pool overlooking Hempstead Bay and was built in such a way that all the rooms overlooked the bay too. Open plan, with light flooring and high open ceilings, giving the place a feeling of space and freedom. The fact it was huge helped, as did the large windows.

"Lottie, where do you want this bookshelf positioned?"

I turn from where I'm admiring the view to admire my husband instead. He's dressed in old jeans and a white tee, which make him look good enough to eat. A growl tears from him as he stalks towards me.

"Don't look at me like that, sweetheart, or I'm going to give the movers out there a show."

I wrap my arms and legs around him as he lifts me in the air, cupping my ass, and twirls me around, making me laugh. "Oh yeah?"

His head nuzzles my neck and I feel my body respond as it always does when he touches me. I'm a slave to my needs when it comes to Linc and he knows how to satisfy every single one of them.

He sinks onto the couch as the sounds of our friends and family moving about helping us get settled in float around me. I'd never imagined this could be my life, that I could be loved and accepted and showered with joy but every day Linc proves to me that I was right to take a chance on him.

Not a day goes by where he doesn't give me a reason to love him more and it has nothing to do with the wild extravagance he showers on me at every opportunity. He's disgustingly rich, with more zeros in his, sorry, our bank account than he could ever spend. He's always whisking me away by helicopter for a meal in an exclusive restaurant or buying me jewels and designer clothes, but it's the small things and the quiet moments that mean the most to me.

Like the night he'd learned to cook Eric's favorite diabetic cookies or the way he'd rub my feet after a long day spent with Audrey at Love Books. That he goes out of his way to buy me the pastries he knows I love, and makes sure the bathroom is always stocked with my favorite lotions and potions without me ever having to ask.

Those are the things that show me who he is. To the rest of the world, he was, and will always be, the cold untouchable billionaire, but to me and those he loves, he's just Linc, a man who'll move mountains for those he loves.

"Where did your head go?"

"I was thinking how lucky I am and how much I love you."

"Did any of those thoughts involve how much you want to give me a blow job right now?"

I snort and shake my head. "Insatiable."

"Only for you, my love, only for you."

Small feet pounding down the hallway have us both turning to the door. I'm straddled over Linc and make no move to get up. We've decided Eric should see love and affection between us and he's so used to seeing us like this or kissing that he doesn't give it a second thought, although we keep it PG around him.

"Linc, Uncle Harry is looking for you."

Eric is bouncing from foot to foot and I know this move to our forever home is as exciting for him as it is us. It was another measure of security in an uncertain world.

"He is?"

"Yeah."

At that precise moment, Harrison walks in looking harried and stressed like I'd never seen before, and he has his phone hanging from his hand.

Linc stiffens beneath me and then palms my ass to move me off him.

"What's going on?"

"I have to go."

"Okay."

I stand, feeling the tension oozing from the normally cool Harrison.

"I have a son."

Linc's eyes go wide, and he moves closer to grip his friend's arm. "What?"

"I just got a call. Apparently, a woman named Norrie Richards was brought in after a serious accident and she has me down as the guardian for her son, who's also listed as my son."

"Jesus. Is she gonna make it?"

"I don't have a clue. But I have to go because if I don't, they'll put him with a foster family."

"Do you know this woman?"

Harrison looks at us, his eyes wide and haunted. "Yes."

"And is it possible she's telling the truth?"

"Yes."

"Then go and take Beck with you. He'll be able to help you with all the medical jargon."

Harrison nodded. "Yeah, good idea."

Linc walks Harrison out and I miss the conversation, but I know it would consist of Linc offering whatever help he can.

I send Eric off to unpack his room and go to find Linc, who's coming back in from the drive. "Is he okay?"

Linc wraps me in his arms. "Yeah, a little shaken but he'll be fine, and he has all of us and I sent my mother with him too."

"Yeah, he does, and Heather was a good idea. She'll keep him calm and offer some support."

Heather and I had cried a lot over the last six months but ultimately there was no blame from either of us. She was as much a victim in some ways as I was but neither of us were victims in the way my mother had been. She doted on Eric and I loved her for it. I knew when the time came for us that she'd be a wonderful grandmother to our children. Linc wanted to get started straight away but I wanted more time with my husband before we had kids of our own, and I knew it would happen.

I rise on tiptoes and kiss my man. "I love you."

"I love you too and don't think I've forgotten about the blow job."

He winks and I swat his ass before running off, looking over my shoulder. "Play your cards right and you might get one in each room later."

I can hear his laughter like a balm ringing through the house and feel excited about our next chapter.

The rest of the day is perfect as we work side by side with friends and family to make this home the fresh start we all need. By eight that night, we'd almost put everything away thanks to our friends help. Even Hudson had stopped by with pizza for us all and, while he and Linc may never be best friends, they have a truce and a mutual respect that eases my soul. Eric is staying with Clark and Gaspard, who'd moved back to the States after everything went down with Charles, and I know how much it means to Linc to have his brother back in his life on a more permanent basis.

The house is quiet except for the sounds of the water lapping the banks of the shore. I hadn't had chance to get out onto the deck today and wanted to enjoy the view with the lights behind it. Linc had shown everyone out and sent me for a long bath, in our deep claw foot tub, which I appreciated after such a long day. I don't bother getting dressed, just slip a short pink silk robe over my naked body. Linc will take it off before the night is out anyway.

"Linc, I'm going to head to the deck."

Silence greets me but I know he's here somewhere; I can always sense when he's close. I know how silly that sounds but it's the truth. We're connected in a way that I know is unusual, a once-in-a-lifetime love made for romance books, and that makes me the luckiest woman in the world.

The pain and doubt of the painful past we share is behind us and only the future matters to me. He made mistakes and he paid for them and learned from us being apart and neither of us ever want to repeat it. I'd had no idea of the burden he carried with his father and hid behind my pain like it was a shield, when I should have pushed it into the light and faced it. I never knew I could be as happy as I am with Linc beside me. He is my best friend, my lover and the man I know will treasure me as much as I do him for the rest of my life. It seems crazy but the man who hurt me is my safe place in this world, because he sees me, he always has and one day when we have children, I know he will be the best father they could ask for because he has lived the alternative.

Moving to the back window, I pull open the bi-fold doors and flick on the lights, wondering where my man has got too. A gasp leaves me. The entire pool is awash with pink rose petals and floating candles. My hand flutters to my mouth and tears prick my eyes. I step outside and see a table set for two with a white tablecloth and flickering candles in the middle.

A movement to my right makes me glance that way to see Linc walking toward me wearing a black tux. My heart skids in my throat as he gives me the sexy smirk that makes me weak. He looks so dashing, so powerful, but it's the way he's looking at me that makes my heart explode with joy. "Linc?"

The words barely leave my mouth before he's dropping to one knee, and I cover my mouth with my hands as my lip wobbles.

His clear blue eyes find mine and I can see the nerves on his face.

"Lottie, since the day we met you've been the one constant in my life. Even when we were apart, your light and the memories of us kept me going. I've loved you since before I knew what the emotion was, and I know I'll love you until the world stops turning. You make me a better man, a better son, a better brother, and a better friend. I want you to continue to make me the best husband, and one day, if we're lucky enough, the best father I can be. We've been through some difficult times, but I believe that they've made us stronger. There is nobody in this world I want to do this with but you. So, I'm doing this how I should have done it the first time."

He takes something out of his pocket, and I step closer to see a stunning sapphire and diamond ring.

"Will you do me the honor of staying my wife?"

I nod as tears run down my cheeks and I sink to my knees in front of him. "Yes."

"I love you, Lottie."

His kiss is demanding, yet sweet and full of the love I know he feels for me. I feel his thumb skim over the pulse in my throat a growl breaking from his throat. My Linc is sweet but he's still him, dominant and possessive and I wouldn't have him any other way.

He releases me long enough to slide the ring over my knuckle and I marvel at how beautiful it is and how perfect. I haven't worn the rings he'd given me on our wedding day and he'd understood my hesitance and said he'd replace them one day, but neither of us had felt the need to rush it.

We were together, building a beautiful life and that was enough but now seeing the ring nestled on my finger, I know that I'd needed this and so had he.

"Now, do you want to eat first or do you want me to fuck you in a pool full of roses?"

"Roses, Linc, always the roses." I step back and let my robe fall from my shoulders as his hungry gaze wanders over my skin. "But first, I promised you a blow job if you played your cards right and this, Linc," I gestured to the scene behind me, "is the perfect hand."

~

THIS IS THE HAPPY EVER AFTER FOR LINC AND LOTTIE. IF YOU WANT TO read what happens to Harrison and Norrie, you'll find their story in *The Consequence*, releasing 07 March 2023.

CLICK HERE OR TYPE HTTPS://BOOKHIP.COM/PANKCNR INTO YOUR browser to receive an extended epilogue and find out how Linc and Lottie cope when they get an unexpected surprise.

Books by L. Knight

KINGS OF RUIN

The Auction

The Consequence

About the Author

Lia Knight is a romance author of billionaire romance with lots of angst, and heat. Her heroes are super rich, demanding and know exactly what they want, so when they set their sights on the heroines in these books you know the chemistry will explode your kindle. Having written over forty books under a different pen name she wanted to give those rich, bossy heroes fighting for a story a chance have their say and find their HEA.

When she isn't writing she is binging Yellowstone, The Big Bang Theory, and Bridgerton from her home in Hereford in the UK.

You can contact me at: lknightauthor@gmail.com

Join my Facebook group to get all the latest updates:
https://www.facebook.com/groups/KnightsDelights1

Made in United States
Orlando, FL
06 August 2024

50030808R00143